"I was never ser~~ious~~... and I never will... airplanes."

Jen gasped. Dan had ~~been~~ perfectly clear. He would never have a serious relationship with a woman as long as he flew. That meant forever, as far as she could see. "You can't mean that."

"I won't risk making a woman a widow."

Now he was making her angry. "Don't you think she ought to have a say in that?"

"No." The man didn't even have the grace to hesitate. "A relationship can't work unless both partners work together. Until I stop flying, that can't happen."

"Why not? Jack and Darcy have made it work."

"Oh?"

That simple question infuriated her. "We are not here because both Jack and Darcy fly airplanes. This could happen to anyone. At any time." That reality finally sank in. "No one can remove all risk from life."

"Perhaps, but I can minimize it. I won't make a woman suffer from losing her husband."

"That sounds to me like you're afraid of losing someone you love."

His expression darkened, all sense of calm gone.

She had finally pushed him too far.

"If that's true, Miss Fox," he growled, "then we both are."

A small-town girl, **Christine Johnson** has lived in every corner of Michigan's Lower Peninsula. She enjoys creating stories that bring history to life while exploring the characters' spiritual journeys. Though Michigan is still her home base, she and her seafaring husband also spend time exploring the Florida Keys and other fascinating locations. You can contact her through her website at christineelizabethjohnson.com.

Books by Christine Johnson

Love Inspired Historical

The Dressmaker's Daughters

Groom by Design
Suitor by Design
Love by Design

Visit the Author Profile page at Harlequin.com for more titles

CHRISTINE JOHNSON

Love by Design

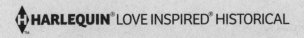

HARLEQUIN® LOVE INSPIRED® HISTORICAL

Recycling programs
for this product may
not exist in your area.

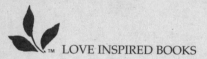 LOVE INSPIRED BOOKS

ISBN-13: 978-0-373-28312-5

Love by Design

To give unto them...the oil of joy for mourning.
—*Isaiah* 61:3

To God belongs all the glory.

My deepest gratitude to Mary Hayes, RN, MS, CNM, who helped me understand the potential problems faced during pregnancy and answered my many questions. Your ideas and assistance were vital.

Chapter One

January 1925

Jen Fox had to pass the test this time. She *had* to.

She nervously tapped the end of her pencil on the tabletop, drawing a glare from the flight instructor who was scoring her written examination. Already the instructor's red pencil had scratched the paper two times. Two more marked incorrect and Jen would fail for the third—and final—time.

"Perhaps you should take a walk," suggested Darcy Hunter, who in addition to serving as proctor was also Jen's instructor and mentor. "Go home for lunch, check on the dress shop or visit one of your sisters. Surely there is something you can do."

Jen glanced out the window of Darcy's dining room. Brilliant winter sun sparkled off last night's snowfall. Despite a cutting breeze that whirled the powder into tiny white cyclones, it would make a fine day for ice-skating or snowshoeing. With her entire future in the balance, Jen had no taste for sport, and she couldn't stomach lunch or casual visits. That left the dress shop. She glanced at her trousers and flannel shirt. Dressed like this, she would not project the proper image at the family business. Her older sister would shoo her away.

"No, thank you." Jen set the pencil in the middle of the table and knit her fingers together so she wouldn't tap them on the tabletop. *Deep breath in. Blow it out.* Still the nerves wouldn't settle. "I'll wait."

Darcy didn't look pleased, but she returned to scoring Jen's examination.

Jen puffed out her breath, lifting the bangs of her cropped hair. "I'm going to pass the test this time. I spent hours and hours studying. I could do the calculations in my sleep."

"Good," Darcy murmured. "Then there's no reason to be anxious."

Still, Jen's stomach tumbled over and over. She had arrived at eight o'clock sharp this morning and spent the next three and a half hours working through the problems. The mathematics in the navigation section gave her fits. She could figure out anything mechanical as long as the machine was in front of her, but angles and vectors and calculations drove her crazy.

Darcy cleared her throat and pointed at Jen's feet. "Quiet would be helpful."

"Oh." She must have been tapping her toe, which was one of her bad habits. She tucked the offensive foot under her chair. "I'm sorry. It won't happen again."

"Good." Darcy resumed scoring at the top of the sheet.

"I think you already did that question," Jen pointed out. At Darcy's glare, she added, "It looked like you were farther down the page."

Darcy sighed. "Why don't you head home? I'll bring the score over when I'm finished."

"I don't think I can wait that long." Jen clenched her hands until her knuckles turned white.

"Then I'll telephone the dress shop. Please. You're making me edgy."

Jen bit her lip. "I'm sorry. It's just that everything depends on passing this test."

Everything was really just one person—Daddy. Jen squeezed her eyes shut. His passing last October had sent her into what aviators called a stall, when the airplane stopped dead in the air. Despite a weak heart, he had survived so many scares that she'd assumed he would continue to rebound. Not that time. When she'd walked into his room and seen him, she'd known he was gone.

Flying had been their dream. They'd talked about it for ages, since they first saw Darcy take to the air over Pearlman. In that moment Jen had seen the future she wanted. Unlike her sisters, she had no taste for dresses or sewing. Daddy recognized that and encouraged her to fly. But then his health had deteriorated, and her savings went toward his care. She'd told herself that she'd take lessons when he got better, but he never did.

Now she owed it to his memory to succeed. With Darcy and her husband, Jack, planning a record flight over the North Pole, she had to get her license now or miss out on the chance to put her father's name into history as her inspiration. Twice already, she'd failed the navigation section. Time was running out.

She rolled the pencil back and forth against the tabletop. Its faceted surface massaged her stiff fingers.

Rrrrrep, rrrrrep, rrrrrep. The rasping sound released tension.

Mother had given her the money for this final attempt, but there would be no more. She wanted Jen to pursue a "reasonable" career like nursing, which could be learned without charge at a hospital school.

Rrrrrep, rrrrrep, rrrrrep.

Nursing? Jen couldn't picture herself in the stiff white cap and uniform.

She bore down on the pencil. *Rrrrrrep.*

Darcy held out her hand. "Give me the pencil."

"I'm sorry." Jen handed it to her. "I guess I am nervous."

Darcy sighed. "Look, Jen, this is going to take a while. I have to check all your calculations. It could easily take me as long to score the test as it took you to complete it. I need complete silence in order to concentrate. Go home. Go to the dress shop. Go anywhere, but let me finish in peace."

"But you don't understand. If I don't pass this time…" She couldn't bring herself to finish the thought aloud.

"It's all right." Darcy clasped Jen's hand. "If you fall short, you can always take the test again."

Except that she couldn't. Time and money had run out.

Darcy must have noticed Jen's stricken expression, for she gave her what was meant to be a reassuring smile. "Trust me. You will be fine, but right now your presence is making it difficult to complete the scoring."

"All right. I'll go." Jen scooted back the chair and decided to ask the only thing that mattered. "If I do pass, will I have a chance at the expedition? Providing I complete the flight training and get my license, of course."

Darcy returned a tight smile. "As you know, that's Jack's decision." Her husband headed the expedition.

"But he'll consider me, won't he? He does know I'm studying for my license."

"Yes, he does." A wistful look crossed Darcy's face. "He still needs a navigator to replace me."

Darcy had taken herself out of the cockpit once she learned she was with child. That open spot was Jen's best hope, but navigation was her most troublesome area.

Would Jack accept someone who had failed that section of the test twice?

Darcy leaned toward her. "You might want to remind Jack of that need while I finish scoring your exam. You can find him at the flight school."

Darcy must be very sure Jen was going pass in order to make that suggestion. Before she could find another error, Jen hurried out into the bitter cold afternoon.

The flight school office was as frigid as an icehouse and just as quiet. Dan Wagner set his Stetson on the battered oak table and took a seat. Across from him sat Jack Hunter, owner of the school, and Hendrick Simmons, owner of the aeromotor factory that he'd read about in one of his aviation magazines. If the article was right, they had an engine that would win him the airmail contract and let him leave stunt flying forever.

After introductions, Dan drove straight to why he'd come across the country in this coldest of months. "I'm looking for an engine that'll run reliably at temperatures well below freezing."

He had already told Simmons that when he visited the factory this morning. Instead of answering, Simmons had brought him to the flight school to talk to Jack Hunter. That name was vaguely familiar, but Dan couldn't quite place the man. Why Simmons insisted on this meeting was beyond his comprehension. Either he had an engine that met the specifications or he didn't. End of story. Bringing in a third party only muddied the waters in Dan's opinion, but Simmons wouldn't back down.

Hunter, a suave sandy-haired man with the look of a first-class aviator, glanced at Simmons before taking the lead. "We've been working on that problem for over a year. Longer, in fact. My wife and I first started puzzling it out after our failed transatlantic attempt. We brought in Hendrick once he had the factory up and running."

Simmons, a man of few words if today was any indication, nodded.

"Transatlantic attempt?" Dan couldn't get past the tidbit that Hunter had glossed over so casually. "I followed all the newspaper reports back in '19, but I don't recall your name. How far did you get?"

Hunter's easy grin told Dan he didn't harbor any regrets. "We never made it to Newfoundland thanks to the icing problems. Solving that is a big part of a successful polar attempt."

"Polar attempt?" Now Dan was truly stunned. In such a small town, he'd never expected to hear the words *polar* and *attempt* in the same sentence. He must have misunderstood. "I thought the navy scrapped their dirigible expedition. Is it back on?" He looked from Hunter to Simmons. If they were making the engines for some as yet unannounced naval expedition, then there was big backing behind Simmons Aeromotor. This was exactly what Dan was looking for. "Or are you supplying engines to Amundsen?" It seemed a far stretch for a company in a tiny American town to send motors to the Norwegian explorer, but he supposed it was possible.

"Nope." Hunter grinned. "We're not helping any other expedition. We're competing."

Dan's jaw dropped at the audacious statement. "You? Attempt to fly to the North Pole?" He raked a hand through his wavy hair. "That takes a lot of logistics and some mighty big funding."

"That it does."

Apparently the man had a lot more backing than Dan had figured. "Who is on your flight crew?" He looked at Simmons. "Do you fly?"

Simmons shook his head violently.

Hunter laughed. "Hendrick's no aviator. My wife planned to come along."

"Your wife?" Dan sat back in shock. Many women flew. Some, like the Stinson sisters or Ruth Law, had done so with unquestioned expertise. Still, a polar attempt was different. Dangerous. Deadly. "You'd risk your wife's life?"

"I wouldn't have had a choice. This was her dream." Hunter's expression softened. "But she pulled herself off the expedition. We're expecting a baby."

"Congratulations," Dan said automatically. "She's a smart woman." He shuddered at the memory of the accident that had ended his season. If a baby had been involved, he wouldn't have been able to live with himself. As it was, he couldn't shake the taste and smell of death. "Some people don't know when to stay on the ground."

Hunter gave him an odd look. "Enough about our plans. Hendrick tells me you want to run in some pretty tough conditions."

The change of topic had to be deliberate. Hunter had mentioned their plans to impress him, not interest him. Fair enough. Dan had plans of his own. "Montana gets bitter in the winter. Snow, wind, blizzards. The airmail route I'm aiming to bid on goes clear to the border. Some of these folks are isolated. Receiving and sending mail would be a godsend. I could even bring in a few supplies. Medicine, food, necessities," Dan ticked off an impressive list. "This isn't just an airmail contract. This is a lifeline for those folks. I need a more reliable motor than what I have now."

The next hour was absorbed by a discussion of Dan's current plane, a modified Curtiss Jenny, and the motor's limitations. Neither Simmons nor Hunter seemed to recognize him. He'd wanted it that way to keep prices down. Most men figured Daring Dan Wagner, headliner on the air-show circuit, had barrels of money. He didn't. His earnings went to keeping the family ranch out of the bank's hands. Every year seemed to bring a new crisis that tapped his funds. This year had been quiet—except for his accident—and he aimed to keep it that way. Daring Dan had made his last death drop.

"I assume you've had problems?" Hunter asked.

"The motor works great in the heat," Dan said, "but I have fits keeping it going in cold weather. I'm hoping your engine will solve the icing problem."

"We're working on it," Simmons said.

That did not sound good. "Are you close? The bids are due by the end of next month."

"We plan to make the next test run as soon as the winds die down," Hunter chimed in. "Could be tomorrow if the forecast is right."

"I'd like to see that flight," Dan said. "Your engine could give me the edge I need to land the contract."

"Fine with me, if it's all right with Hendrick."

Simmons nodded. "We couldn't produce another engine in time for your deadline, but we could get it done in, say, three months."

"That'll have to do." Dan hoped a letter to that effect would sway those making the decision. "First we have to make sure it does the job."

"It will." Simmons seemed confident.

Hunter was less so. "Even if this engine takes care of carburetor icing, how do you plan to combat icing on the wings and fuselage?"

Dan was impressed. Hunter had nailed the next biggest problem right on the head. Wing icing was deadly. Any pilot worth his salt knew it. "You're the one planning a polar attempt. You must have come up with some ideas."

Hunter shook his head. "Weather will be an issue. Too cold, and the engines won't start. Too warm, and moisture ices the plane."

"Then you haven't found a solution."

"Not yet."

Dan sensed opportunity. "Surely bright minds like ours can come up with something."

Simmons looked skeptical. "How? There's not a material out there that'll prevent icing."

"Not that anyone has discovered yet." Dan looked each man in the eye. "But we have to try—for both our projects. I'd stake my reputation on the experience gathered in this room." He sat back with a grin, waiting for one of them to admit they'd recognized him. When neither did, he hinted, "I do know something about flying. Perhaps you've heard of me."

Hunter echoed his grin. "I'd be a fool not to know who Dan Wagner is. Altitude, distance and speed records, not to mention the number of downed enemy planes over France. I don't suppose you'd consider—"

The office door burst open, drawing Hunter's attention away from his question and toward a tall woman with the brightest hazel eyes Dan had ever seen.

"Jack, I wondered if—?" The woman stopped midsentence when she noticed Hunter was not alone.

Her flustered confusion sat so awkwardly that Dan suspected she was seldom at a loss for words. She obviously didn't care about public opinion, because she wore men's trousers, a flannel button-down shirt and a ragged mackinaw. Her cracked and scuffed men's leather boots dripped muddy snow on the floor. Her cropped brown hair stuck out in all directions, as if she'd just yanked off a knit cap. She wasn't at all the type of woman that usually attracted him, so the tug in his gut came as a big surprise.

"I'm sorry." She looked around the small room, pausing when she reached him. "I didn't realize you were in a meeting."

Her cheeks, already pleasantly flushed from the cold, got even pinker. Dan was surprised to feel his pulse quicken with the hope that he was the cause of that blush.

She squared her jaw and thrust a hand toward him. "You're new in town. I'm Jen Fox."

He allowed a slight smile. "Pleased to meet you, Miss Fox." He noted her frown. "Not much for formalities, eh? Well then, I'm Wagner. Daniel Wagner." That was a test. Did she recognize Daring Dan by his full name or was she just another gal who swooned over aviators?

She matched his smirk. "Pleased to meet you, Wagner."

He shook her hand. Her grip was as firm as that of a vigorous man. He flexed his fingers when she let go.

She cocked her head to the side, as if assessing him. "Are you a new instructor at the school?"

Hunter snorted and then pretended to cough.

Dan grinned. This gal was definitely not an aviation devotee. She could use a little brushing up on the social graces and a decent wardrobe, but her directness was refreshing. "No, I'm not."

"Oh. You look like a flight instructor."

"I didn't realize flight instructors had a certain look."

"Oh, yes." Her head bobbed emphatically. "They're confident, almost arrogant, as if they think the world revolves around them."

Hunter didn't succeed in covering up his laugh this time.

"Except Jack, of course," she added hastily.

Dan was surprised at the informality. Clearly the pair knew each other. Perhaps some relation of Hunter's wife.

Hunter chuckled at Miss Fox's backtracking. "I'll admit that there's some truth to what you said. We are an overconfident lot."

Mollified, she turned back to Dan. "Then, Wagner, if you're not an instructor, you must be a student." Her hazel eyes twinkled, as if enjoying some unknown joke. "Sorry, but the flight school doesn't open until March."

That sent Hunter into unbridled guffaws.

Miss Fox drew back. "What did I say? Why else would anyone be here in January?"

Since Hunter was laughing too hard to speak and Dan didn't want to spoil the fun, Simmons ended up explaining, "Dan Wagner is interested in the cold-weather engine we've been testing."

Her eyes widened. "Dan Wagner? *The* Dan Wagner?" She clapped her hands to her cheeks. "I thought you looked familiar."

Dan groaned. From the impudent upstart, she'd turned into the dreaded ingenue. He sank back in his chair. "Afraid so."

Her cheeks glowed red, but apparently not from embarrassment. "You should teach stunts. Shouldn't he, Jack? Everyone wants to learn them. The loop-de-loop, the death drop—"

"No." Dan cut her off. "I retired from stunt flying."

"Retired?" Her shock mirrored that of his former manager.

The man had nearly wept when Dan delivered the news. Then he had pleaded, even offering to decrease the number of appearances or raise the fee they demanded from air-show sponsors, but Dan could not be swayed. As much as his manager had glossed over the accident by calling it a casualty of aviation, that single event had changed everything. His stunt flying days were over.

"But you're famous," she exclaimed.

"I'm alive," he said dryly. Surely she'd read about the crash. The newspapers had seized the story and blown it into something even more horrific than it had actually been, if that was possible.

The office door opened again, ushering in a lovely brunette, clearly with child. Must be Hunter's wife. Though more conventionally dressed in a wool dress and pretty by anyone's assessment, she didn't have Jen Fox's spunk.

She smiled at her husband and then addressed Miss Fox, "Jen, let's go to the classroom."

"The classroom?" Disappointment briefly flashed across Miss Fox's face before being replaced by trembling hope. "Did I pass?"

Mrs. Hunter smiled and pointed to the door. "To the classroom. We have to work out a schedule for flight training."

"I passed! I passed!" Her whoops could have been heard clear to the train station. "You know what that means, Jack."

Hunter squirmed in his seat. "Congratulations."

She must have taken that as confirmation of whatever she expected from him, for her smile outshone the electrical lighting. When she next turned it on Dan, unexpected pleasure surged through him. "Pleased to meet you, Wagner. I hope you stay in Pearlman for a while."

"That will depend on the test run of the new engine." Yet as he said it, Dan found himself hoping that the winds stayed too strong for the test flight, at least for a day or two.

* * *

Jen could hardly rip her gaze from Dan. Just think. Dan Wagner. Daring Dan Wagner was right here in Pearlman at Jack and Darcy's flight school. Sure, some aviators got bigger newspaper headlines, but in her estimation Daring Dan was the top flier in the country—if not the world.

It didn't hurt that he was incredibly handsome. Wavy auburn hair. Brilliant blue eyes. A commanding jaw and that absolute confidence she'd spotted at once. Sure, a pale scar slashed across his chin, probably from the horrible crash he'd suffered in November, but it only added to the legend. She tried to recall the details of that accident. Somebody got hurt, she thought, but she'd been too distraught at the time over Daddy's passing to concentrate on newspaper articles.

Dan Wagner!

Her knees wobbled as she left the office. She was glad to sit down in the classroom, but the cold wooden chair couldn't diminish her excitement. Finally, for the first time in ages, something truly exciting was happening in Pearlman. In addition, it meshed with her dreams. A pilot the caliber of Dan Wagner could teach her stunts. Even if he wasn't flying air shows anymore, he could talk the sponsors into hiring her. Maybe he could not only teach her, but he could also become her manager. The possibilities were endless.

"Thank you, God." She'd never received a better answer to prayer.

"For what?" Darcy asked as she took the seat across the table. "That Dan Wagner is here?"

Jen hadn't intended anyone to hear that. "I'm thankful that I passed the examination."

"Of course." Darcy grinned. "But you do seem taken by Mr. Wagner."

"No more than I would be for any other star aviator." Jen stared at the chalkboard, which was still covered with notes from last fall's classroom sessions. "This is my dream. Why wouldn't I get excited to see the best pilot in the world?"

"The best in the world?" Darcy chuckled. "Some might debate that, but he's certainly accomplished."

"He can do everything. Don't you see? It's the perfect opportunity to learn from the best." Jen frowned. "But Jack said he's not an instructor. And Mr. Simmons said he's only here to look at the new engine. Do you really think someone like Daring Dan Wagner would come all the way to Pearlman just for a motor?"

"I have no idea, but there isn't a lot for a pilot to do this time of year other than the exhibitions in Florida and California."

"And he said he's done with air shows."

"He did?" Darcy seemed as surprised as Jen had been. "Interesting. The crash must have gotten to him. I can see why. Jack was pretty shaken up by our crash. It took a lot of nerve to get in a plane again."

"But he did. And so did you. Wagner doesn't seem like the type to run away."

"Wagner?"

"That's what he told me to call him."

Darcy shook her head. "Oh, Jen."

"What do you mean by that?" Though she knew perfectly well that Darcy thought her hopeless when it came to men. Many a time Jen's friend had counseled her to give a man a chance, but Jen had yet to meet someone who made her pulse race.

Darcy smiled coyly. "You must admit that he is a handsome man."

Jen's stomach fluttered despite her attempt to appear aloof. "I suppose some might think so."

Darcy laughed. "Your reaction reminds me of when I met Jack. I remember noticing how handsome he was—and how arrogant. The man annoyed me to no end. Did you know that at first he refused to teach me to fly?"

"He did?" Jen had never heard that part of the story.

"Oh, yes. I thought he considered women incapable of flying an airplane, but then I learned he was afraid I'd get hurt."

"But he did teach you."

"With a little persuasion." This time Darcy's laugh tugged up the corners of her mouth. "I didn't give him any choice. Remember that, if Mr. Wagner proves to be as frustrating as Jack was."

"I don't think he's going to stay. The way he talked about seeing the test flight makes me think that's the only reason he's here."

"Hmm. That's not much time to get to know him," Darcy mused, "Nor is a test flight the best place to show your finer qualities."

"Why would I want to show him my finer qualities, whatever those are?"

"A woman should always show a man her best side, especially when that man could help her achieve her dream."

Jen sucked in her breath. "You read my mind. He could teach me stunts and get me in air shows."

"He could. Did he seem interested in teaching you?"

"I didn't ask," Jen admitted.

"Then we'll need to arrange an opportunity to do so. The engine test won't do. He won't want to talk about anything but the motor." Darcy's dark eyes twinkled. "I'm thinking a dinner invitation might be in order. We can celebrate your success at the same time. Say six o'clock?"

"Tonight?"

"Why not? We can't afford to wait a single day."

Jen's pulse accelerated. Dinner with just the Hunters and Dan Wagner. Darcy would make sure she had plenty of time to talk with Daring Dan. She would start by asking him to show her a stunt or two on one of the school's planes and work up to the rest. "I'll be there at six o'clock sharp."

"Oh, Jen?" Darcy touched her arm in the same manner her older sisters did when they were about to suggest something they knew she wouldn't like. "You might want to wear a dress."

Chapter Two

"What did you say?" Jen's oldest sister, Beatrice, stood rooted to the slate floor of her foyer, her jaw dropped.

"I need to borrow one of your dresses." Jen thought she'd stated that plainly the first time. "I need a dress, and you're closest to my size." It also didn't hurt that Beatrice had a sizable wardrobe of fine gowns, courtesy of marrying into the most prominent local family. True, they'd hit hard times lately, but even an outdated gown from Beattie's closet was better than anything in Jen's.

"You need a dress? You? What on earth for?" Beatrice asked. "You only wear dresses to church and special occasions, like weddings and...um, dances and such."

"I have a dinner engagement."

"Dinner engagement?" Beattie echoed, still shocked. "Such as with a gentleman?"

"Such as at the Hunter's house."

"Darcy and Jack won't care if you wear a dress or not."

"They're not the only ones who will be there." Jen hesitated to reveal that Dan Wagner would be in attendance. Beattie would leap to the wrong conclusion, thinking Jen was sweet on him, which she wasn't. She was only interested, in a general and businesslike sort of way.

"Ohhhh." Naturally, Beatrice still assumed a man was involved.

"It's not what you think. It's just a dinner."

"You need to borrow a dress for that? Surely your Sunday best would suffice."

"It's old and worn." Jen gritted her teeth. She would not feed Beatrice's matchmaking inclinations. "Besides, I think Jack and Darcy are inviting others, people interested in the expedition and whatnot. I don't want to ruin the night for them."

"Oh." Beatrice's hopeful expression fell. "I suppose I could find something that would do, but none of my gowns are in the latest fashion. We haven't been able to… um…afford many new things lately."

"Old is fine. It's bound to be in better shape than mine."

"All right." Beatrice flinched at the screeching and squealing coming from the nursery upstairs. "Excuse me." Her heels tapped across the slate to the thick carpet at the base of the staircase. "Branford! Tillie! That's enough. Your Aunt Jen is visiting."

"Auntie Jen, Auntie Jen," Jen's nephew and niece cried in high-pitched voices. The squeals of delight were soon followed by the clatter of two sets of small feet racing down the stairs.

"I'm sorry," Beatrice apologized, though she knew full well that her children would come running the minute she mentioned Jen was here. "You know how much they love their aunt's company. I'll look for an appropriate gown while you spend time with them."

Seconds later, five-year-old Tillie and three-year-old Branford grabbed Jen by the hands and dragged her upstairs to the nursery. Books and dolls and wooden blocks were strewn across the floor. After Jen played a game of jacks with her nephew, ensuring he won, she received an invitation to a tea party from Tillie. Thankfully Beatrice returned before Jen had to join her niece and three dolls for the formal affair.

"I've laid out a few gowns that I think might work," Beattie said as they walked across the hallway to the bedroom. Five dresses were lined up on top of the quilt. Every one of them was covered with lace or ruffles or bows.

Jen cringed. "These aren't exactly my style."

"You want to look nice for all those expedition supporters, don't you?" Beattie's tone made it perfectly clear that she doubted even one subscriber was invited.

Jen saw no reason to confirm her sister's suspicions, even if it meant wearing a ghastly dress covered in ruffles. She looked for the least frilly gown. "Maybe we are celebrating something else."

"Oh! I almost forgot. Today was the day you were taking the examination, wasn't it? Darcy mentioned it earlier this week when she stopped to look at Branford's and Tillie's old baby clothes. So, how did it go?"

"I passed."

"You did?" If at all possible, Beattie looked more surprised than when Jen had asked to borrow a dress. "Congratulations." The automatic response lacked warmth.

Beattie had never liked airplanes. She didn't understand her friend Darcy's interest in aviation and couldn't believe she continued to fly after crashing twice. From the first time Jen had mentioned her desire to fly, Beatrice had tried to talk her out of it. The reasons varied—unladylike, too dangerous, unbecoming—but the message was always the same.

"Flying is safer now," Jen reassured her.

Instead of responding, Beattie picked up a garnet-colored velvet gown. "This one would suit your coloring."

Despite the hideous gown, Jen was glad for the change of subject. "It has lace. You know I don't like lace."

"There's only a little."

"There must be ten yards of it around the waist and neck and hem."

Beattie, the fair beauty of the family, pursed her heart-shaped mouth. "When did you say the dinner was? If there's enough time, you could ask Ruth to remove the lace."

"The dinner is tonight." Jen tossed down the gown she was holding. "These are all too frilly for me. Do you have something…plainer?" That was probably a futile hope. Beatrice had always chosen the most elaborate, feminine styles.

"My everyday maternity dress."

"Definitely not." She held up the garnet-colored gown. Though it was a couple years old, it had the dropped waist currently in fashion. With Jen's greater height, it fell at exactly the right length. Beattie was right about the color suiting her, but she would feel ridiculous with all that lace.

Beattie shooed away Tillie, who had come to watch the spectacle, and turned back to Jen. "Perhaps you could cover the lace. A sash around the waist might help. Or a cardigan. It is winter. A sweater would not be out of place except at the most formal occasions. Is this formal?"

"No." Darcy and Jack Hunter definitely would not host a formal dinner. Given that Dan Wagner wore an old Stetson and Levi's to the flight school, she doubted he'd appear in a tuxedo or tails. "Maybe I should wear my Sunday dress."

"Take this one, too. If you decide not to wear it, nothing is lost. At least you'll have a choice." Her blue eyes twinkled. "Who is he?"

Jen felt a flush of heat. "No one." What was wrong with her? She never blushed. Never. "I didn't say anything about a gentleman coming to dinner."

"You didn't have to. The fact that you want to wear a pretty dress says it all. Come now, you can tell me."

"Like I said, it's just a dinner. And a celebration."

"Mmm-hmm. And who will be sharing that celebration?"

Jen sighed. Since Darcy was Beattie's closest friend, she'd find out soon enough. "Dan Wagner."

"Dan Wagner?" Beatrice frowned. "Who is that?"

"Daring Dan? Surely you've heard of him."

Beattie shook her head.

"He's only the top stunt pilot in the world."

Beattie blanched. "Stunt pilot? Like Jack?"

"Jack doesn't do stunts. As far as I know, he's only been a test pilot and a flight instructor. Nothing as exciting as doing loop-de-loops and the death drop."

"Death drop?" Beattie gasped.

Jen closed her eyes and envisioned doing the death drop with Dan Wagner. "That and so much more."

"I see." Beatrice's voice hardened. "I thought you had grown up."

"What do you mean?"

"That you'd stopped playing around with dangerous preoccupations."

"This isn't a preoccupation." Jen fought back. "This is my dream."

"What about Mother? Do you ever think about her?"

"Of course. She's the one who gave me the money to study for the examination."

Beatrice frowned. "What about the rest of the family?

We need you. We couldn't bear another loss." She paused, probably to swallow the same knot that had formed in Jen's throat. "You need to focus on the right priorities. Flying stunts is foolish."

"No, it's not. Daddy wanted me to learn to fly. It was our dream."

"Daddy isn't here anymore."

Jen reeled at her sister's insensitivity. "Maybe that's why I have to do this. Maybe I'm going to do something really important, like join the polar expedition."

"Are you quite out of your mind? That's even more dangerous. Think of Mother. She's just lost her husband and best friend. Do you want her to mourn the loss of a daughter, as well?"

Jen brushed aside her sister's ridiculous fretting. "I don't intend to die."

"I doubt Daddy did, either."

"I'm not listening to this." Beattie would never understand. "We disagree, and that's that. I'm sorry I asked you for anything." Jen tossed the garnet gown on the bed. "I'll wear my Sunday dress."

Beattie's eyes misted as she picked up the gown. "I'm sorry, Jen. I know you're hurting. You were so close to Daddy. We all miss him, but you must miss him most. But think of Mother. Promise you'll keep her in mind?"

"I always do."

"And take the dress."

"No, thank you." Jen forced a smile for Tillie, who still stood in the doorway, a stricken expression on her face. They shouldn't have argued in front of her. She knelt before the little girl. "Don't worry. Your mama and I just disagree on some things, but we still love each other, and we always will." She kissed Tillie's forehead. "I'll see you tomorrow for that tea party, all right?"

At the promise, Tillie's expression brightened, and she hurried back to the nursery. If only Jen's spats with her sisters could be fixed so easily.

"I'm sorry," Beatrice whispered. "I shouldn't have said anything." Her lip trembled, and her eyes brimmed with tears.

"Oh, bother." Jen threw her arms around Beattie. "You only want the best for everyone." She had to keep in mind how much Beattie had suffered this past year with her husband's arrest and subsequent trial. Though he had avoided jail in exchange for testifying against the bootlegging ringleaders, his reputation had been tarnished. Beattie bore the shame. "I'm sorry I upset you."

"I'm sorry I said anything." Beattie wiped her eyes with a lace-edged handkerchief. "Will you forgive me?"

"Forgotten."

"Oh, Jen, I just don't want anything to happen to you."

"I know."

Beattie placed the garnet dress in a garment box. Then Jen linked her arm around her sister's, and they walked downstairs.

After Jen donned her coat, Beattie handed the box to Jen. "Whatever you wear, I hope he notices."

Jen opened the door.

Beattie stopped her with a touch. "And I hope he's worthy of your notice."

Dan figured a home-cooked meal would be a welcome break from eating at restaurants. That was before he got the news from home.

When he reached the boardinghouse, the plump proprietress handed him a telegram. The minute he saw that his pa had sent it, he knew it was bad news. Pa never wired for any other reason. Congratulations and pats on the back could wait until they could be given at no cost. Disaster couldn't.

His father kept it brief.

Thirty head lost. Stop.

Dan sat apart from the other boarders in the cluttered Victorian parlor and read the message again. It wasn't clear. Were the cattle missing or dead? If the latter, Pa would need money, but he was too proud to ask outright. Dan scratched his head.

If the ranch had telephone service, he would place a call, but wires hadn't been run out that way yet. Even if they had, Pa would resist. He figured a real man stood on his own, and these newfangled contraptions made a man weak. Dan's brothers favored progress. Eventually the younger generation would win out, but for the moment Pa's stubborn independence ruled the day.

On the other hand, it left Dan in a tough spot. Pa expected him to come home to clear up the problem. That meant packing up and heading back across the country before getting an answer on the new engine.

"Great stars," he muttered as he folded the telegram and tucked it in the pocket of his waistcoat. If his father had spent a little extra to explain the situation, Dan wouldn't have to throw away this opportunity.

He blew out his breath and considered the alternatives. He could place a call to Joe Portco at the feed store and hope he knew what was going on out at the Wagner ranch. Between Joe and his wife, no local happening went unreported. Joe might know enough to buy Dan time to examine the engine and see it in action.

"Supper is served." The boardinghouse proprietress,

known by all as Mrs. Terchie, bustled through the parlor rounding up the boarders.

Dan stood. "Excuse me, ma'am, but I need to place a long-distance telephone call. Do you know where I might find the exchange?"

"Now, don't you go running all the way downtown. Use the one out front," she said with a wave toward the front hall.

"That's mighty kind of you, ma'am." Dan pulled some bills from his wallet. "This ought to cover the cost."

After protesting sufficiently, she jammed the money in her apron pocket. "Ain't you the gentleman, Mr. Dan?"

"And I'll be eating elsewhere tonight."

Her cheery smile vanished. "You not like my food?"

"No, ma'am," he hurried to assure her. "That is, I do favor your cooking. Why, it's the finest I've tasted in years, but I'm obligated. I expect the food I'll get tonight won't come close to what I could've had here."

The woman beamed at him before following the boarders into the dining room.

Once the door closed behind her, Dan pulled out the telegram. It was a couple hours earlier back home. The feed store would be open. He could catch Joe.

For a moment he considered sending his regrets to the Hunters. He had no taste for dinner parties. They inevitably included the overbearing and the clinging sorts. Considering Hunter was planning a costly polar expedition, he would no doubt invite potential subscribers. Rubbing shoulders with Daring Dan Wagner would bring in the financial support.

The whole thing made him feel like an organ grinder's monkey, doing tricks to line other men's pockets. He hadn't figured Hunter for that sort. He'd seemed a straight shooter whose interests happened to align with his. Since Hunter had been working on the engine for years, his expertise couldn't be overlooked. Dan needed that engine. So he'd go to the party and play the famed aviator for Hunter's potential subscribers.

For a moment he wondered if the lively Miss Fox would attend. She didn't look as if she had two pennies to her name, but Dan had been misled by looks before. After she and Mrs. Hunter left the room, Jack Hunter had told him that Miss Fox aimed to fly air shows. That meant she had enough money to afford costly flight time and instruction. It also meant he had to nip her aspirations in the bud. That spunky gal was just crazy enough to attempt dangerous stunts. She was too young and too full of life to end up like Agnes Finette.

The pall of memory pushed down on him, heavier than the burgundy brocade drapes shrouding the darkened parlor windows. The gathering gloom could not blot out the memories that raced through his mind like scenes from a tragic film. Agnes had laughed and turned back to look at him. Her bright red lips opened wide. She reached for him. The plane dipped. He pushed on the pedals. They wouldn't respond. She screamed and crawled out of her seat. And then...

Panting, he hurried from the parlor and grabbed the earpiece on the wall telephone. When the operator answered, he prayed she wouldn't hear the tremor in his voice.

"Would you like to place a call?" A woman's voice scratched over the line.

"Yes, please." He cleared his throat. "I'd like to place a long-distance call to Boynton, Montana." He reeled off the number.

"One moment, please."

While waiting, he leaned against the papered wall and

breathed in slowly, eyes closed, until his heart stopped racing. *I have to make it through this. I have to repay the debt.*

One life saved might assuage the guilt, but many lives helped would erase it.

When the call connected and Joe assured him that the thirty head were missing in a blizzard and might still be found, he could stay for the engine test run.

"Call here if things get worse," Dan said. "I'll pay the charges."

"I'll put 'em on yer tab," Joe answered before the connection broke.

Dan took a deep breath. The first life he'd save belonged to one spunky gal with dreams too big for her ill-advised britches. Another starstruck girl would not die before her time. Not if he had anything to do with it.

Despite telling her oldest sister that there might be expedition supporters in attendance, Jen had expected an intimate supper. She was horrified to find Mayor and Mrs. Kensington chatting with Dan Wagner in the Hunter's small parlor.

"I'm sorry," Darcy mouthed, nodding toward her husband to indicate he had invited the prominent pair.

It didn't take long for Jen to figure out why. Although he had refused to pay off his only son's debts—consequently hurting Beatrice and the children—Mr. Kensington had given Jack a considerable amount toward the polar expedition. Now he blustered on about the adventure to Wagner.

Jen wanted to join that conversation. She took the tray of punch glasses from Darcy and angled toward the men, but Mrs. Kensington artfully stepped in her way.

"I'll take one of those." After plucking a glass from

the tray, Mrs. Kensington looked Jen up and down. "That is one of Beatrice's old gowns, is it not? I believe I remember it from three Christmases ago."

Mrs. Kensington clearly intended to embarrass her, but Jen didn't care two pins what the woman thought.

She lifted her chin and put on the most lethal smile she could muster. "Why, yes, it is. How perceptive of you to notice. In my opinion, it's better to use a garment than stuff it in a closet, don't you agree?"

Mrs. Kensington's pinched lips tightened. "That might be the case if one has no need to make a good impression."

The first comment had been a veiled insult. This barb was out in the open. Though Jen was tempted to accidentally dump the tray of punch glasses down the front of Mrs. Kensington's navy suit, the ruckus would ruin Darcy's party and cost Jack a big subscriber. It wouldn't impress Dan Wagner, either.

So she pretended not to understand. "How true, and I have you as an inspiration."

The woman's gaze narrowed.

"More punch?" Jen asked with excessive cheerfulness.

"Don't think for a minute that I didn't understand your rude comment. If your sister wasn't married to my son, I would make the hosts aware of your insulting behavior. As it is, I suppose we should be grateful that you at least wore a dress." Having delivered her crowning blow, Mrs. Kensington glided off to offer advice to Darcy.

Though Jen was thoroughly miffed, at least the pretentious woman's departure gave Jen a chance to join the men. Naturally, Mr. Kensington dominated the small group, shoulder to shoulder with Jack and Dan Wagner, who looked perfectly at ease with the statesman and town father. Wagner made a joke. Mr. Kensington belly-laughed and clapped him on the shoulder.

"You should have seen the one I shot back in '09," the mayor chortled. "Big as a locomotive."

Jen could only imagine. Mr. Kensington had gone on game hunts out west. He'd traveled from one side of the country to the other and loved to tell anyone and everyone about it. He owned half the property in town and a handful of the businesses. He'd served as mayor most of Jen's life. Yet his only son had managed to run amok without the slightest notice.

Wagner, however, couldn't know that, so he laughed and traded tall tales, each one more outlandish than the last.

"Punch, anyone?" Jen thrust the tray in front of the men.

Mr. Kensington took a glass without breaking the flow of conversation. Jack nodded his thanks, but Dan Wagner winked.

Winked? Jen drew back, jiggling the remaining glasses on the tray.

"Nice dress." Dan's grin revealed perfectly aligned teeth. "You clean up pretty good."

Jen's stomach fluttered again. Her mind turned to mush. "Uh, thank you."

Thank you? Was that the best she could muster for a man who'd winked at her and paid her a compliment?

His attention had returned to Mr. Kensington's tale of landing a thirty-pound trout in the midst of a thunderstorm with the rising waters tearing him from his feet.

"I don't wear them often," Jen blurted out, drawing puzzled looks from all three men.

Oh, no. That was just about the most idiotic thing she could have said. Moreover, she'd interrupted Mayor

Kensington's story to inform them that she seldom wore a dress.

She forced a smile that probably came off more like a sick grin. "What do you think of the flight school, Mr. Wagner? It's got everything a student could need, right, Jack?"

Jack grimaced.

"Sure." Wagner examined his dusty boots.

As she'd suspected, he hadn't bothered to change, though he'd left the Stetson at the door. Considering the Hunters also dressed informally and the Kensingtons wore everyday attire, Jen stuck out like a sore thumb in Beattie's holiday dress. Moreover, the cardigan didn't match and hid little of the frilly lace.

"I'll get more punch." She scooted away, drawing only Wagner's notice.

He winked again, and she nearly dropped the tray of bright red punch. According to the reflection in the mirrored glass of the china cabinet, her face was nearly as red as the punch. The little glass cups jiggled against each other, drawing a sharp glare from Mrs. Kensington.

"What do you think of our Jack, Mr. Wagner?" Kensington bellowed, his exuberant voice impossible not to hear. "Flying to the North Pole. Quite an endeavor."

"Yes, it is," Wagner said slowly, "but with the right backing, planning and personnel, it can be done."

Jen set the tray next to the punch bowl before she dropped it.

"My thoughts exactly," Kensington said. "Seems like an accomplished aviator like you would be chomping at the bit to come on board."

Jen's pulse raced. If Dan Wagner joined the expedition, he would stay in Pearlman. He could help her hone her navigation skills and supervise her flight training.

"I already have obligations," Wagner said.

"Come now, this kind of opportunity happens once in a lifetime." Mr. Kensington seldom took no for an answer. "It'll never come around again."

Jen lifted her gaze only to find Dan watching her.

"My family depends on me," he said.

Family? Dan Wagner had a family? He couldn't be married. The newspapers followed each new lady friend with avid attention, speculating if she would be the one to capture the elusive aviator.

"You're not married," she stated.

Wagner's chin tucked back, and his gaze narrowed.

In fact the entire room grew embarrassingly quiet.

His gaze locked on her. "No, I'm not, but that doesn't mean I don't have family. They depend on my income to keep the ranch running."

"Oh. You have a ranch." Her head spun. Family. Ranch. That sounded a great deal like the sort of family that involved children. "Are you widowed? Or divorced?"

Mrs. Kensington gasped. Jack squeezed his eyes shut and shook his head. The mayor guffawed.

Dan Wagner didn't bat an eye. "Neither. My parents, brothers and their families run the ranch. It's beautiful land but tough to eke out a living."

Darcy attempted to rescue Jen by steering the conversation in another direction. "Is that why you want the airmail contract? Jack told me you're trying to get the contract for a route in Montana. I didn't realize the Post Office was offering routes to individual pilots. Or did they hire you?"

"They're still running the service, but they're beginning to turn over some routes to qualified contractors. It's the perfect opportunity to return home." Though Dan answered Darcy, his gaze never left Jen. "Family is more important than records or fame. They come first, and they could use the extra income."

"Why didn't you say that, son?" Kensington said. "If money's the problem, I can ease your mind. A top-notch aviator like you commands top dollar. Name your price."

That drew Wagner's attention away from Jen. "Are you offering to hire me?"

"Didn't I just say that, son?" Kensington looked at Jack. "Back me up, Hunter. You could use someone like Wagner here on your side."

"Sure could. In fact, we're in need of a navigator."

"What?" Jen squeaked. That's the position she wanted, the one she'd worked so hard to get.

The men didn't hear her.

"A navigator, eh?" Wagner smoothed a thumb across his lower lip. "If the pay's right—"

"I'll make it right," Kensington interrupted.

"If the pay's right," Dan Wagner reiterated slowly, "I don't know how I could turn it down."

"That's what I want to hear," Kensington bellowed.

The two men shook on it, and, in the matter of a moment, the dream that Jen and her daddy had shared slipped quietly away.

Chapter Three

Dan had figured Kensington for a blustering fool until he offered to pay him to join the polar expedition. Then he *knew* the man was. No one hired an expedition crew. Either a crewman paid his own way or gathered support from home in exchange for the privilege of risking his life in the pursuit of glory. Financial rewards came later, if at all.

Even with the generous wage, Dan would have hesitated to sign on if not for the look on Jen Fox's face. She wanted to fly on that expedition. He'd heard that squeak of dismay she'd let out when Hunter asked him to join as navigator. She must think she deserved the position. From what he'd heard earlier, she must have passed some sort of written exam, even though she hadn't yet started the flight training. Passing a written exam did not qualify her to fly on the polar expedition. She had no flight experience. None. No one—man or woman—belonged on a risky flight unless he or she had a lot of experience in the air. It took massive accumulated experience to deal with unexpected changes in weather, fickle air currents and fallible machinery.

Dan had carried the lifeless body of one overconfident

novice off the airfield. He would not be party to another woman's death. Since Kensington threw in more than enough to cover the cost of thirty lost head of cattle, Dan had to snap it up. This time of year he had few options to raise funds, and he'd already plunked down most of his reserves modifying his plane for cargo service. The rest would go to a reliable engine. The airmail contract could wait. If this expedition succeeded, he would make a fortune selling the story to newspapers and on the lecture circuit. If it failed, he could bid on another route.

The meal had been awkward. Clearly Mrs. Hunter had placed him next to Miss Fox so they could converse, but the gal sat stiff as a railroad spike and was just as silent. Any fool could tell she was angry. His attempts to placate her fell short. He put on his best manners and went out of his way to compliment her hair.

That drew a steely glare.

"I hear congratulations are in order," he threw out. "I understand you passed the written flight exam."

She nodded curtly but wouldn't look at him. Then she asked Mrs. Hunter to pass the potatoes.

Mrs. Hunter gave him a sympathetic look that said to give it time.

Dan Wagner was patient with family, finicky engines and weather delays. He drew the line at sulking women. Life was too short to waste effort trying to talk reason into someone who didn't want to be reasonable. Soon enough he'd be elbow-deep in expedition preparations. Miss Fox could pout all she wanted. He would stick to what he knew best.

He asked Hunter how many he planned for the flight crew.

"Two."

"Both pilots?"

Hunter grinned. "You and me. Do you think we need more?"

"I would have someone for backup."

Miss Fox brightened.

He corrected himself. "An experienced aviator, of course. A lot can happen before and during the attempt that might take a man out. Sickness. Injury. Even if the conditions are perfect, the cold is going to take a toll on the people and machinery on such a long flight."

Miss Fox gave him an icy glare.

Dan tried to concentrate on the task. That was another reason not to include women. They had a way of distracting a man that could lead to disaster. He stared at the white linen tablecloth until his head cleared. What had he been about to say? White. Snow. Cold. Ice. That was it. "We might have to deal with ice."

"Probably will," Jack said. "That's why we're working on the engine."

"That's not what I meant." Dan glanced at Jen to see if she had perked up.

She turned to Mrs. Hunter.

"I don't see a solution for wing icing other than watching the weather," Jack said.

"I meant the runway or whatever spot you have for taking off. Do you plan to use skids or wheels?"

"I planned skids. What's your opinion?"

They debated the merits of each form of landing gear as well as the best places to use as a takeoff location. Though Alaska and Greenland were temptingly close, Point Barrow wasn't accessible until late summer. They could get to Etah, Greenland, by the first of August, but Spitsbergen Island was accessible by April. The latter made the most sense, but getting the plane across the Atlantic would be costly. Dan hoped Hunter didn't plan to fly it there. Transatlantic flight was as difficult as it had been in 1919. Doing so in spring would be almost impossible.

The conversation should have fascinated anyone interested in the expedition. It certainly held Mayor Kensington's attention, but Jen Fox looked away every time he glanced her way. That disappointed him more than it should have.

Dan returned his thoughts to the expedition. "How much flying have you done in subfreezing temperatures?"

"As much as the weather allows," Jack answered.

"Any in subzero?"

Jack shook his head. "It hasn't gotten that cold yet this year."

That was a problem. "Then the new engine hasn't been put through its paces yet."

Hunter admitted that was true.

"It's a good engine," Jen blurted out.

Dan grinned. In return, she pointedly turned away. That woman was definitely not worth the effort.

Again he focused on the status of the engines. "If the engine isn't ready, then I assume the plane isn't, either."

Hunter shook his head, and a bad feeling gnawed at Dan's gut. Why was Hunter waiting to run the tests? Without testing they wouldn't know if the engines could perform under the rigorous Arctic conditions.

"As soon as the wind drops, we'll take her up," Hunter said.

It took a minute for Dan to calculate what Hunter was saying. "Are you telling me the new engines are on the plane already?"

Hunter grinned. "That's exactly what I'm saying."

Dan whistled. No wonder Hunter was holding back. It

was one thing to lose an engine, but crashing the whole plane meant the end of the expedition.

By the time the evening ended, Dan had a good grip on the status of preparations and no grip at all on Miss Fox, whose initial spunk had vanished behind a wall of ice. It shouldn't have bothered him. After all, she wasn't his type. Nothing about her fit the kind of woman that usually attracted him. Her hair was too short. She had no feminine grace and almost no social skills. She was moody and strong-tempered and spoke her mind. She had unfounded confidence in her abilities and an irrational idea that she belonged on a dangerous expedition. In short, she offered nothing but trouble.

Yet as he walked the short distance back to the boardinghouse, he couldn't stop thinking about her.

The next day Jen sat across from her sisters at the dress shop's worktable, the place where the three of them generally ended up working out problems. With the flight school closed and the winds high, Jen had nowhere to go but home and the dress shop. Both were filled with memories of their father, but at least at the shop she didn't have to endure her mother's pointed questions.

"How will you pay for the flying lessons?" Mother had asked as Jen headed for the kitchen door.

Jen didn't have a good answer. Flight time cost a dollar and a half a minute, and that was the discounted rate that Jack and Darcy extended to her. She needed hours and hours of practice. With no job this winter and no savings, she couldn't hope to pay for a single fifteen-minute session.

"I'll figure something out," Jen had answered as she donned her coat.

"Consider nursing," Mother had urged for the umpteenth time. "It will only take two years. Doctor Stevens thinks you have the perfect temperament for it."

Jen had shut the door on the conversation, but she couldn't put that neat an end to the problem. She had to find a source of income sufficient to pay for flight lessons. All the hospital nursing programs Mother had promoted lasted two years. It might as well be forever. By the time she finished, every aviation milestone would be conquered, including reaching the North Pole.

So she looked to her sisters for ideas.

Her older sister, Ruth, and younger sister, Minnie, both worked at the family's dress shop. Ruth managed it along with her husband, who was in the back room placing orders at the moment. Minnie helped with the sewing and oversaw the shop's new upholstery service, at least until she got married in May.

Both worked while Jen recited the events of last night. "Can you believe Jack would ask Dan Wagner to be the navigator? He wasn't even interested in joining the expedition until Mr. Kensington offered to pay him."

"Mmm," Ruth mumbled around a mouthful of pins. She was putting together a new dress, which, based on the sketches, was just the type of gown Beattie would love.

"In one shot, they killed my dream," Jen mourned. "What am I supposed to do now?"

Minnie cocked her head. "It seems to me that you're the one who is always telling us to fight for what we want."

"That's true," Ruth agreed as she finished pinning a panel on the dress form. "You told me to go after Sam, and look what happened." She gazed at little Sammy asleep in the cradle by her side. "Everything my heart desired and more. I agree with Minnie. You need to fight for what you want. Tell Mr. Wagon—"

"Wagner," Jen corrected.

"Wagner. Tell him that you want to be the navigator."

"I can't do that."

"Then tell Jack."

"I can't." Jen's sisters meant well, but they didn't understand. "Jack offered it to Dan. He accepted. Mr. Kensington is paying him. Moreover, he's a professional. He has his license. He's experienced. He has set dozens of aviation records. How can I compete with that?"

"You're a friend of Darcy and Jack's," Ruth said, as if that made any difference. "Friends always come first."

"Not with something this important. Besides, even if Jack changed his mind and gave me the spot, what would Mr. Kensington say? He's paying Dan, not me."

Ruth lifted an eyebrow. "Dan? Do you realize that's the third time you used his first name?"

"Wagner, then. But that's not the point. No one ever gets paid to go on an expedition. They sure wouldn't pay me."

"You don't have the license," Ruth pointed out.

"I know that, but I intend to get it as soon as I get my flight time."

"Then do that," Minnie said.

"I can't afford it. Mother only gave me enough for the written lessons. Moreover, it's winter. By the time the weather clears, the expedition will be headed to someplace called Spitsbergen. It'll be too late."

"It's never too late." Ruth fit another panel to the emerging dress. "Not if you're following the Lord's will for your life."

"That's the hard part," Minnie chimed in. "Figuring out where you're meant to be. I thought I wanted a life of glamour until I realized I was much happier with Peter." Her expression softened when she said her fiancé's name.

"None of this helps at all." Jen spun a pincushion between her hands. "Didn't you hear what I said? Dan Wagner is going to be the navigator for the polar expedition, and there's nothing I can do about it. I'll never be the navigator. It's hopeless."

Ruth looked at Minnie, who grinned back. Together they said, "No, it's not."

"If anyone can do it," Minnie said, "you can. Look at how much you know about engines. You spent half your time at the aeromotor factory watching them build the motors for the plane. Peter says Hendrick told him you even came up with some good suggestions."

"He said that?"

Minnie nodded vigorously.

"Use the talents God gave you," Ruth seconded. "Maybe it's not navigation. Maybe it's not in the cockpit. But you have other, equally valuable, talents. Understanding how machines work, the ability to inspire people, determination, creativity. Use what talents you do possess."

The fog that had engulfed Jen since last night's dinner party began to lift. "Maybe there is something I can do for the expedition. They will need lots of mechanical help. And logistics. Ordering and organizing the supplies is a huge task. I do it all the time for the flight school. There's a lot I can do."

"That's right," Minnie said. "Besides, there's nothing like working alongside a handsome man to lift your spirits."

Jen glared at her little sister.

"Very true," Ruth seconded. "I heard that Mr. Wagner is most handsome."

"Maybe," Jen snapped, "if you like arrogant, self-centered cowboys."

"Aha." Ruth chuckled.

"No *aha*. No anything. My dream has nothing to do with Mr. Dan Wagner's looks. He could go back to Montana today as far as I'm concerned."

"Is that so?" Ruth's smug smile was beginning to grate on Jen's nerves. "What do you think, Minnie? Shall we?"

Minnie nodded.

"Shall you what?" Jen asked. Whatever they were up to, it wasn't good.

Ruth pointed to Jen's hands. "I do believe that's the very pincushion we all touched when we vowed to help each other find husbands."

"That's right," Minnie agreed. "You can't duck out of that vow now, after helping Ruthie and me. Now it's our turn to get you married."

"Wait a minute!" Jen dropped the pincushion like a hot brick. "I'm not looking for a husband."

Minnie smirked. "Sure you are. Didn't you once say that everyone wants to get married?"

"I said no such thing."

"Oh, no, you don't." Minnie wiggled her finger at her. "Nothing you can say will change our minds. We aren't about to let you down, right, Ruthie?"

"Right. Who knows, maybe the Lord has a more interesting expedition in store for you."

"Stop it!" Jen threw a wad of cotton at her sister. It fell harmlessly at Ruth's feet and sent both sisters into spasms of laughter.

"Stop it this instant." Jen stomped a foot for emphasis. "I am not looking for a husband. Understand? And even if I were, it wouldn't be Dan Wagner. He's arrogant and prideful and thinks he knows everything. He's not interested in me, and I am definitely not interested in him."

For some reason that made her sisters laugh harder.

Chapter Four

Jen wanted to talk to Jack Hunter right away, but she couldn't find the expedition leader anywhere. The flight school was locked. No one answered her knock at their house. She even checked the aeromotor factory. The Hunters seemed to have vanished into thin air.

All that walking around did give her ample time to think. By the time she'd received the same negative response at Simmons Aeromotor, a brilliant idea came to mind. Her steps grew lighter along with her heart. If Jack agreed, she would get her flight lessons. Though she could not find him today, the proposed barter would still be good tomorrow or a week from tomorrow.

Since she'd promised Tillie she would attend her tea party, she headed back across town for her oldest sister's house. Main Street was busy. Jen hunched against the knifing wind. As always, she looked at the window displays. Most stayed the same for weeks at a time, but the department store, mercantile and drugstore changed often. The brand-new cowboy hat in the mercantile window would look a lot nicer on Dan than that battered old thing he wore. On her, it would make her look like the sharpshooting Annie Oakley.

After a chuckle, she moved on. That's when she spotted the Hunters in Lily's Restaurant. Dan Wagner was with them. They huddled around a table, engaged in deep conversation. Jack was writing on a piece of paper and gesturing as he talked. Darcy watched her husband with a contented smile, but Dan Wagner looked as if he would hop off his chair at any moment. He leaned over the table, stabbing at the piece of paper with his index finger. Darcy nodded, but Jack clearly disagreed with whatever he'd just proposed.

Jen glanced at the clock on city hall. Twelve-thirty. Tillie was probably eating lunch. Tea could wait long enough for her to talk to Jack.

She pushed open the door to the diner and waved at Lily before pointing to Jack's table. "I'm joining them."

"Coffee?" the restaurant owner asked even as she picked up a cup.

Jen checked her jacket pockets. Empty except for a wadded-up handkerchief and a penny.

"No, thank you," she said to Lily. "I won't be staying long."

"Sure, you won't." Lily plunked the steaming cup down at the empty spot on the square table.

"But I don't have any money."

"I'll put it on your account," said the proprietress with her gravelly voice. "Stop by and pay on it sometime. Do you want something to eat?"

"No, thanks. I'll be by later to pay you back."

"Sure you will, honey," Lily said over her shoulder as she headed back to the kitchen. "I could use a dishwasher tonight."

"I'll keep that in mind." Jen shot back.

By now they had their parts down pat. Jen never had money on her. Lily always gave her food or drink, and

Jen would pay when she got another paycheck, which wouldn't be for a long time unless she worked off her debt by washing dishes.

"Jen," Darcy and Jack said nearly at once.

It was amazing how often married people did that. She'd noticed Ruthie and Sam saying the same thing at the same time, too.

Dan Wagner looked less enthused, but he rose along with Jack. "Miss Fox."

"Wagner." She loved his expression when she called him by his last name. He always flinched and then turned up his nose as if he'd just sniffed a cow pie. "Sit down. I won't take up much of your time. Jack, I have a proposition for you."

His eyebrows rose in surprise while Dan's tugged down to match his scowl.

She didn't give either of them a chance to shoot her down. "I can help you with the expedition."

That low growl of displeasure had definitely come from Dan.

Jack, on the other hand, took her offer in stride. "We can use all the volunteers we can get."

She didn't miss the stress he put on the word *volunteer*. Well, until Wagner, no one got paid. She sure wasn't asking for money. "Good. I figure with my experience at the flight school and all the time I've spent learning about the engines, I can at least help out with the supply lists and ordering."

"That's true," Darcy seconded, though her sly smile indicated she figured Jen had an ulterior motive that was centered on one arrogant stunt pilot.

Jen was just about to correct her assumption when Jack added, "But we can't pay you."

That was her opportunity. "Maybe you can. Not in cash but in flight time."

"Flight time?" Jack looked lost.

"I need flight training to get my license. I'll exchange work for training." It made perfect sense to her, but Jack looked less than enthused.

"It costs us fuel and oil every time we take the planes up. You know that."

Jen stuck to her plan. "It's a fair exchange, and I'll only use the minimum amount needed to get my license."

Jack tugged a hand through his hair. "I don't know."

Darcy, however, backed Jen. "It's a good trade-off. Jen understands all the terminology. She knows a plane inside and out. She's familiar with our filing system and knows all the suppliers. Any other volunteer would take hours of training."

Jack still looked concerned. He whispered something to his wife.

Jen couldn't hear what he said.

Darcy countered her husband's misgivings. "We won't be able to start flight training for a couple months. By then, we'll have student deposits."

A couple months? Jen fidgeted. That was the traditional start of the flight school, but by then it would be too late to join the expedition. She would have to train for weeks and weeks. "Are you sure you couldn't start sooner?"

Darcy looked sympathetic, but she didn't give her approval. "You know that it depends on the weather and a whole host of other issues. The training planes are all laid up for the winter. Taking any of them out of storage means fitting them out and then laying them up again if the temperatures drop too low."

"It's January," Jack pointed out. "Snow and ice make

flying difficult for professionals. I'm not comfortable with the risk, especially since there's no reason for it."

But there was. Her whole chance at the polar attempt rested on getting her license now. She could be that backup aviator.

"But there are occasional days perfect for flying. Calm. No precipitation," Jen pointed out. "Couldn't we start then? After all, I'm here. The school is here."

"You wouldn't build up any continuity," Jack insisted. "That's no way to learn to fly. I'd never send a student out in the worst weather." He cast a tender look at his wife. "Darcy might disagree, but without a good reason, the risk just isn't worth it. I promise we'll start as soon as the conditions warrant."

Jen heaved a sigh. "Then there's no hope."

Jack looked perplexed, but Darcy understood.

"Jen wants to learn the basics in case she's needed at any point leading up to the expedition."

"The expedition?" Dan Wagner blurted out. "You can't seriously expect an inexperienced student to take part in a risky flight into bitter cold conditions."

"That's why it's important to learn now, in the winter," Jen pointed out.

Dan shook his head. "You can't possibly get enough experience in that short a time. Any flight instructor with an ounce of self-respect would never risk a student's life."

"I expect a flight instructor to use proper caution," Darcy countered, "but Jen has a point. If the weather is fair, why not take advantage of the situation?"

"Because I will be testing the expedition airplane," Jack answered bluntly and turned to his wife. "And you are grounded. That means no lessons until the weather is good on a consistent basis."

Under those criteria, Jen wouldn't be flying until May. By then, they'd all be gone to Spitsbergen.

Darcy must have noticed her consternation. "Perhaps Mr. Wagner would be willing to train Jen. From what I've heard, he is quite the cold-weather aviator."

"What?" His face darkened along with his scowl. "You can't be serious. I was hired on to a polar expedition, not to fulfill some starry-eyed woman's daydreams. No. Never. Impossible." He stood and tossed some money on the table. "It's not going to happen. If I have to teach, the deal is off."

Instead of looking threatened, Jack grinned. "All right, but I do need you to work with Jen on the supply lists."

Dan looked as if he might refuse that, too. Instead, he turned and stomped out of the restaurant without another word.

Teach Miss Fox to fly. In the winter, no less. Dan fumed all the way back to the boardinghouse. He had his bag packed when the proprietress, Mrs. Terchie, knocked on the door to his room.

"Mr. Dan? Message come for you."

Dan whipped open the door and took the handwritten note. "Long-distance telephone call?"

She nodded. "Joe Something-or-other."

"Portco. Joe Portco. He runs the feed store back home." He had no idea why he was blathering except that he was still furious with Jack Hunter. The man might let his wife take a plane up in bad weather, but Dan sure wouldn't risk a young woman's life just to fulfill her whim. "Thank you, ma'am."

She looked past him with a frown. "You leaving?"

Dan sighed. He might have overreacted. After all, he had a verbal contract. And the train only left this small town once a day. He couldn't storm out of here at a moment's notice. "No, ma'am. Not just yet."

Her plump cheeks rounded above her broad smile. "That good, Mr. Dan. I glad to hear it." Her smile vanished. "Sorry about the bad news."

Then she toddled off down the hall, broom in hand.

Dan closed the door and looked down at the note. Mrs. Terchie's handwriting was a little peculiar, and the spelling was poor, but he could make it out.

> Blizerd kilt cows. More then 30. More like 50. Woovs got em.

He figured Joe had told her the wolves ate the carcasses. Wolves, coyotes, dogs. It didn't much matter what got to the cattle. Fifty head were lost. They wouldn't make one cent off them. Moreover, Dan would have to replace them come spring.

He growled. Why couldn't his pa corral them at the ranch during the winter like his neighbors? Why was he so stubborn about doing things the way they'd always done them? Every time Dan argued with him about it, his pa would point out that the land was made for grazing. It had once supported hundreds of thousands of bison. The natives didn't pen them up. They didn't pen their cattle now.

Tradition, Pa called it.

Dan had no use for tradition when it meant unnecessary loss.

When Pa added to that his confidence that God would see them through, it took all of Dan's patience not to point out that his air-show money was the only thing seeing them through. Without that, the ranch would have gone on the auction block years ago.

He'd counted on his brothers to bring Pa around, but Dale and David didn't like to stir up controversy. Dale's wife had backbone, but over time she'd swallowed Pa's ideas to the point that she was spouting them, too. David's new bride was too shy to speak up. That left Dan.

He crumpled the note and tossed it in the wastepaper bin. Then he unpacked his bag. There would be no backing out of his contract now.

"Can you believe that?" Jen sputtered to Minnie as they ladled stew into bowls for supper. "Wagner refused to teach me to fly. Ever."

"I thought you said he wasn't a flight instructor." Minnie took the bowl from Jen and carried it to the table.

"That's beside the point. He acted like Darcy had asked him to commit a crime."

"Aren't you overreacting?" Minnie had stiffened, and Jen realized she shouldn't have mentioned anything to do with criminal activity.

"Maybe I shouldn't have used those exact words." After her youngest sister's brush with a bootlegging ring last year that nearly got her killed, she was a little sensitive about anything illegal. "I meant that he was appalled."

"I know. I've just learned how easy it is for good people to get caught up in a bad idea."

Jen had, too. Both Minnie and Beatrice had watched their beloved men fall victim.

Minnie returned to the stove, and Jen scooped some potato-laden stew into a bowl and handed it to her.

Minnie peered into the bowl. "This one doesn't have any salt pork."

"How can you tell? Salt pork looks the same as potatoes."

"No, it doesn't. Just add some, all right?"

Jen fished out a chunk of pork and dumped it in the bowl. The meat was pretty meager. It was getting close to the end of the month. Their credit must be running low at the mercantile, as it had every month since Daddy died. The Kensingtons would extend more credit, but Mother refused to fall any deeper into debt. In a couple weeks, the dress-shop receivables would start coming in, and then they could pay down their bills.

"The bread smells wonderful, Mother," Ruthie said from around the corner, where she was nursing little Sammy. "You must have baked it today."

"Yes, dear," Mother said absently.

Her attention was riveted on the newspaper, which was unusual. Daddy had been the one who devoured every news story. Mother had constantly chided him to set aside the paper during meals. Now she was doing the very same thing.

"I don't see what the problem is, Jen," Ruthie said as she returned to the kitchen and burped the baby. "The flight school is closed. Jack and Darcy never fly this time of year."

"But they will for the expedition." Jen slopped stew into another bowl. "And if I don't get my license before spring, I'll never be able to go along."

"Go along?" Ruthie exclaimed. "Why would you go with them? Even Darcy won't be able to, not with the new baby." She held up a hand. "I don't care what she says now. Once the baby arrives, her whole world will revolve around him." She leaned down and kissed Sammy's forehead before cooing and holding out a finger for him to grab.

Sammy giggled and squealed.

Jen rolled her eyes. Babies were fine and all, but she would never give up something important, like the polar expedition, in order to have a baby. Not that Darcy had a choice. She'd been married for years, after all. A baby was bound to happen along, and with this being their first she was extra cautious.

"What I need to know is how to convince him," Jen mused. "Darcy said Jack didn't want to teach her at first, but she was able to persuade him. She might have some idea how to change Wagner's mind."

"Wagner?" Minnie said, holding out her hands for the next bowl. "No more Dan?"

Jen made a face at her little sister. "That was a slip of the tongue, when I was feeling more charitable. Ruthie, is Sam eating with us?"

"Yes, but don't dish up any stew just yet. He had to place a telephone call to New York. It could take a while. He said to start without him."

Jen carried her own bowl to the old wooden table. It was battered and stained from years of use. Everyone sat in their usual places, leaving Daddy's place empty, as they had since he'd moved to the parlor. At first, she'd figured he would return as soon as he recovered his strength. But he never recovered. Still, the empty place remained.

When Sam arrived, he would sit in Beatrice's old spot. Jen ran a finger over the holes she'd poked into the wood when she refused to eat peas and had to sit at the table until dark. The battle of wills had lasted until bedtime, when Mother finally let her go to sleep, but in the morning, Jen found the peas in her breakfast bowl. She'd swallowed them whole with large gulps of milk rather than go hungry.

The stain in the center of the table happened when a jar of beets exploded after removing it from the home canner. Even Mother had jumped and shrieked. Then they'd all laughed at their squeamish reaction when the red juice ran all over the table like blood. Though they'd cleaned up the mess, the stain remained and over the years became a treasured memory.

"Oh, my." Mother sighed. She closed the paper and set it aside while they waited for Ruthie to finish wiping Sammy's face. "Such a terrible story. All those little ones without any hope of help."

Ruthie laid Sammy in the cradle. "What little ones?"

"In faraway Alaska. There's a diphtheria outbreak and no antitoxin." She shook her head. "They are shipping some by train from Anchorage, but apparently this town is hundreds of miles from the railroad lines, and there's no way to get it to those little ones."

"An airplane could take it," Jen said.

Ruthie shook her head. "If airplanes can't fly here because of the weather, how could they possibly fly in Alaska?"

"If they can get the engines running, there's no reason a plane can't do it."

"What about snow and wind?" Ruthie countered.

Jen had no answer for that. It was exactly the problem Simmons Aeromotor had been working on with Jack and Darcy. What if the weather wouldn't allow them to make the polar flight? Then all that cost and effort would go for nothing.

"That's enough, girls." Mother put an end to the discussion. "Let's bow our heads and give thanks to Our Lord for all the blessings He has showered upon us."

Jen wasn't so sure about blessings. Her father was gone. Dan Wagner recoiled at the thought of teaching her. Children in Alaska were sick without hope of life-saving medicine. And their stew didn't have much meat. Yet one by one, her mother and sisters listed blessing after blessing. Then it was her turn.

Jen could think of only one thing. "Thank you for letting me pass the written flight examination."

Minnie rolled her eyes, and Ruthie sighed, but Mother ended the prayer with "Amen" just as Sam stomped through the kitchen door with a blast of cold and snow.

Ruthie looked up expectantly.

He nodded, his expression glum.

Ruthie's hopefulness changed to concern.

Mother looked from Ruthie to Sam, who'd shed his coat, hat and boots in record time, and then went back to her daughter. "What is it? What happened?"

Ruth shook her head.

Sam took the lead. "My father suffered a setback."

"I'm sorry to hear that," Mother said. "I know you've had your differences, but he is still your father."

"Yes, Mom." Sam dished some stew into a bowl.

Jen found it fascinating that he called her mother by such an informal endearment—and that she allowed it. She had never been anything but Mother to Jen and her sisters.

"How is your mother faring?" Mother asked as Sam took his seat. "Caring for an ailing husband can be stressful."

Sam bowed his head to give thanks and didn't answer until he'd finished. "It's definitely a challenge for her." He took a slice of bread. "Father is used to giving orders. I suspect he's doing the same thing at home, though my mother would never admit it." Again he glanced at his wife.

Ruth gave an almost-imperceptible nod, as if she understood exactly what he didn't say aloud and approved it.

"She's not a strong woman," Sam said after swallowing a bite of stew. "Not like you, Mom. Sometimes I think the only thing holding her together is her faith."

Mother gave him a reassuring smile. "That will carry her through, Sam. During tough times, the Lord is our strength. I'm glad to hear she's leaning on Him."

Sam smiled, but not with confidence. Again he looked to Ruth. This time she shook her head.

Ruthie turned conversation to business at the dress shop. Mother and Minnie seemed glad to discuss the latest projects, but Jen wasn't fooled. There was a whole lot more going on than Ruth and Sam were letting on.

Chapter Five

"Ready?" Hunter yelled.

Dan gave the thumbs-up.

Hunter released the brake and the airplane rolled from the barn.

The morning had dawned clear and cold and calm. Perfect for the test flight. If Dan had left yesterday, he would have missed this. Maybe some good could come out of bad news after all. Fifty head of cattle was a big loss for a small operation like his pa's. Dan would come through as he always had, but it would cut into his savings and his future. If this polar attempt got off the ground, he stood to make it all back and a whole lot more. A newspaper or magazine exclusive could pay in the tens of thousands of dollars.

Hunter taxied the plane toward the head of a grass and gravel runway, which in late January was more ice than grass or gravel. Good thing, considering the plane had the skids on instead of the wheels. Dan sure hoped Hunter could stop the plane after they landed or they'd have a quick trip into the snowbank at the end of the runway. The fuselage had a sturdy frame, but that kind of impact would damage any airplane.

With every bump, Dan's nerves inched a level higher. He hadn't set foot in an airplane since the accident. Now he didn't even have control. Yes, the plane had dual controls, but Hunter was flying. Dan wasn't to take control except under direction or in an emergency. The copilot's wheel was right there in front of him, but he couldn't touch it. He flexed his fingers, anxious to grab on to something and opted for the clipboard. His job was to log every second of the flight, from instrument readings to weather conditions to engine operation.

Hunter had installed every instrument available for an airplane, but some things still fell to chance even here. Near the pole, magnetic and gyroscopic compasses would operate differently, making them useless for finding direction. The flat white landscape and twenty-four-hour sunlight erased the horizon and gave no landmarks. Snow blindness, drift and imprecise means of direction-finding made for a treacherous trip. That didn't even take into account weather issues—fog, updrafts, downdrafts and blizzards. Every element worked against them.

Today's winter flight would give them the tiniest taste of what they'd face, except this landscape offered landmarks in buildings and trees, a blue sky and working compasses. The conditions were perfect. It was cold enough to tax the engines, yet calm and clear. If something did happen to one of the motors, this big plane would be a challenge to fly on a single engine. Many years of flying meant Dan knew every little thing that could go wrong. He usually scoured every inch of his plane before takeoff. He knew each strut and bolt. He knew which tended to loosen and which held fast. He didn't know this plane.

For years, Daring Dan had ignored danger, had reveled

in the thrill. Minor problems hadn't fazed him, but causing someone's death? That was something else entirely.

He glanced over at Hunter. The man exuded confidence despite the crash that had ended his transatlantic attempt. If not for the coming baby, he would have let his wife in the cockpit for the polar attempt. Dan didn't understand that reasoning. He would never again put someone he cared for in peril. Agnes had been his latest in a long line of gals. Like the rest, she hadn't touched the heart that he kept locked in its hangar. But he hadn't thought twice about agreeing to teach her to fly, and look what happened. Never again.

He was not going to put Jen Fox in the cockpit of any airplane.

Hunter pulled the plane into line with the runway and accelerated. The roar of the huge twin engines literally hurt. Dan was glad he'd stuffed cotton into his ears, but he'd need more than that for the long flight to the North Pole.

The brake released, and they sped down the runway, bouncing and sliding on the skids. The plane was large and heavy. Was the runway long enough? Dan pressed back on the seat as the end loomed closer and closer. At the last second, Hunter nosed the plane up, and she cleared the snowbank and climbed into the crystal-blue sky.

That's when the exhilaration rushed in. That feeling of invincibility had driven Dan to the skies over and over. Up here, the world and its troubles looked small. Up here, he had control. The initial thrill of rising on nothing but cloth and wood soon wasn't enough. He'd learned stunts from fellow aviators, watched them crash and bettered the trick. Daring Dan did not fail. He hadn't until November's crash.

Today's flight made him edgy. He had to write constantly to avoid the impulse to seize the wheel. Dan did not like giving the controls to anyone, but as they circled the tiny town and came back down for the landing, he had to admit Hunter knew his craft. He slowed their airspeed to just above what would send them into a stall. Then he dropped the plane to the runway. The skids hit, bounced and hit again. The claw brake dug in, jerking Dan forward, and they slid to a comfortable taxiing speed.

When Hunter turned the plane for the taxi back to the barn, Dan saw her. With her arms waving in that ragged mackinaw, Jen Fox grinned wider than a country mile.

"That was perfect," Jen crowed after Jack killed the engines and crawled out of the plane.

She'd heard the plane take off on her way to the flight school to start her volunteer assignment and had run the three blocks so she didn't miss a minute of the flight. The big bird had soared high against the rising sun, circled slowly overhead and then made a perfect landing. The engines didn't hiccup once.

It had coasted into the big barn that they were using as a work area this winter since the school's hangar was full of training airplanes and other equipment. The barn was also smaller and easier to heat. She'd hurried up the shoveled path between the school and the barn, arriving just as the pilot and copilot disembarked.

Jack hopped to the ground and removed his helmet, but instead of acknowledging her cheers, he met Wagner behind the tail. "Great run. A little touchy on takeoff, but she made it."

Wagner had peeled off his helmet, pulling his auburn hair into a mass of curls. "Takeoff? That was a breeze compared to landing. That runway's not a foot too long. Had me grabbing for the brake."

Jack laughed. "Must feel strange not to have the controls."

"You're right about that, but I was there for you if anything went wrong."

"I know you were."

The men chattered away as if she wasn't even there. Just like at the dinner party. What was it with men, anyway? Get them together over something mechanical, and everyone else might as well not be there.

Jen tromped across the barn, ignoring the poofs of years-old straw dust that rose with each step. A workbench and tables filled the extra space. Tools littered every tabletop. A handful of crates were stacked along the barn wall.

She stopped within reach, but they still didn't notice her.

"Good flight!" she yelled.

That drew their attention.

"Jen." Jack tugged off a glove and pushed back his jacket sleeve to check his wristwatch. "I didn't expect to see you here this early."

"I saw the plane take off and had to watch. Great flight."

"Thanks." Neither Jack nor Wagner was as jubilant as they'd been with each other.

"Great day for flying, isn't it?" she hinted. "Practically anyone could take a plane up on a day like today."

Wagner frowned. "Not a student."

That man was going to be a thorn in her side. If she didn't change his negative opinion, he was going to convince Jack not to let her train until summer. "Why not?"

"The field is solid ice," Wagner shot back. "We're fortunate we didn't end up in the snowbank."

"You're skilled. Between the two of you, there was never a doubt." Though Jen knew her odds of flying the expedition plane were slim, she wasn't about to let Wagner win the argument. "That's why Jack is such a great teacher. He can handle any conditions. Besides, students start with grass cutting." That first step used a governor on the motor to keep the student pilot on the ground. "They don't even get into the air. An icy runway won't make a bit of difference."

Wagner laughed. No, it was more like a derisive snort. "That shows how little you know, darling. On ice, you can do some serious damage grass cutting. I doubt Mr. Hunter is eager to lose one of his training planes before the season begins."

She could have stomped on his finely honed superiority. Darling, indeed. She was not and never would be his darling. "Since you know so much, Wagner, maybe you'd like to demonstrate the proper way to practice on ice."

His gaze narrowed.

Jack chuckled. "Enough of this, you two. I'm not bringing any of the trainers out of storage, Jen, so you can forget that crazy idea of yours. Flight lessons can wait until the weather breaks, so you might as well go home."

She felt the disappointment clear to her bones. If she couldn't get her license by April, she would have no chance at the backup spot for the polar attempt. Handling supplies might be a necessary part of an expedition's success, but those people didn't get their names in the record books. Her father wouldn't be remembered as the source of her inspiration. No, she would not give up.

"But I can't go home. I'm here to start on the expedition preparations, just like I said I would."

"That work is back at the flight school." Jack jerked a thumb in that direction and turned back to Wagner, who was looking at her with a very peculiar expression.

"You're going to have to show me what to do," she pointed out.

"To begin, I could sure use your help sorting out the supply orders. I brought Dan up to speed earlier this morning. He'll show you what to do."

Jen's stomach tightened. "You want me to work with Wagner?"

"Actually, he'll be a sort of supervisor," Jack said.

Jen balked. "But I know my way around the school. I've worked with suppliers and placed orders for years."

Jack gave her a dazzling smile. "That's why we're so glad you're helping out. Thanks, Jen. You're the best. Dan, why don't you take her on over? I'm going to check the engines and then talk to Hendrick about their performance today. I'll take that clipboard off your hands."

At least Wagner looked as upset with this arrangement as she did. He gave over the clipboard with a lot of reluctance.

"I should go with you over to the plant." Dan pulled cotton from each ear. "I took a lot of notes, listened carefully. I might have noticed something you didn't."

Jack scanned the paper on the clipboard. "Nope. Makes perfect sense. If Hendrick has any questions, we'll come on over to the school." He tucked the clipboard under his arm and headed for the open barn doors.

Jen glared at his retreating back. She and Wagner were expected to obey, as if they were in the military—or primary school. Though she'd never been good at following orders, this was Jack's expedition. He had put out a lot of time and effort and funds. That gave him the right to call the shots. If she wanted to be part of the end result, she'd better learn to follow orders.

She shoved her hands in her jacket pockets and followed Jack.

"After you, then," Wagner snipped, apparently still perturbed at being shuttled off to supplies. He plunked that tattered old Stetson on his head and never broke a scowl.

That made her grin. Dan Wagner's unhappiness was her joy.

"Why, thank you," she said with her best imitation of Beatrice's cultured elegance. "I do so appreciate good manners in a gentleman."

She was pretty sure she heard him growl behind her.

That gal was going to drive Dan crazy. Not only had Jen Fox pulled him away from following up on the engine test, but she threatened to disrupt the entire expedition with her single-minded determination to get in the cockpit on the polar attempt. Sure, it started with lessons, but a reasonable student understood that training couldn't begin until spring. No, her agenda clearly pointed to the expedition.

She sure didn't like hearing that he was going to supervise her work. Dan had suspected that would be the case when Hunter proposed it earlier that morning, but the aviator had brushed off his concerns, saying she understood the situation completely.

Apparently, Hunter was the only person who did *not* understand the trouble he was bringing on board by agreeing to Jen Fox's proposal. That gal would not let up until she got what she wanted.

As Dan pulled the barn doors closed and locked them, Hunter got into his old Model T and putted off to Simmons Aeromotor. That left Dan alone with Miss Fox. Her arms were crossed over that old mackinaw. The trousers bagged at the knees. Given her disheveled appearance, the pink-and-green knit hat looked so out of place that he had to scowl to keep from laughing.

She eyed him with a mixture of indignation and curiosity, her expressive mouth twisted into a smirk, as if she figured she had the upper hand. Since she apparently worked for the Hunters when the school was open, she probably did. That didn't mean he was going to let her stomp all over him. Dan liked challenges. He intended to break through that crusty shell of hers to discover if there was a woman inside.

"Well?" Her hazel eyes sparked in the sun, defying him to say just one thing that would set her off again. He opted instead for a little Western gentility.

With a tip of the finger to his Stetson, he nodded toward the flight school. "Why don't you lead the way, miss? You're more familiar with the layout around here than I'll ever be."

His statement was ridiculous. Not only had he already received a tour of the facility, but she knew he'd gone over the paperwork with Jack earlier. Moreover, even an addle-brained gal would notice that only one path led from the barn to the school. Jen Fox was far from witless. Thus far she'd proven a tenacious opponent. Still, she seemed to appreciate that he'd let her take the reins.

Her expression softened. A little. "I also happen to know a whole lot more about ordering supplies than you ever will."

He choked down a retort. He wasn't a novice who'd never seen a plane before. He'd done his fair share of locating aviation parts. The owner of an airplane had to know suppliers. A squadron commander in the Great War learned how to claw parts out of anyone and anywhere. But pointing out his experience would only irritate her, so he swept out an arm.

"All right, darling." He threw on the cowboy charm that worked wonders on most women. "I'll put myself in your capable hands."

She looked a little suspicious but must have decided to take him at his word, for she headed toward the school at a rapid pace.

Dan stayed right on her heels. "Worked here long?"

"A few years. In season, of course. I volunteered before that, once I got out of high school, that is."

He didn't care to guess how long ago that might be. She looked fairly young but not a girl, maybe in her early twenties. "Is that when you got interested in flying?"

"No."

The path widened, so he hustled to walk by her side. She didn't spare him a glance.

"Then what did grab your interest?"

"Darcy." Her pace slowed a fraction. "Jack's wife. My father and I—" She turned her head, clearly battling emotion. "We saw her fly the very first time. I wanted to learn how."

Dan was glad to see the woman had some feelings other than anger, but her statement didn't quite add up. "My understanding is that Mrs. Hunter learned to fly before the transatlantic attempt. That was quite a few years ago." He calculated exactly how much. "At least six or seven years. What took you so long?"

Her shoulders tensed. "First of all, I was still in school. Then I couldn't afford lessons, all right? That's why I didn't do it before now. I was setting aside money, but then—" She broke off and ran to the door of the flight school.

What a peculiar woman—confident and defiant one moment; upset the next. Dan made a mental note to steer clear of the subject in the future. Apparently the shabby clothes weren't a front. Finances were a problem. Lessons cost plenty, but that was only the start. The cost of buying an airplane had come down with the flood of army surplus Jennies on the market after the war, but it still required a healthy bankroll. Jen Fox clearly didn't have enough resources.

Dan followed her into the building. The flight school was just as cold as it had been the day he met Jack Hunter. Dan rubbed his hands together as he followed Miss Fox into the office. She switched on the electric lighting, and after a bit of humming, they came to life. By then, she was already digging in the filing cabinet.

Dan pointed to the table. "Jack already got out the files."

Her head jerked up. After spotting the folders on the table, she pulled another one from the cabinet. "He forgot the old supply lists."

"You've done this before?"

She tossed the folder on the table. "Darcy kept the lists from their transatlantic attempt. We still have some of the items. I figure we can go through the lists to see what might work and what won't. I'm guessing that leftover gear is what's in the crates stacked in the barn."

Dan couldn't help but notice that her cheeks were pleasantly flushed and the green in her eyes had retreated into the warm brown. She had tugged off that knit hat, and her hair stuck out in every direction again. He resisted the impulse to smooth it. Nothing would get him a quicker and more deserved slap.

She leafed through the folder and pushed a couple

pages his way. "Have you ever prepared for an expedition?"

Though it grated on him to admit any deficiency, he hadn't. "That's what interests me about this project. I've done pretty much everything that can be done on the air-show circuit. Even danger gets tiresome after a while. At that point, the smart man knows to walk away. The foolish one ends up dead."

"You were in a crash, weren't you? I remember something about it." Her brow scrunched as she thought back. "I didn't follow the newspaper stories, but one of my sisters mentioned it."

He breathed a silent sigh of relief. If she didn't know much about the crash, she wouldn't ask questions. To divert even the possibility, he took the conversation in a different direction. "Sisters? You have more than one?"

"Three. Two of them are older. They're married. And my younger sister is getting married in May. That leaves me."

If that was a hint, he wasn't going to bite. "You have other plans."

For the first time since Hunter left, she smiled, and it was as if a cloud had drifted away. Jen Fox had a dazzling, engaging smile. Breathtaking. As if he was the one-and-only person in the entire world that she wanted to see.

"…then I'm going to set a record," she was saying.

Dan had missed most of it, but he suspected she was talking about flying. "Noble goal."

She beamed. "Especially since it will fulfill our dream."

Our? She'd lost him.

"We talked about it all the time," she continued. "He found every aviation story in the newspaper and saved them especially for me." The emotion returned, and she blinked furiously. "It's important. That's all. Now you know why I have to get on the polar flight." She beamed at him again. "I knew you'd understand once I explained everything. You can talk Jack into it."

"W-What?" Dan spluttered. How had a pleasant conversation turned into an assumption that he would help her? Though he'd missed the bulk of what she'd said, he had no doubt she wanted him to talk Hunter into teaching her to fly so she'd be ready for the polar attempt. He would not, could not, put any inexperienced pilot on a dangerous flight no matter how many tears she shed.

She restated her case without the slightest degree of shame. "You can talk Jack into giving me flight training right away so I can be your backup for the polar flight."

Dan set his jaw. "That is not my call. It's Jack Hunter's expedition. He makes the assignments."

"I thought you understood." She hardened, but at least she didn't pout or resort to tears.

He raked a hand through his hair. Somehow he had to get out of this without spurring her anger. "Whether or not I understand doesn't change things. I'm just a hired hand, so to speak."

"You're Daring Dan."

"I *was* Daring Dan," he corrected.

Her anger eased into curiosity. "Don't you miss it?"

"No. A man has to know when to move on."

"Because of the crash?"

"That's part of it." He hadn't admitted that even to himself. "It got hollow."

"Hollow?"

He had a tough time putting this thought into words. "What good does an air show do in the grand scheme of things?"

"What do you mean? Air shows thrill the crowds. They show people what airplanes can do. They made you famous."

That was the kind of response he should have expected from a woman who saw aviation as a romantic adventure filled with glamour and daring.

He tried again. "Why do people go to air shows?"

"To see amazing stunts."

"To see crashes."

Her eyes widened. "That can't be true."

"It is." Better she know the bitter truth now. "Promoters want more and more dangerous stunts. Crazy things. Stunts that get men and women killed. Why?" That's what stuck in him like a thorn. "If a man's going to die young, it should be for a good reason, not just to entertain folks."

Her brow had pinched into a frown. "I never thought of it that way."

"That's why I wanted to run an airmail route."

She looked up, interested again. "So you could bring mail to people who might have to wait weeks or months otherwise."

"Mail, food, supplies. That could make a difference in folks' lives."

"Then why join the polar attempt?"

She had a point, but it was one he'd thought through. "To learn how to fly in the worst conditions. Maybe we can discover a way to keep planes in the air in frigid cold or excessive wind or even snowstorms."

"So you can bring the needed supplies no matter what the weather is," she finished for him. "Like the diphtheria outbreak in Alaska. I told my sisters that they should use planes to bring the antitoxin to the village."

"They can't." Dan had read the same newspaper article, and he knew a little about the obstacles they faced. "First of all, there's the distance that needs to be traveled. Nome is hundreds of miles from the closest airplanes. Secondly, the weather is too bad. Too cold. Too windy. A storm is headed in. Even if the airplane engines started and they had a way to refuel along the route, they would have trouble running into that weather. If they crashed, the antitoxin would be lost."

Jen considered it carefully. "It would be faster."

"If airplanes could battle the elements or if the weather relented. I'm hoping Simmons' new engines will solve at least part of the problem. That's why I want to test them under the worst conditions before beginning airmail service." He had explained this need to accomplish something worthwhile to fellow pilots and even Agnes. None of them understood why he would give up the fame and money of air shows to "cart mail into the wilderness." Dan waited for Jen to express similar sentiments.

Instead, that expressive mouth of hers curved skyward. "That's a flight worth risking your life to complete."

She understood.

Chapter Six

Dan Wagner might be arrogant and pigheaded, but he apparently had a heart. Jen mused over his dream of flying mail into remote areas while they reviewed the old supply lists from the transatlantic attempt.

The tedious work spanned several days. First of all they discussed if the item would be useful for the polar expedition. If so, then they had to track down if the item had been used in the past six years or if it was in one of the crates in the barn. If it was in a crate, was it still in good condition? Jen wished she'd kept exacting records, even though she hadn't worked with the Hunters until a couple years later. No one had. When Jack or Darcy needed something, they used it. No note. No crossing it off the original supply list. That meant extra work now.

She groaned as she and Dan lifted one crate off another.

He gave her that overprotective look she was beginning to recognize. "I can get Jack to help me."

"Did I say it was too heavy? I'm just thinking about how much work we would have saved if we'd kept track of everything through the years."

"You have a point there." He removed that ragged old

Stetson and mopped his forehead, a gesture that must be habit since it wasn't at all warm in the barn. "But aviators aren't known as the best record-keepers." He plopped the hat back on.

"Why do you wear that old hat? It looks like it's going to fall apart at any moment."

He grinned and ran a hand over the worn crown. "I've had this baby since my first cattle drive."

"Then you really are a cowboy. I thought it was all show."

He shook his head, but that grin never faltered. "My folks have a ranch out in Montana. That's home. Big, open spaces. Sky so wide and blue that the possibilities seem endless."

"Mariah says there are mountains in Montana."

"Mariah?"

"You met Hendrick Simmons, the owner of the aeromotor plant. Mariah is his wife. She traveled out there with him a few years back. She said the same thing as you, except for the mountains." Jen thought back to the stories that had enthralled her. "She said you can see for miles."

"That's true. The ranch is a long distance from the mountains, but you can see them hanging on the horizon like a cloud."

"I'd like to see that one day."

"Maybe you will."

The way he said that sent a flutter of excitement through her. "You could take me."

He stared at her, clearly shocked.

Oh, dear. She'd gone and blurted out what she was thinking again. "Forget I said that." She stuck the crowbar under the lip of the crate's lid. "I'll get there on my own."

He had the audacity to laugh. "You probably will."

She wasn't sure if that was a compliment or not. "Do you miss it?" She leaned on the crowbar, and the lid popped up.

"Sometimes, but not this time of year. The cold and wind bites into you so deep that all you want to do is sit by the fire." He removed the lid.

Jen stared at the jumble of gear inside. Some things she couldn't identify. Others might work for the expedition, like an inflatable rubber raft, radio and dry cell batteries. She tugged out a corner of the raft. "Oh, no, the mice ate it."

"Or some other critter." He shook his head. "We can cross this off the list."

"You don't think it can be fixed?"

"Do you want a patched raft if you have to ditch the plane?"

Jen thought a second. "If I have to ditch the plane at the North Pole, a raft won't do me much good. Isn't it all ice and snow?"

"That depends where you go down. In some places, there's open sea."

"Then it might be useful." Another thought occurred. "And on snow, it could be used as a sled for food and gear."

Dan's eyes widened with appreciation. "You're right."

That had to be the first time he'd ever said she was right. It felt good. The fact that he smiled at her didn't hurt, either. Maybe Dan Wagner wasn't such an arrogant, unfeeling man after all.

"Thanks," she murmured.

He laughed. "Hey, I'm willing to admit when I've been bested."

She doubted that, but for the first time she noticed the twinkle in those blue eyes. He was teasing her. The thought made her nervous and excited all at the same time. Minnie would jump right in, but then she'd gotten hurt by her rash decisions. Jen was cautious. Men were friends and nothing more. She didn't dare cross that line with Dan.

"Is something wrong?" he asked. "Dirt on my face?" He rubbed his cheek.

"No." She gulped and looked away. Those eyes of his weren't twinkling anymore. They'd softened along with the hard lines of his face. Jen had never been in love, but she'd seen the way a man looked at a woman. She'd also seen how a man could hurt a woman, and Dan Wagner was notorious for both. Why did she react this way to him? She knew better.

"Something is bothering you."

"No. Not at all. Just a stray thought." And a feeling that had best disappear if she wanted to join this expedition. Most men thought women had no place on an expedition team. Too many accommodations had to be made. It was too risky. Too dangerous. The reasons went on and on. Jen knew one thing for certain. Romance would crush any hope of convincing Jack she should be included.

"Not sure I like that stray thought, since it took your smile away."

The sweet sentiment only made her insides churn more. If Ruth and Minnie knew what had just happened, they would pull out all stops to match the two of them. She couldn't let them know. They could ruin everything.

Dan touched her shoulder, and she jumped.

He looked at her with real concern. "Something is wrong. Did you hurt yourself?"

She shook her head. No one had ever affected her like this. Dan Wagner made her giddy and angry. He brought her to the point of tears. Jen Fox did not cry. Ever. She squeezed her hands until the fingernails stabbed into her palms. Pain always conquered weakness.

"Help me spread out that raft," she barked, slipping away from his comforting touch.

The conversation had gotten too personal. From now on, she would keep strictly to business.

Dan had no idea what had just happened. One minute Jen had been talking and laughing. She had seemed genuinely interested in Montana, the ranch and his dreams of airmail service. The next, that wall went up again. It couldn't have been that he instinctively reached out to comfort her.

Sweet stars, it had to be.

Most women liked a man to hold them. Jen Fox was definitely not like most women.

For the umpteenth time that week, he wished he was doing this project alone or with another man. A man wouldn't insist on patching an old rubber life raft. A man wouldn't question his assessment—well, maybe a man would do that. Maybe that's what irritated him most about Miss Fox. She didn't act like a woman, at least most of the time. She did get misty-eyed for a second but throttled that back in a hurry. He was used to women weeping and falling into his arms. Not her. That gal was prickly as a porcupine.

"The mice only chewed through the rubber in two spots." She pointed to the obvious holes.

"That doesn't mean the raft isn't compromised in other places. The rubber is old. It might be brittle."

"It doesn't feel brittle."

He was getting tired of having every statement contradicted. "Fine. Fix it." He threw up his hands in defeat.

Her gaze narrowed. "Now you're mad at me."

Why did any discussion with a woman end up at an emotional impasse? "We have a job to do," he snapped. "Let's stick to business."

Her delicate jaw jutted out. "My thoughts exactly."

Something about that pixie face and wild mop of hair was endearing. He suspected she used the dismal attire and woeful hairstyle as a barricade, just like her pointed barbs and ceaseless questioning. Underneath that hard exterior was a sensitive woman who didn't want to get hurt. That meant she'd been hurt in the past, so much so that she couldn't bear going through it again. If Dan hoped to break through that exterior, he couldn't do so through argument. That just fed her fire. He'd have to charm her, tease her and put her at ease. In short, he'd have to treat her like the little sister he'd never had.

He tipped the brim of his hat up so he could catch every nuance of her expression and leaned casually against the barn wall. "All right, Madame Foreman, now that we have that straight, what is the first order of business?"

She looked suspicious but answered. "Find the rubber repair materials. We have rubber and cement for repairing tire tubes in the flight school hangar. It should work."

"You want me to get that now?" It made no sense to interrupt their inventory for a futile repair unless she was just trying to get rid of him.

She considered a moment and then shook her head. "Let's get through the rest of this crate in case we find something else that needs repair."

Dan grinned. That gal had a head on her shoulders.

She squinted up at him. "What was that for?"

"For surprising me, which you seem to do on a regular basis."

That made her laugh, and he was surprised how good

it made him feel. What was wrong with him? First he'd relinquished command and now he wanted to please her. Dan shook his head. He was getting soft. No doubt about it.

After that momentary vulnerability, Jen got along with Wagner much better. She made sure not to look into his eyes. The cut of his strong jaw, the rugged high cheekbones and the wavy auburn hair were a fine sight. The broad shoulders and trim waist weren't too bad, either. He wasn't a tall man, but he did top her by a couple inches. If they were ever to dance, which was not going to happen, they would be well matched. She had to keep her distance.

For the next few working days, things went smoothly. They finished the inventory of old expedition supplies, and he even repaired the raft and a few other items. When the raft held air overnight, she didn't crow over the victory. When it gradually deflated in the next two days, he didn't point out that he'd been right. She stayed away from asking personal questions, and he did the same. They stuck to business.

The first week of February brought a thaw that set her to thinking about flight training again. If the snow and ice melted off the runway, Jack wouldn't have any excuses. He'd have to take her up. After all, she had fulfilled her part of the bargain.

She whistled as she reworked the list of items they would need to purchase. Jack had given her a budget, which fell a couple hundred dollars short of the amount needed. Wagner hadn't shown up today, meaning something else had come up, maybe another test flight. She'd waited for the drone of engines but heard nothing.

When he pushed open the office door at a little before

noon, she looked up with surprise. "I figured you must have done a test flight."

"No."

She didn't miss his scowl. "What happened? Are the motors not running?"

"It has nothing to do with the engines." He tossed his hat on the table, sending a couple papers flying. He bent to retrieve them. "Sorry. I'm just irritated by what's going on back home."

She took the papers from him. "Does that mean you'll have to leave?"

"You'd like that, wouldn't you?"

"No." She looked down, shocked she'd said that and hoping he didn't hear her.

"No?" He leaned his elbows on the table until his face drew close to hers. "Are you saying you'd miss me?"

"I wouldn't go that far."

"Oh, darling. You sure know how to wound a man." He thumped his chest in mock agony.

She couldn't help laughing. He had a way of bringing out the craziest emotions in her. One minute laughing and the next fighting tears. "I try."

"Ouch!" But he laughed, too, that warm inviting chuckle that meant he'd enjoyed their little sparring match. "Figured I'd check in on you, but it looks like you have things handled here."

"Wait a minute, are you saying you're not going to help?"

He propped his chin in his hands again, his lips mere inches from hers. "Darling, I'm all yours."

Someone gasped. It was definitely feminine—and not her.

Jen shot to her feet, face flaming, to discover her sister

Minnie standing in the doorway. "What are you doing here?"

Minnie held out a small basket. "You forgot lunch."

"Oh. Set it on the table." Jen knew she was being unreasonably harsh, but she could just imagine what Minnie had thought she'd seen. Dan's mouth had been only inches from hers. "Nothing was going on, right, Wagner?"

He had the most irritating smirk on his face. "Nothing at all and that includes work."

She could have slapped him.

Minnie, however, looked from him to her and back again. "Jen's really nice once you get to know her."

"Is that so?" Dan said drily.

Jen gestured for her sister to stop matchmaking.

Minnie didn't. "She's a lot of fun and will try anything. If you ask me, Jen is the bravest person I know. She is going to fly over the North Pole. She's wanted to fly airplanes her whole life, and she'll be even better than Mrs. Hunter. All she needs is someone to teach her." That minx smiled coyly. "She's pretty, too, don't you think? She's the only one of us who inherited our father's coloring."

Jen was dying. "Don't you need to get back to the dress shop?"

"Oh, no." Minnie played the innocent. "Ruth gave me a whole hour for lunch."

Jen was not deceived. Her sister hadn't come here just to bring lunch. She was making a very calculated visit.

"But I don't want to interrupt you," Minnie added slyly. "You looked like you were deep in conversation."

"No, we weren't, Miss…uh, Fox?" Dan stammered.

"This is my *baby* sister, Minnie," Jen said. "She is heading home, aren't you?"

Dan chuckled. "Pleased to meet you, Minnie. Don't mind Jen. I know exactly how an older sibling can act, since I'm the oldest of three boys."

Minnie shook his hand. "And I'm the youngest of four girls."

"So I understand." He scooped up his Stetson and plunked it on his head. "Don't mind me. I was heading out, anyway. Have some business to take care of. Ladies." He nodded farewell and left.

"How could you?" Jen choked out after she heard his footsteps die away.

"Oh, I almost forgot." Minnie pulled a newspaper from her coat pocket. "The first batch of antitoxin reached the children in that Alaska village. Page four. Sorry, but I have to go now."

Before Jen could reprimand her, Minnie danced out of the office. Jen slammed down the newspaper and followed. That girl needed to learn that she should never do this again.

"Come back here, you little scamp!"

Minnie squealed, but she was also quick. She slipped out of the school before Jen had crossed the hangar. By the time Jen stepped outside, Peter was pulling away in the old Model T he had fixed up last fall. Minnie sat beside him.

Jen kicked at the melting snow. She would kill her sister, but it would have to wait until later. She eyed the airfield. It was still firm, but a couple more days of this thaw would turn it into a muddy, sloppy mess. She blew out her breath and was about to head back into the school when she noticed the barn door was ajar. Maybe Jack was there. Maybe she could ask him to take her grass cutting before the field got soft.

She hurried along the path. The sun was warm, but

the breeze was icy. She wished she'd put on her mackinaw. When she reached the door, she started to slip inside when she heard the murmur of men's voices.

In years past, she could have looked between the boards to see inside, but Jack had sheathed the interior to retain heat. Though she'd lost that vantage point, she could still see through the narrow gap where the door met the siding. Dan stood with his back to her, facing Jack. He punctuated his point with a stab of his finger.

Jen held her breath, straining to hear.

"If you put her in the cockpit, I'll quit the expedition," Wagner said.

"Don't worry." Jack clapped Dan on the shoulder. "I don't know where you got the idea I would put an inexperienced aviator in the cockpit for such an important flight. Jen can talk all she wants, but she'll be staying safe at home."

Jen stumbled backward. And then she ran. Where, it didn't matter. She just had to get away from that traitor, Dan Wagner.

Chapter Seven

Once Jen reached the road, she slowed her pace to a walk. That's when she realized she'd forgotten her coat. The cold bit into her.

After retrieving coat and lunch basket, she headed for the dress shop. Ruth would know what to do. Then she remembered that Minnie would be there. Ruth had probably sent her on the matchmaking mission. After all, Minnie wasn't one to pack a lunch basket. No, she couldn't get advice from Ruth. Jen's older sister would say that Dan was only trying to protect Jen. Well, she had not asked for protection, especially from him.

Mother would not sympathize, either. She had given Jen the money for the written flight examination, but only because Daddy would have wanted it. Her insistence that Jen find a more traditional occupation was proof that she, too, did not want Jen to fly.

The only person in Pearlman who might understand was Darcy. She had told Jen that it took some convincing to get Jack to teach her to fly. Well, if Darcy could do it, so could Jen. She just needed to know how.

After eating lunch on an icy bench in the park, she

headed for the Hunters' house. Jack's car wasn't there, so he wasn't home. She knocked on the door.

"Come in," Darcy called from inside. "The door is unlocked."

That was unusual. Darcy always greeted visitors, even family and close friends. She must feel poorly indeed. Maybe Jen shouldn't bother her. Then again, Darcy could have ignored the knock or sent her away.

Jen pushed open the door. "It's me. Jen."

"Come in. I'm in the parlor."

Jen kicked off her boots, set down the empty lunch basket and slipped out of the mackinaw. Then she walked stocking-footed into the small parlor.

"It's so good to see you." Darcy sat under a blanket on the sofa with her legs stretched out. She looked a little pale and fatigued.

"Are you feeling all right?"

Darcy waved off Jen's concern. "Just the normal rigors of carrying a child. Weight gain and nausea. Nothing I can't handle. Now, what can I do for you?"

Jen perched on the edge of a chair. How could she put this so Darcy didn't think she was sweet on Dan?

"Nervous?" Darcy pointed to Jen's feet.

Sure enough, her foot was tapping at a rapid rate. "Irritated is more like it."

"Let me guess. Does it have anything to do with Dan Wagner?" This time Darcy's smile reached clear to her generous heart.

From the first time Jen approached her, Darcy had supported her desire to fly. She had understood when Jen needed to use her savings for the family rather than flight lessons. She had hired Jen before the school had many students and probably before they could afford it.

Jen owed Darcy Hunter a great deal. It was terribly self-ish to burden her with Dan's interference.

"It's nothing important."

Darcy sighed. "You didn't come here for no reason. Spit it out."

Jen had to smile. That was her friend, straight to the point and always positive. "I'm hoping you can give me some advice. You mentioned that you had to persuade Jack to teach you to fly. How did you do it?"

"Ahhh. Mr. Wagner won't teach you to fly."

"Not only that, but he made Jack promise not to take me on the polar attempt."

Darcy's gaze narrowed. "Do you mean in the cockpit?"

Spoken aloud, the idea sounded ridiculous.

Jen stared at her hands. "Wagner mentioned that they should have a backup in case someone gets sick. I figured I could be that backup. Why not? Wouldn't it be better to have someone they know, someone who has been working with those engines from the start?"

"You've never flown. You haven't even taken flight training yet."

"Yes, but I can be ready if only someone would teach me. The weather conditions are perfect. They could easily pull one of the trainers out of the hangar and take me up."

Darcy had started shaking her head midway through Jen's reasoning. "It's not that simple. They are busy men with a lot on their minds. They don't have the time to train anyone. Even if they did, you wouldn't have the experience for that kind of flight. I'm sorry to be blunt, but that's the truth."

Jen had not expected Darcy to stand against her. She shot to her feet. "Well then, why do I even bother? If I can't be involved—"

"I didn't say you wouldn't be involved."

"If I can't fly on the polar attempt," Jen restated, "then there's no use learning to fly." She stomped toward the door.

Darcy stopped her with a single question. "Why do you want to fly?"

"For my father." A clot formed in her throat, and the next words came out ragged. "It was our dream."

"It needs to be your dream," Darcy stated, "and no one else's. Dreams demand a high cost, and no one but you can pay it."

When it rains it pours, or in this case, snows. Dan stared at the old wall telephone in the boardinghouse, wishing that for once it could bring good news.

The day had started off badly, with a written reminder of the deadline to submit bids for the airmail contract. The US Post Office must be struggling to get bids if they were soliciting him based on an initial inquiry. The fellow handling the bids had written personally. The letter had raised doubts in Dan's mind. Was he making the right decision? An airmail route offered a comparatively secure future. The polar attempt—headed by a man who'd failed in his transatlantic attempt—was a long shot. The prudent man would choose the airmail route. Daring Dan had never been known as prudent.

On top of that, with calm winds and clear skies, he'd expected another test flight only to have one engine toss a valve when they started it. The next layer came when Jen snapped at him as if it was his fault that her sister had decided to play matchmaker.

The long-distance call from Montana was the cherry on the ice cream sundae. Apparently the blizzard had drifted so much snow onto the old barn roof that one end collapsed. They'd salvaged the feed and straw, but a new roof had to be built. That meant more money, which Dan didn't have.

"Can't it wait?" he said when Joe stopped long enough for him to get a word in edgewise.

"What? Are you out of yer mind? The feed'll rot if it's not covered."

"I thought you said they got it into the other half of the barn."

"Yes, but the roof's gone. The snow's blowing in as we speak. You need to git a roof up, son, or that herd'll starve."

Dan did a double take. "I thought the herd was on the range."

"Nope. Yer pa brung 'em down to pasture once the blizzard let up. Didn't want to lose any more, I figure."

Only that could have changed Pa's mind. Dan had suffered through a bout of measles without the benefit of a doctor, but let one cow go off her feed and Pa would call out the troops. *Cattle are money*, his pa had said. *Without cattle, we don't eat. Plain and simple.* Even though Dan had sunk fortunes into the business, his contributions didn't compare to working the herd.

"You still there?" Joe's voice crackled over the line.

Dan snapped back to attention. The connection could drop at any moment. "Yes, sir. I'll see what I can do."

"Yer pa's not gonna like that answer."

Dan fumed. His pa never liked Dan's answers. "I'll find some way to get together the money for the roof. You tell Pa to go ahead and get the work done."

"Thanks, Dan. Yer pa'll be mighty glad to hear that." The static increased, obliterating half of Joe's words. "… mighty proud…"

The connection broke, and Dan hung up the receiver.

His only choices were sending the savings he'd set aside for setting up the airmail route or begging Kensington for an advance. He fingered the letter in his pocket. The airmail route was his safety net in case this unlikely polar expedition didn't get off the ground. No, he wouldn't sacrifice that parachute.

He would beg.

The last time he'd seen Kensington was at Hunter's party. The man had blustered and boasted like the best politician. Dan hadn't heard much of it, because his attention had been captivated by a pretty woman in a dark red dress. Maybe it was her discomfort, maybe her total lack of artifice, but he could not look away.

How different Jen Fox was in her own surroundings. The flight school was home to her. She knew where every little thing was located. She could put her finger on the last detail. She wanted the impossible and was just determined enough to talk her way into it.

Securing Jack's promise that she would not be in the cockpit during the polar attempt had been the one good thing that came out of the day.

Wagner didn't show up at all on Friday, which was just fine with Jen. She could manage the supply operation without his supervision and distracting conversation. It also kept her sisters away. Though she'd scolded Minnie over that ridiculous matchmaking attempt, neither Minnie nor Ruth had shown any remorse.

When Jen arrived to help close the dress shop late that afternoon, any customers had left. Minnie and Ruth were deep in conversation. They looked up with a decidedly guilty expression.

"What's going on?" Jen prodded.

"Nothing," her sisters said in unison.

They then looked at each other. Minnie mouthed something. Ruth shook her head.

Jen had no interest in their scheming as long as it didn't concern her. "Where's Sam?"

Ruth's husband often worked in the back room, unless there were customers. Some women preferred to do business with him, which would have irritated Jen to no end but didn't seem to bother Ruth at all.

Jen's older sister waved a hand but also didn't meet her gaze. "He had some errands to run, and then he planned to check the post."

The post office also happened to be the telegraph office and telephone exchange, all of which were manned by the biggest gossip in Pearlman.

Jen glanced around the shop. Other than one of Ruth's design projects, it looked overly tidy. Judging by the slim stack of orders, no customers had stopped in. She recalled the same three orders on the metal spindle yesterday. Jen had never stitched so much as a hem, but she knew that meant trouble.

"Is that all the work you have lined up?"

Ruth glanced at the spindle and shrugged. "It's always slow this time of year. Those are waiting for fabric to arrive."

Jen frowned. In the past, Ruth would have fretted over the lack of business. Now she didn't seem to care. "How much trouble are we in?"

"Trouble?" Ruth blinked. "None at all, thank you."

That response came too quickly. Jen turned to Minnie.

"It's slow," her baby sister admitted, "but we should get some alterations and repair orders before and after the Valentine's Day Ball."

Jen had forgotten about the annual soiree for the Pearlman elite. "That's only a week away. Shouldn't you have gotten orders by now?"

"Genevieve Fox," Ruth exclaimed, "since when have you cared about business at the dress shop? You only come here to talk or when I ask you to watch the shop because Minnie and Sam and I are busy."

Jen cringed at the use of her detested given name and raised her hands in surrender. "All right. I don't know a thing."

But she still suspected things were not as rosy as Ruth let on. If business plummeted at the dress shop, they were all in trouble. Jen didn't have a paying job this time of year. Minnie had dropped all her housecleaning clients now that she was also helping her fiancé, Peter, at the motor garage by doing the billing.

Again Ruth looked at Minnie. This time they both nodded.

"The more important matter is the Valentine's Ball," Ruth said far too cheerfully. "Minnie and I have been talking, and we decided you need a new gown."

"Whatever for? People like us don't get invited to the ball. Minnie used to work at it."

Jen's baby sister made a face. "Thanks for the reminder."

That might have been an unwarranted jab, but Jen did not need or want a dress. "The point is, I wouldn't go to that ball even if I was invited, and I won't be. You and I both know that. The ball is for the people who live on the Hill." The wealthy part of Pearlman had been dubbed the Hill due to its location on the large hill overlooking town.

"I heard it's going to be different this year," Ruth said with a dramatic pause.

"You heard? Oh, from Sam."

Ruth had married into a wealthy family, though Sam's

father had disinherited him for marrying her. He still would know what the social elite had planned.

"Not from Sam." Ruth grinned at Minnie. "In fact, I'm surprised you didn't know, considering you're working on the polar expedition."

Now Jen was confused. "What does the expedition have to do with the ball?"

"I understand that everyone involved with the expedition is going to receive an invitation," Ruth said triumphantly. "Since you're involved, you must be invited. That means you need a new gown. That ghastly Christmas dress that Beatrice loaned you won't do. Aside from being horribly out of date, it's not suited to your temperament at all."

At the thought of receiving an invitation, Jen's pulse accelerated. She had to admit it would be fun to walk in the shoes of the elite if only for a night. Moreover, Wagner would be there. Though she was still angry with him, a dance might be entertaining. She could stomp on his toes. On the other hand, Ruthie designed glamorous, overstated gowns. Those were definitely not to her taste.

"My temperament would like a leather coat and boots," Jen countered. "I don't suppose you had that in mind."

Minnie giggled. "Don't be silly. Ruthie designed the most beautiful dress for you. It's perfect. Not a bit of lace or anything frilly. You'll love it."

Ruth slipped a sketch across the worktable.

Even in the dull light of the oil lamp, the dress took Jen's breath away. Minnie was right. It didn't have any ornamentation beyond a simple sash gathered at the hip. The handkerchief hem and sweeping boyish cut were the height of fashion. Ruth had even drawn a short-haired model. A sleek band encircled her head, sporting a small feather.

"With your coloring, a deeper, more russet red would work well." Ruth laid a sample fabric on the table.

Jen fingered the airy material. "It's silk. We can't afford silk."

Ruth looked at Minnie. "It's something we found lying around in the shop. What do you think? Do you like it?"

Jen ran her hand over the fabric one more time. "It's beautiful, but I can't." She pushed the sketch and fabric away. "Wagner will get invited but not me. I'm just working on supplies, part of the support crew. The crew is never included."

"I'm sure you're wrong," Ruth whispered, "but even if you're right, this gown won't go to waste." Again she looked to Minnie.

"That's right," Minnie gushed. "You can wear it for my wedding. I want you to be my maid of honor."

Ruthie pressed her hands together. "Isn't that wonderful?"

Jen did not enjoy weddings. Each one reminded her how far she was from ever finding the sort of man she would want to spend a lifetime with. They also reminded her of Daddy's promise to one day walk her down the aisle and how that would never come true now. She must have let the moment of sorrow show, for Minnie's excitement changed to a stricken look.

"Say you'll do it?" Minnie's wide blue eyes begged for Jen's agreement. "Please? It would mean so much to me. You're the only one I even considered."

How could Jen deny her baby sister? That day wasn't about Jen's dashed hopes or broken dreams, it was about Minnie. She smiled as broadly as she could manage. "Of course I will."

Minnie screeched and threw her arms around Jen. "Oh, thank you. Thank you."

"Then it's settled." Ruth snatched up the sketch and fabric. "We will make the dress."

"All right. I'll wear it to the wedding." Jen extricated herself from Minnie's enthusiasm.

"And to the ball. I know you will," Minnie insisted. "From the way Dan Wagner was looking at you yesterday, I have no doubt he will ask you to go with him."

Jen's sisters were so excited with their plotting and planning that she couldn't disappoint them. Soon enough they'd learn that even if Dan Wagner did ask her to the ball, she would never accept.

Chapter Eight

Jen had trouble focusing on the conversation at supper that night. Minnie chattered on and on about her wedding plans, but Ruthie and Sam were unusually quiet.

Before the sisters closed the dress shop, Sam had arrived with the mail and a glum expression. He and Ruth had vanished into the back room. Perhaps he had received bad news from home. Sam's father had suffered a stroke of apoplexy, much like the ones that had gradually weakened Daddy. Jen expected Sam or Ruth to reveal what had happened once they were all gathered around the table, but thus far they had remained silent. Maybe the problem wasn't with Sam's family but something else entirely. If the lack of orders on the spindle was any indication, the dress shop was struggling financially. If only one of them would spill what was wrong.

Instead, Minnie told Mother that Jen had agreed to be her maid of honor before dancing off into a discussion of flowers, decorations and other uninteresting aspects of getting married. If Jen ever wedded, she would elope and forget all this fuss.

Much more interesting to her were the looks that Sam and Ruth gave each other. Somehow they managed to ask and answer questions without saying a word. It only ended when the baby started fussing and Ruth got up to check on him.

Then Sam turned his attention to Jen. "Did you read the article in the newspaper about that diphtheria outbreak in Alaska?"

"Is there another update today?" Jen eyed the newspaper, carefully folded beside her mother's plate. Mother wouldn't let her read it during the meal, but maybe later. "I thought it was all settled."

"Apparently they need more antitoxin up in Nome than the dogsleds brought the first time." Sam tore a piece of bread in half and dipped it in the bean soup. "They're trying to decide how to send it this time. I thought you'd be interested to know that they might try airplanes."

"That's smart. If the weather's good, they should be able to do it."

"Hmm. Apparently the government has gotten involved in the matter. Some think the debate over how to transport it has gotten too political."

Jen read disapproval in his comment. Though Sam had been raised in the cradle of capitalism, he now espoused a community-centered approach that placed people's welfare first. Jen didn't disagree, but she believed progress could bring the same result. "All that matters is getting the serum there by the fastest means. If an airplane can get it there in half the time, then they should use airplanes."

"I don't suppose there's any chance you're biased." His grin betrayed he was teasing.

"Not at all," she shot back.

"I understand that the new man on the polar expedition is a whiz with cold-weather flying."

"He knows a lot," Jen admitted. His description of how

the weather would affect the plane on a polar attempt had stuck in her mind. "But he doesn't know everything. He came here to see the new expedition engines."

"And stayed on for the expedition."

Ruth returned. "Or maybe he had another reason for staying."

Jen felt an uncomfortable heat creep into her cheeks and shoveled soup into her mouth so she wouldn't have to respond to Ruthie's prodding.

Mother must have finished discussing Minnie's wedding, for she chimed in. "I heard at the Ladies' Aid Society meeting that Mr. Wagner is getting paid. Are they paying you, too?"

Jen choked on a mouthful of soup and coughed into her napkin. She had to swallow half a glass of water before she could talk, but she did shake her head hoping to stop this line of inquiry.

"Why not?" Mother asked.

"Because they don't pay crew." Jen gulped another mouthful of water.

Ruth handed her a piece of bread. "That will help calm your throat."

Jen took a bite. At least she wouldn't have to answer while chewing.

"Well, they should," Mother said. "Crew perform an important job. Jen, I insist you ask the Hunters for your usual wage."

"I can't."

"Of course you can. You work for the flight school when it's open. They value your work."

"No," Jen said. "You don't understand. We already have an agreement. I'm working on the expedition in exchange for flight lessons."

Mother's lips pressed into a line of disapproval before

she shook her head. "Then you're determined to go forward with this nonsense."

"It's not nonsense—"

Mother raised a hand, silencing her. "How will you afford an airplane? How will you even afford fuel? I should never have encouraged this foolish idea by giving you the money to take the flight examination. If your father hadn't insisted, I would never have done it. Now look where it has led, to precisely where I told him it would. This course has no future, Genevieve. You need to stop dreaming and start living." She pushed the newspaper down the table.

Jen glanced at the page. It wasn't folded to the front page or even the article about the diphtheria outbreak. No, it was carefully folded to an advertisement by a hospital in Grand Rapids.

"Accepting students for the nursing program," Jen read.

Mother nodded. "An honorable and necessary profession."

"But I don't want to be a nurse."

"Genevieve, growing up means doing things you don't want to do. A woman takes responsibility for her life and her family."

Jen flinched. Maybe Ruth and Sam's somber expressions did center on the decline in business at the dress shop. Maybe the family needed a steady income. She stared at the remainder of her soup, no longer hungry.

Mother threw out the winning card. "Your father would be proud if you became a nurse. If not for nurses, he would have suffered greatly. He always said that he owed his life to their care. It's a noble calling, Genevieve, one you should seriously consider."

Jen bit her lip. "I'll think about it."

"Pray upon it," Mother counseled. "Spend some time seeking the Lord's guidance, and in the meantime, write a letter of application. It won't hurt, and it will give you the option to enter the program should the Lord lead you in that direction. I believe the advertisement says students can enter the program in March. Letters of application must be received by next Friday. That gives you a few days to compose and send the letter."

Mother was dead serious this time. Jen could only change her mind if she could get Jack to pay her for her work on the expedition. He would never do that. Neither would the chief subscriber. Mr. Kensington might pay for a first-rate pilot to join the expedition, but he would never pay for a supply clerk.

She would have to write the letter of application to appease Mother and pray the program would not accept her.

The next day, Dan and Jack Hunter attempted the test flight again. The clouds hung low on the unseasonably warm day. They lifted off without trouble and made a broad circuit before the left engine coughed. That put an abrupt end to the flight. Jack brought the big plane down without incident and rolled her into the barn, but they discovered icing when they tore into the carburetor.

The right engine, on the other hand, had no icing at all.

Hunter wiped his forehead. "I don't know what's going on."

Dan didn't, either. "The conditions were perfect for icing. Temperature just above freezing at ground level, low clouds and mist. Either they both should have iced or neither of them."

"Exactly." Hunter crawled off the ladder and tossed the wrench on the worktable. "Why just the left engine? It makes no sense."

"Maybe we consider this an anomaly and test it again."

Hunter gave him a sharp look. "Maybe you want to risk your life, but I don't. Both could ice next time. Then we end up splattered on the ground. I escaped one of those crashes and don't want to try it a second time."

Dan was beginning to wonder if this expedition would ever get off the ground. Thanks to the roof collapse on his father's barn, he was into Kensington for a lot of cash. On the air-show circuit, Dan Wagner either delivered, or he took no fee. If weather or airplane trouble grounded him, he refused any money above expenses, much to his manager's irritation. That unwritten rule had garnered Dan the overwhelming support of promoters, though.

Since he'd already drawn an advance from Kensington, he either had to deliver the promised polar attempt or repay the man. That meant draining his savings and heading back to the air-show circuit.

"Are you calling a halt to the polar attempt?" He blew out in frustration. "I have a lot riding on this. There's still time to get a bid in for the airmail route." He'd have to do it without the new engine, but it was better than stunt flying.

Hunter wiped his jaw with the rag. "It wouldn't hurt to send in a bid. If we can't get the engines working properly by the end of the month, you can pull out."

"I doubt Kensington will accept those terms."

"Kensington doesn't have to know. It'll only come into play if this project collapses."

This time Dan scrubbed his chin. "I suppose that's the safe route, but I already got an advance from Kensington. I'd have to pay that back, and I wanted to put my savings toward a new engine."

"Tough decision. Hendrick and I will do our best to

figure out this icing problem, but I can't make any guarantees."

"That's the trouble. No guarantees. Not here or anywhere." Dan groused about the situation, but he would play it safe and prepare a bid. If they got the engines working, he wouldn't send it in. "Now let's figure out this icing problem. The left engine's carburetor iced. The right engine didn't. Why?"

"They're not running at the same temperature." That feminine voice belonged to Jen Fox.

Dan felt a quickening of his pulse and the irrational desire to know if she'd come here to see him or if she was just interested in the engine test.

Hunter swiveled toward her. "What are you doing here on a Saturday?"

"Watching your test flight." Her expressive hands were tucked in the pockets of that ragged mackinaw. "The engine started sputtering when you reached altitude."

"I adjusted the fuel mixture," Hunter said.

She shook her head. "It's not the fuel mixture. That sounds different."

"Sounds?" Dan asked.

"The cough from a bad fuel mix is different from when the engine is starved for fuel. It's more like too lean a mix, but not quite the same."

Dan looked at Hunter. He must think Jen was crazy, too. There wasn't a difference in the sound. That was all her imagination. "They sound the same to me."

"That's because you're in the plane." She looked at him as if he should have known this. "It's hard to hear the difference when those engines are roaring in your cotton-stuffed ears."

Cotton-stuffed ears indeed. She probably figured his

head was stuffed with cotton, too. "I can hear perfectly well."

She rolled her eyes and put her efforts into convincing Hunter, who for some reason seemed to find this amusing. After a long explanation, she reiterated her observation that the left engine must be running too cool. "If you'd been here, you would have heard it."

"What do you suggest?" Hunter said. "I can't be in the plane and on the ground at the same time."

"Have Wagner take it up, then. I'll ride copilot."

"You?" Dan sputtered. "You haven't even done grass cutting yet. What qualifies you to ride copilot?"

"I know the engines."

"Then you should be on the ground," he insisted. "Not in the air where, as you just said, you wouldn't be able to hear the engines correctly." If she thought she was going to talk him into giving her flight lessons, she was mistaken.

She crossed her arms and tapped her toe. "Jack asked how he could hear it. Since you don't believe my report, I'm giving you an alternative."

"A lousy alternative." He crossed his arms, too. "If you know so much about the engines, then you'd also know what the problem is."

"Maybe I do."

"Then tell us." He was getting tired of this game.

"I will if you'd give me a chance."

Dan snorted. "I've given you every chance in the world, and you've led us on some wild-goose chase over how an engine sounds different depending on the problem. All right, Miss Fox. Tell me what's wrong."

"The cowling."

"The what?" Dan and Hunter said at the same time.

"Have you checked the cold-weather cowling? Maybe

the one on the left engine isn't quite the same as the one on the right."

"Brilliant," Hunter muttered. "I'll get Hendrick on it right away."

Dan had his doubts. The cowling looked perfectly fine. No dents or dings. Nothing that would point to a problem.

"Thanks, Jen." Hunter patted his leather jacket. "That reminds me. I've got something for you, Dan." Finding nothing, he went over to the worktable and hunted around until he located a greasy envelope. He tossed it toward Dan.

He caught it. Who would be writing him? Then he noticed it hadn't been stamped or postmarked. In fact, only his name was scrawled on the small ivory parchment envelope. He ripped it open and pulled out an invitation.

"Valentine's Day Ball?" he asked Hunter.

The pilot nodded. "We're both invited. It's an annual event for the well-heeled. A good chance to rub elbows with potential subscribers."

Dan groaned. "I don't dance."

"No one will force you." Hunter grinned. "It is a great opportunity, though. Mayor Kensington is inviting several interested parties. It would mean a lot to me."

Dan had no choice but to accept, though the evening would be deadly dull. "It's not my cup of tea, but I'll do it for the sake of the expedition."

"Great." Hunter's grin expanded. "It won't be that awful, especially if you invite someone interesting, like, say, Miss Fox."

Dan instinctively glanced in her direction. She had backed away, scowling, but the moment he spotted her, she darted into the office and slammed the door.

Hunter laughed. "Not many would take on that challenge."

"I can see why," Dan observed. "In addition to having more bristles than a porcupine, she apparently has uncanny hearing."

"Could be, but sometimes the tough ones bring the best reward."

Dan eyed Hunter. "Are you speaking from experience?"

"Absolutely."

Jen hadn't been invited. That much was obvious. No invitation had arrived in the post, and Jack had suggested Wagner invite her. Naturally, he hadn't.

That shouldn't have stung as much as it did. She detested formal affairs, which oozed with unwritten rules of behavior. Jen's sister Beatrice knew them inside and out. She didn't. The last dance Jen had attended had taken place almost two years ago when she and Minnie tried to get Ruth and Sam together. She had not danced. As soon as her mission was complete, she'd left.

Then why did she care about some highfalutin, overrated ball? As Jack said, they'd only been invited to talk to potential subscribers. Dan said he didn't dance. He had no reason to bring a guest, yet the thought of another woman on his arm agitated her in the worst way.

When she first arrived home, no one was downstairs. Minnie was probably seeing Peter, but Mother had been watching the baby while Ruth and Sam manned the dress shop. She must be upstairs. Jen climbed the stairs and noticed Ruth's bedroom door was closed. Muted voices drifted out. Jen could pick out Ruth and Sam talking.

"Are you certain?" That was Mother, and she sounded upset.

"It's the right decision," Ruth said.

Then baby Sammy started crying, and Jen scooted

back downstairs. What decision? What was going on? Whatever it was, Mother wasn't pleased.

That observation was confirmed when Mother descended. Her eyes looked puffy.

Jen lowered the newspaper. "Is everything all right?"

"Of course." She joined Jen at the kitchen table. "Your sister tells me she's making a gown for you for the Valentine's Day Ball."

That was a deliberate change of topic. Mother apparently would not discuss this. "It's for Minnie's wedding. I'm not invited to the ball."

"I understand that Mr. Wagner has shown interest."

Jen flinched. Her sisters were relentless in promoting this impossible match. "Minnie and Ruth are making a lot out of nothing. We work together. That's all. Besides, even if he did ask me, I wouldn't accept." That wasn't quite true. Despite his arrogance, she couldn't refuse an evening on Daring Dan's arm.

"I see." Mother's tone made it perfectly clear she didn't believe Jen.

"Well, maybe I would, but he is so arrogant and manipulative. He went to Jack and made him promise not to let me fly in the polar expedition."

"Apparently Mr. Wagner has a great deal more sense than my daughter. Passing a written examination can't possibly qualify you to fly an airplane on a dangerous mission. You have never even taken a ride in one. The heights might make you ill."

"I'm not afraid of heights."

"Mrs. Shea said Darcy had to have hours of practice before she was qualified to fly an airplane."

Jen gritted her teeth. "Yes, but I don't have the time for hours of practice."

"Genevieve Rose. You have put ambition above common sense."

"But Daddy—"

"Your father would not approve of this foolishness, either." She placed her hand over Jen's. "Patience, dearest. Use the intelligence God gave you and stop trying to force things that aren't meant to be."

"How do you know it's not meant to be?" Jen jerked her hand away. "Maybe the polar crossing is my destiny."

To her credit, Mother didn't scold. "If it is, then everything will fall into place."

Jen couldn't agree with such a passive approach. Anything worth accomplishing took struggle and perseverance. The British pilots credited with the first transatlantic flight had overcome their share of problems and barely reached the coast of Ireland. Success didn't depend on circumstances falling into place. It depended on overcoming setbacks.

But before Jen could respond, Ruth and Sam came down from upstairs and Minnie rushed in with a blast of cold air and a burst of excitement.

"Mariah said her parents are going to give Peter enough money to set up the wood shop that he's wanted for ages." Minnie tugged the cloche hat from her head.

"Why would they give Peter money for a wood shop?" Even though Mariah was married to Peter's foster brother, Jen couldn't understand why her parents would step in financially.

"It's for the apprentice program, so Peter can train the older orphaned boys to work with their hands." Minnie beamed with pride at her fiancé's project. "They're going to build the wood shop on the land next to the orphanage. Can you believe that Mr. Coughlin is donating the property? Mariah says that goes to show that the Lord can work wonders in the most unlikely places."

Mr. Coughlin had been a mean old hermit for years after his wife died and his son ran off. He had softened a bit in recent years, but this was an enormous change of heart. In the past he'd built a fence to keep people from straying onto his land.

"What wonderful news," Mother said. "When do they expect to build?"

While Minnie outlined the plans to start building as soon as the ground thawed, Jen noticed Ruth and Sam giving each other looks that meant they'd come to an unspoken consensus.

"Well, I suppose we ought to get supper on the table," Mother said.

Jen hopped up. "I'll do it." She was restless anyway, and the chicken and dumplings smelled delicious.

"Please sit, Jen," Sam said.

She couldn't. Whatever was happening, she couldn't hear it sitting down. Jen crossed to the cupboards and removed a stack of plates.

Sam looked to Ruth, who nodded.

"While you're all here," he began slowly, "we have news of our own to announce. It has to do with my…" He drew a shaky breath and swiped at his mouth.

Ruth touched his shoulder with a combination of gentle compassion and unwavering strength. No matter what had happened, she would stand by her husband. At this moment, that meant she took over explaining what had happened. "Sam's father has suffered a setback, and his mother needs help caring for him. After much prayer, we've decided to go to New York so we can help her."

Jen didn't understand. She set the plates on the table. "Wouldn't it be better to hire a nurse?"

"Sam's mother suggested that." Ruth squeezed her husband's hand. "But we feel this is an opportunity for reconciliation. We can't let it pass."

Sam nodded. "You know how my father reacted to our marriage. He refused to speak with me. Now he can't speak. The latest stroke took that from him, but Mother says he can hear and understand. It's probably the last chance I have to mend the breach between us."

"We understand," Mother said quietly.

Sam wasn't finished. "In addition, I vowed long ago to look after my mother if ever the need arose. It has. She needs my help." He squeezed Ruth's hand. "Our help."

"Then Minnie will run the dress shop?" Jen asked. Without Ruth, there was no one else. Mother hadn't sewn in years, since Daddy's health began to decline.

Minnie blanched. "But I planned to help out Peter."

"I expected you would," Ruth said calmly. "That's why we are closing the dress shop in Pearlman and moving it to New York."

Jen dropped into a chair. "You're what?" The muted voices and Mother's questioning now made sense. But closing the shop? "What will we live on? How will we pay the house mortgage?"

Mother took the lead with her usual firm hand. "I plan to sell the house."

"But—" Jen choked as she realized that once Ruth and family left and Minnie married, only two of them remained at home.

Mother continued, "After Minnie's wedding, I will join Ruth and Sam in New York."

Jen's head spun. Her entire world was coming apart. "Then…" She didn't need to finish. The result was obvious.

In less than three months, she would be homeless.

Chapter Nine

No wonder Mother had pushed and prodded Jen to apply to nursing school. Even though the final decision had likely come today, she must have known for some time that Ruth and Sam were considering closing the shop and leaving Pearlman. Sam's father's stroke had turned speculation to certainty.

Understanding what had spurred the decision didn't make Jen feel any better. "But why sell our house? This is our home. We all grew up here. This is where Daddy sent us off to school and read us stories at bedtime. This is where he spent so much of his life." And where he'd died.

"Your father isn't here," Mother responded with characteristic firmness. Once she set her mind on a course of action, there was no changing it.

"But our memories are."

"Your memories live in your heart." Any shakiness or doubt had vanished from Mother's voice. "They can't be found in wood and plaster. This is too big a house for one woman."

"But I'm here."

Mother cast her an understanding yet firm smile. "It's

time someone else raised a family here. It's time to move on, Genevieve."

But moving on hurt. The fatal spin of a stalled airplane could not feel worse. Everyone else had determined a course and filed a flight plan. Jen alone stood on the ground while her dreams flew away.

Unable to stomach the excited planning, she finished supper and retired to her room to study the nursing program advertisement. Now she had no choice. After Minnie's wedding in May, she must stand on her own. Since marriage was not on the horizon, she had to find a job that would pay enough for room, board and—someday— flight lessons. Jack and Darcy couldn't give her that. No job in Pearlman could.

She drew a sheet of paper from the desk that she and Minnie shared. Taking a fountain pen, she poised it over the paper. What should she write?

The entire course of her life had changed. Instead of honoring her father's name in the record books, she must grind out a living as a nurse. This was not the life she had envisioned. Mother would say it was the life set before her, that she must accept the opportunities that came her way, but everything inside Jen rebelled at the idea of becoming a nurse.

No matter what Mother said, Jen wasn't nurse material. Nurses did not neglect their patients. They did not run off to the flight school to fetch study materials when they were supposed to be watching a patient. A nurse did not leave a sick father when he needed her most.

Jen swiped away an angry tear. What kind of daughter was she? All she had to do was spend time with her beloved father, but the moment she'd thought he was sleeping, she'd left. By the time she returned, he was gone.

The pain surfaced raw as a fresh wound. It was her fault. Her fault.

She'd thought that fulfilling their dream would solve everything. By passing the written examination, that horrible guilt would go away. By honoring her father with a record flight, he would live again.

That would never happen.

She must become a nurse. She must save others to pay back the sin of leaving her father when he needed her most.

She touched the pen to the paper and wrote the application letter.

If Jen Fox hadn't scowled at the mention of that Valentine's Day ball, Dan might have asked her to accompany him. Seeing her in an evening gown would be worth the sparring sure to follow.

He chuckled. She sure wasn't like any other woman he'd ever known.

Spunk? In barrelfuls.

Opinionated? All the time.

Sure of herself? Seemed to be, but that might be an act. He ought to know. He'd put on a show of confidence ever since the accident. No one knew his palms sweated when the plane took off. No one suspected the internal battle every time he stepped into a plane. If he flew alone, no problem, but as soon as another person entered the plane, he choked. Make that other person a woman, and he couldn't squeeze a breath into his lungs.

That's why he wouldn't put Jen in any plane he flew. Nor would he be party to any effort that would put her in danger. If she wasn't so mule-headed, she'd realize that her requests were impossible. Learn to fly now? In changeable weather? Ridiculous. Sit in the cockpit on the dangerous polar attempt? She must be out of her mind. Didn't she know how many pilots died in less risky ventures? And they were experienced. She wasn't.

Monday morning he sat in the flight school office waiting for Jen to show up. It wasn't like her to be late. She was always there before him, arching an eyebrow and commenting on his tardiness. Something must be wrong.

He arranged the supply lists from oldest to newest. He leafed through the list of suppliers. As the clock inched past the nine o'clock hour, he could wait no longer.

He picked up the telephone and got the operator. "Please connect me to the Fox house."

There was a slight pause. "I'm sorry, sir, but the Foxes don't have a telephone at their house. Would you like me to connect you to their business?"

Jen tromped in, shook the snow off her mackinaw and threw her gloves on the table.

"Never mind," Dan told the operator before hanging up the receiver. "Miss Fox. Glad to see you could make it this morning."

She shot him a scathing glare. "I happened to have business. Considering this is a *volunteer* position, it hardly matters if I am here early or not. You, on the other hand, are being *paid*, a fact you seemed to have forgotten on Friday when you didn't work at all."

"Ouch!" Dan mimicked being struck by an arrow. "You know how to wound a guy."

She peeled off the mackinaw despite the fact that the office was freezing. "So, what did you get done?"

"I rearranged your supply lists."

"You did what? Those were already in perfect order. Now you've gone and made more work for me." She grabbed the lists and one by one slammed the papers down on the tabletop, lining them up in an order that only she understood.

Dan had been mistaken when he described her as a prickly porcupine. She was something a whole lot more dangerous. A warthog came to mind. Maybe a charging bull. Or a grizzly mother protecting her cubs. Best to steer clear.

"You could *do* something," she spat.

That sounded like a challenge he'd better not ignore. He surveyed the remaining stack of papers. "What order do you want those in?"

She glared. And didn't answer.

Fool that he was, he tried again. "Something bothering you?"

"No!"

That woman was definitely upset. He'd weathered his share of pouts and tears. Anger was refreshing. "I can't help if I don't know what's wrong."

"Who said I wanted your help?"

He couldn't help it. He laughed. "That's my girl."

She slammed the papers down and glared at him, hands on hips. "First of all, Wagner, I'm not your girl. Secondly, I didn't ask for your help. Third, you couldn't help even if I did tell you what's wrong. It has nothing to do with you, all right?"

Dan did his best to hide the belly laugh that was building inside him, but it was tough not to grin. He did love a gal who could speak her mind.

She stabbed a finger at him. "Stop smirking, Mr. High-and-Mighty. You won't have to deal with me much longer."

"What do you mean?" He slid from his perch on the corner of the table. "Did Hunter call off the expedition?"

"No. I'm leaving."

The announcement hit with the force of a bad landing. "Leaving? Why?"

"Because I have to make money, that's why. I'm not rich like you. In a couple months, I'm going to lose my home. It's time I grew up and took responsibility for myself."

"Admirable," he murmured, but that picture she'd painted didn't make sense. "What do you mean you're going to lose your home?"

"My mother is selling it and moving to New York with my sister Ruth and her family."

That explained the short temper. He'd be upset, too.

He drew in a deep breath. "I couldn't imagine losing the ranch." That's why he'd propped it up all those years, and why he'd gone out on a limb asking for an advance from Kensington.

She stared at the papers, which she kept shuffling. "Yeah, well, it's not pleasant to lose the only home you've ever known, but I guess no one can stop change."

"I suppose not," he said slowly. "What do you plan to do?"

She shook her head. "Nursing school."

"You?" He tried to swallow that image. Jen Fox was strong and sure of herself, but she was not the nurturing sort.

"Yes, me," she snapped. "Do you have a problem with that?"

"No, I suppose not." He rubbed his jaw. His quick reaction had put them on opposite sides when he wanted to get on the same side. She was clearly upset over the decision but felt she had no choice. If he said she couldn't do it, she would go ahead just to prove him wrong. He needed a different tactic. "I was just surprised. I hadn't heard you mention an interest in nursing."

Her scowl wavered. "It's a job."

"It's a demanding profession."

"A nurse might have saved my father," she whispered.

Her words sent a shiver deep to his gut. That was why she wanted to become a nurse. "That's a noble reason to join the profession."

"No, it's not."

Now he was confused, but she didn't explain further.

She turned away and began slapping down the papers again. "I don't want to talk about this."

"All right." He didn't want to talk about the crash, either. "Maybe you'd be interested to know that the governor in Alaska ordered airplanes to take half of the second batch of diphtheria serum to Nome. The other half will go by dogsled."

Her tension eased a little. "Do they think the planes will get there?"

"Some do, but it'll depend on the weather."

"You mean there can't be any storms or fog or snow."

"Or too much wind," he added. "Then if it's too cold, the engine might not start."

She nodded, determination setting in. "Then we need to get to work and get the new engine running properly. That's the answer, not just for the polar expedition, but for emergencies like this diphtheria outbreak. Lives depend on it."

There was the passion Dan hadn't seen in her when she declared she was going to nursing school. If only he could make her see that her dreams didn't have to die. She might have to adapt a little, but nursing school wasn't the way.

"We could use your help," he said softly.

She looked at him, her hazel eyes luminous in the electrical lighting. Dreams battled duty. He watched it play out on her face. How could he make her see?

"You have a knack for figuring out problems." He swallowed that part of him that didn't want to admit a gal knew more than he did. "You were right about the left engine. Hendrick Simmons confirmed the cowling was off just enough to lower the running temperature."

For a moment, she looked pleased. Then she set her jaw. "All the more reason to go into the nursing program."

The connection was obvious. Jen could never craft a place for herself in aviation without bringing something unique to the table. Until this moment, she'd only been considering the dream she and Daddy had shared. Etching their names in the record book would secure his legacy and her career. Maybe there was another way. Maybe flying could do more than thrill crowds and draw fame. Maybe it could accomplish something worthwhile.

Painful as it was to admit, she had Dan Wagner to thank for that. His initial enthusiasm for running an airmail route to remote Montana melded with the diphtheria outbreak and nursing school to add up to a breathtaking new direction.

"Are you sure?" Dan looked skeptical. "Nursing is hard work. You won't have time to learn to fly."

"I will train on my time off." She paced across the room and back again. "There must be breaks to go home. The college students I know come home often."

"You're attending college?"

She shook her head. "A hospital nursing program. If they accept me."

"I'm sure they will. You strike me as someone who excelled in her studies."

All except advanced mathematics. "If accepted, I will

start on the second of March. That means I should get a break in June or July. That'll be a perfect time to learn to fly."

"Isn't June when they plan to make the polar attempt?"

"Yes, but Darcy isn't going, and her baby is due in April. By June, she'll be ready to teach again."

He had returned to his jaunty perch on the corner of the table, as if sitting atop a corral fence. He'd taken his cowboy hat off, and a wavy lock of his auburn hair stuck up just enough that she wanted to smooth it down.

She shook herself. Where had that come from? She might be feeling a little generous toward Wagner since he'd given her the idea that saved her dream, but that didn't mean she was going to swoon over the man simply because he was handsome and famous.

"Penny for your thoughts," he said with the engaging grin that dimpled his chin.

"Not for a dollar."

He laughed. "That doesn't surprise me."

"Are you saying I'm closemouthed?"

He held up his hands in surrender, though that grin stayed in place. "Not at all. I can always count on you to speak your mind—when you want to."

She wasn't sure if that was a compliment or not. "All right. You win. Here's what I was thinking." Not about his dimple or wavy hair, but about what was really important. "You plan to run an airmail route."

"Yes?" He clearly wasn't making the connection.

"You said that you can bring both mail and supplies to people who don't have much contact with the outside world."

"I did, but why are you thinking about that?"

"Don't you see? Consider that doctor in Nome. He

needed medicine. So might the people on your airmail route."

He nodded. "That's possible."

"They might also need a nurse."

She saw the exact moment he understood what she was saying.

His eyes widened and then narrowed. His brow furrowed, and the grin turned to a scowl. "If they're ailing, they'll need a doctor, not a nurse."

Jen could have snapped out a retort over that assumption, but it wouldn't further her cause. She took a breath. "Maybe there isn't a doctor available. Maybe a nurse can do the job."

"A nurse is not a doctor."

"Yes, but—"

"No buts. No anything. I know what you're getting at, Miss Jen, and I'm not carting you around on an airmail route."

"But you could use a copilot," she pointed out, "and if I get my flight license and my nursing certificate, I can prove doubly useful."

"No." He stood and plopped the hat on his head. "This is not a partnership proposition. You live here. I live in Montana. This would never work."

"I can move to Montana. Mother and Ruthie are moving to New York anyway. If they can make a fresh start, so can I."

"No. Period. I can't afford to take on a partner, and there's no place for you to stay."

"Maybe your family would let me stay on the ranch. I could sleep in the barn."

He looked as if she'd just suggested she move into a speakeasy. "No."

"I'm not asking you to make a decision now. The nursing program will take two years. Just keep it in mind as a possibility."

The icy wall that had risen between them melted just a bit. "Guess anything could happen in two years."

She suspected that meant he was dismissing her idea out of hand, but Jen Fox did not give up that easily. "I will find you, Dan Wagner. You can count on that."

He laughed, and the last of the cold wall fell away. "That's what I like about you. Once you get hold of an idea, you never let go."

"I'll take that as a compliment."

His blue eyes twinkled. "I don't suppose you'd care to spell out that idea of yours to potential expedition subscribers."

Now he'd lost her. "What do you mean?"

"Fame and glory are a powerful draw for some men, but others like to know that the money they're investing is going to a cause that is, shall we say, a little more philanthropic. This expedition could not only set a record, but it could open the way for safer aviation in bitter weather. That means commercial—and philanthropic—possibilities. Your idea of bringing medical care to remote communities is something they could sink their teeth into. With your enthusiasm, they're bound to sign on."

Since Ruth's announcement, Jen's spirits had sunk to subterranean depths. Dan had just lifted them into the stratosphere.

"Me? You want me to talk to expedition supporters?"

"You would do great."

"When? Is Jack hosting another dinner party?" She had a tough time imagining Darcy being up to it, considering how she'd looked the last time Jen had seen her.

"No, darling. At this Valentine's Day ball that I'm expected to attend."

She blanched. "I'm not invited."

"You should have been."

She gazed into his eyes looking for any sign that he didn't mean what he'd just said and found only sincerity.

"You're a big part of this mission," he added. "Without your work, we would never be ready on time. I understand the first shipments should be coming in next week. Hunter's fortunate to have you."

The warm glow that had begun deep inside expanded until she thought she would burst. "You're not just saying that?"

He laughed. "Trust me. I don't give compliments unless they're deserved."

She did trust him. She did.

"Then you'll attend with me?"

With him. That sent a delicious shiver from the tips of her fingers to the bottom of her feet. He wanted her to go with him. No man had ever asked her to attend a social function. Ever. Baseball games and adolescent boys didn't count. This was a ball, the Valentine's Day Ball, the biggest social event of the winter.

"Say you'll go," he urged.

She could only manage a nod.

His mouth spread into a grin that crinkled the corners of his eyes and welcomed her into a world she had only dreamed about, a world both foreign yet oddly familiar. More than a firm handshake, it was an arm around the shoulders, a "welcome to the club" kind of grin. He was glad that she'd agreed to go with him. Of all the pretty women in town, he had chosen her, Jen Fox. Fatherless, poor and soon to be displaced. As far from feminine as the jungle was from the Arctic. Short hair, badly dressed Jen Fox.

He tipped a hand to his Stetson. "I'll be back to help in a couple minutes. I need to touch base with Hunter."

Only after he left did the implications hit. Ruth was leaving, and the dress she'd promised to make for Jen wasn't done. The ball was this Saturday, and she didn't have a gown.

Jen placed a telephone call to the dress shop.

Chapter Ten

"You must wear pearls," Beatrice insisted.

"No pearls. No jewelry at all." Jen was standing firm on that point.

It was bad enough that all three sisters insisted on helping her dress for the ball. Her bedroom was small enough with just Minnie and her. Add in Beatrice and Ruth, and there wasn't room to breathe.

Mother had the sense to stay downstairs with Ruth's baby and Beattie's little ones. The men had vanished the moment Beatrice and her husband, Blake, arrived. That much femininity in one house was apparently more than Sam and Blake could handle. Jen wished she was with them.

Instead she had to endure the combined efforts of three sisters determined to find a swan in her ugly duckling. Beatrice attempted to slip the long string of pearls over her head. Jen ducked away.

"They're not real," Beatrice said, "so don't worry if the strand breaks."

"I'm not worried about losing them," Jen insisted for the umpteenth time, "I don't want to wear any jewelry."

"Your pearls aren't real?" Minnie looked up from

stitching the feather more securely to the headband. It had come off the moment Jen attempted to put the head-piece on. "I always thought they were genuine."

"We sold those." Beattie sighed. "These look nearly the same and cost so much less."

"That's very prudent." Ruth's eyes brimmed with sympathy, while her hands threaded a needle. "We don't need nearly as much as we think we do."

That was just like Ruth to put a positive twist on a difficult situation. Beatrice's husband, Blake, had racked up large gambling debts. When his father, the mayor, refused to pay them off, Blake had turned to a bunch of criminals who promised to settle the debt in exchange for Blake's help securing a bootlegging corridor from Detroit to Chicago. When that fell through and Blake was arrested, he had testified against the gang and avoided prison. He and Beatrice had come out of the mess poorer and humbler. To cover costs, Beatrice had sold many of the expensive furnishings and jewelry they had purchased on their wedding tour. Though no one mentioned that difficult chapter, Beattie still carried the weight of shame. Wearing her necklace might be a symbolic return to her glorious past.

"All right, I'll wear them." Jen reached out for the pearls.

"Stand still," Ruth ordered. "With the tiniest adjustment, the back will lie perfectly flat."

"It's fine as is," Jen insisted, but none of the sisters would listen to her tonight.

Minnie held a faux pearl bracelet against the headband. "Wouldn't this look elegant draped down like so?"

"No!" Jen snapped. "I'll wear Beattie's pearls, but that's it."

Minnie made a face. "You're no judge of fashion. What do you think, Beattie?"

Their oldest sister considered Minnie's suggestion, delicate fingertips to her lips. Beatrice had always been the prettiest of them by far. Ruth was just as lovely but in an understated way, especially since she needed spectacles to see properly. Minnie's blond hair was darker than Jen's older sisters, but her petite stature and sparkling smile drew people's attention. Jen didn't look much like any of them. She was the only one who had inherited Daddy's brown hair and coltish frame. Her square jaw and prominent cheekbones would never be considered beautiful or even very feminine. She was the closest Daddy had come to having a son.

"I think the touch of pearls could work if done just so." Beatrice demonstrated, and Minnie began to stitch them to the headband.

"Stop," Jen cried. "If you put even one pearl on that thing I won't wear it."

"Of course you will." Ruth snipped the thread. "There, it's done."

"What a lovely gown." Beatrice sighed.

For the next several minutes, Jen's sisters exclaimed over the dress.

"It's just an evening gown." At Ruthie's hurt expression, Jen added, "A stunning evening gown, mind you, fit for First Lady Grace Coolidge."

Her sisters stared a moment before descending into chatter again.

Jen tapped her toe, anxious to get this over. "Are we done?"

"Of course not," the sisters exclaimed in unison.

"Poor Genevieve is nervous." Beatrice sighed. "Do you remember how to dance?"

"First of all, I'm not nervous. Secondly, I'm not dancing."

"But you must," all three sisters insisted.

"He doesn't dance," Jen tried to tell them, but of course they weren't listening.

"Sam and I fell in love while dancing," Ruth mused. "I stumbled, and he caught me. That's when I knew he was the perfect man for me."

"He was in love with you long before that," Minnie said.

"Be that as it may, we are not here to reminisce." Beatrice pulled them back on task. "We are here to ensure our dear sister creates the best possible impression for her beau."

"He is not my beau," Jen insisted.

None of them listened. Instead they descended into a debate over how to style her hair and if she should don the headband now.

Jen had had enough. She snagged her hairbrush and tugged it through her short hair. "There." She grabbed the headband from Minnie and pushed it onto her head. "I'm ready."

Beatrice gasped, hand to mouth. Ruth pulled the headband off Jen's head.

Minnie headed for the door. "I'm fetching the hair iron. It should be good and hot by now. I put it on the stove ages ago."

Jen clapped her hands to her head. "No curls. Promise me you won't curl my hair."

Ruth pried her hands away. "We will make no such promise. You must look your best, and a little curl sweeping below the cheekbone will create a stunning modern look."

Ruth demonstrated, and Jen stared at her image in the

mirror. That did look elegant, very much like a moving-picture actress.

"You will look beautiful," Ruth said, "and Mr. Wagner will fall in love."

"I don't want him to fall in love. I want to convey an image of confidence so Jack can get additional subscribers for the expedition."

Ruth dismissed that motive. "Do you remember helping me the night of the Grange hall dance? You and Minnie arranged everything and made sure I looked my best."

"That was different."

Ruth shook her head. "It was exactly the same, and look what happened. Sam and I fell in love and married." Her eyes misted. "It was the most important night of my life."

Could Jen attract Dan Wagner in the same way? She stared at her reflection. No matter how her cropped hair was arranged and how many pearls she wore, her jaw was still square and her face too plain. Daring Dan had always chosen the most beautiful women—actresses and singers, heiresses and famed adventurers. She was none of those.

"What if something goes wrong?" she mumbled.

"It won't," Ruth assured her. "You are always so confident and poised. You'll do wonderfully."

"I don't mean just tonight. What if he does like me? What then? According to what I've read, he doesn't stay with anyone for very long." Jen bit her lip. "I don't want to end up a fool."

Ruth smoothed Jen's unruly hair. "I think Mother said it best. We enjoy every minute of every day that the Lord gives us and leave the rest to Him."

That made sense in theory, but life was messier. Jen wasn't sure she could handle that kind of rejection. A plane crash would be easier.

"Smile," Beatrice said. "Enjoy the evening, and don't place too much importance on it. When a match is meant to be, a false step here or there won't matter."

Jen blew out her breath and refocused. "It's not that I want a match." After all, she was still angry with him for making Jack promise not to put her in the cockpit for the polar attempt, even though it had always been unlikely. Tonight wasn't about romance; it was about propelling the expedition forward. Dan had made that quite clear. "I just don't want to do or say anything to hurt the expedition. Dan thinks I can help. I don't know why, but he has a lot of faith in me."

Beattie and Ruth grinned at each other.

"Not because he likes me," Jen insisted. "Because he thinks I can convince people to invest." The words made sense, but her flaming cheeks betrayed her true feelings.

She did care what Dan Wagner thought of her. She hoped he would find her passably pretty and charmingly witty—two qualities she had never mastered but he apparently expected in his female friends. That's what twisted her stomach into knots. That's what prevented her from eating a bite. She had to transform herself. Her sisters were doing their best to make her pretty. Jen had to find both charm and wit buried somewhere inside her.

Minnie darted in the room, hair iron in hand. "He's here already."

Jen pressed a hand to her mouth. Time had just run out.

Dan knew Jen had four sisters, but he hadn't expected to find all of them and their families gathered in the small house. He sauntered up the shoveled walk in the borrowed tuxedo and overcoat. Some relation of Simmons, being the correct size, had donated to the cause.

The jacket was a little tight across the shoulders, but it buttoned and the trousers were long enough. He couldn't complain.

Two dark-haired gentlemen greeted him from the front porch. One was quite tall and completely at ease.

A smile came readily to his lips as he extended his hand. "You must be Dan Wagner."

"I am."

"Sam Rothenburg." The man's handshake was firm, confident. "I'm Ruth's husband."

"Rothenburg. I've heard that name before. Don't tell me." Dan thought a second, but the sign on the back of the building visible above the houses gave him the clue he needed. "Hutton's Department Stores."

"The same, though I'm no longer with them." Rather than explain why he'd left the family business, Sam introduced the shorter man. "This is Blake Kensington. He's married to Jen's oldest sister and manages the mercantile."

Dan knew the Kensington name well. Blake echoed some of the mayor's features, though he was considerably thinner and more subdued. "Pleased to meet you."

Kensington's handshake wasn't quite as firm. "Likewise. Ready to run the gauntlet?"

"Gauntlet?" Dan wasn't sure he liked the sound of that.

"Four sisters and their mother." Rothenburg laughed. "It's a gauntlet, all right."

Dan had always managed to avoid meeting families. By the time a lady got serious enough to invite him to meet her parents, he had moved on. This wasn't at all like that. "I only asked Jen to join me since she's working on the expedition."

Rothenburg grinned. "That might be your reason, but those women don't see it like that at all."

Dan's stomach churned. "Jen does. She's perfectly aware that this is a business matter. Jack expects to meet potential subscribers and wants everyone there to explain the project and answer questions." He didn't mention that Jen hadn't been included in that plan.

Kensington's lips curved into a wry smile. "I'm sure my father is involved in that."

"I think Jack Hunter did mention him," Dan confirmed.

"Of course he is," Blake said. "Daddy loves to throw money at other people."

Dan didn't know what was going on, but the mood had definitely gotten chillier. "Well, I suppose I might as well get it over." He eyed the front door, its yellowed ivory paint peeled off near the bottom. The Fox family clearly was not well-off. He grabbed the old iron door knocker. It jiggled and tilted. One screw was missing.

Rothenburg stopped him. "No need to knock. They're expecting you, but do keep one thing in mind. Jen's father passed away last October. Mrs. Fox is still in mourning. They all are in their own way."

Dan recalled Jen's wistful expression when she gave her reason for going to nursing school. She seemed to think a nurse might have saved her father's life. That sobered him. "I'll keep that in mind, but I'm more concerned about Jen's sisters."

Rothenburg clapped him on the back. "You can do it."

Dan wasn't so sure. He suspected that pulling out of a stall ten feet from the ground would be easier. Nevertheless, he'd invited Jen. He had to go through with this. He straightened his shoulders, put on the smile that charmed ladies of all ages and cracked open the door.

A woman squealed. That was followed by the clattering of footsteps and the cry, "He's here!"

Then silence. No one approached.

Rothenburg chuckled. "They probably figure since we're out here that we'll show you in."

"They're probably not ready," Kensington suggested. "Knowing Beattie, she's making her sister change this and that until everything is just right."

Dan was skeptical. "Jen doesn't seem like the type to primp."

"You haven't seen the four of them together," Rothenburg said. "There'll be plenty of primping. And chatter."

Kensington nodded. "Holiday dinners are crazy. Beattie supervises the decorations and what everyone is going to wear. Ruth's in charge of the kitchen. Minnie watches the little ones. They all talk nonstop."

"And Jen?" Dan was having difficulty seeing how the tomboy fit into this picture.

Both men shrugged.

Rothenburg spoke. "Since I met her, I noticed she spent a lot of time with her father, dreaming up wild adventures. Blake, is that how she was before I arrived?"

"When she wasn't sticking her nose into her sisters' plans," Kensington said.

Dan laughed. "That sounds like Jen." He glanced at the door. "Maybe I should stay out here."

"Not a chance," Rothenburg said with a laugh. "You'll have to face the gauntlet like the rest of us."

The door opened, and a stately matron with silvered hair and the black dress of a widow surveyed Dan from shined shoes to brushed felt fedora.

"Mr. Wagner? Please do come in."

Her smile was kindly, and the broad sweep of her hand welcomed him.

Dan smiled back. "Mrs. Fox? It's a pleasure to meet

you. He handed her the lavender sachet he'd purchased at the drugstore.

She looked startled. "For me?" A delicate rose colored her fair skin. "Oh, my." She backed from the door, clearly flustered. "No one has ever been so thoughtful." She lifted the cover of the small box and sniffed the sachet. "Ah, lavender is my favorite. God bless you for your thoughtfulness."

"Good job," Rothenburg whispered along with a nudge of his elbow. "Wish I'd thought to do that."

Dan stepped into the small house. Despite fading wallpaper that had begun to curl and pull away at the edges, it exuded a warmth and comfort reminiscent of his parent's ranch house. Four embroidered samplers, from highly skilled to poorly executed, hung on the wall. The foyer opened immediately into a living room. A doorway on the opposite side of the room led to other rooms.

"Genevieve will be down shortly," Mrs. Fox said, still cradling the gift.

Genevieve? She must mean Jen, but Dan would never have guessed that was Jen's full name.

A pint-size shriek split the air, followed by a yelp. Then two children flew through the opposite doorway to plead their case before Mrs. Fox.

"Grandma, Grandma," the girl of perhaps five years old cried. "Brannie hit me."

"She hit me first," the younger boy countered.

"Branford, Tillie," Kensington barked. "I expect you to behave. That means no running indoors and no hitting each other. Understand?"

The children's exuberance vanished. "Yes, Daddy."

They slunk out of the room.

The sound of footsteps clattering down a staircase was followed by the appearance of the petite young woman who had visited Jen at the flight school last week. "Sorry, Mother. I meant to get down here sooner." She beamed at Dan. "Jen will be down in a moment. Wait until you see her." After a final grin, she disappeared into the room with the children.

Kensington checked his wristwatch. "They're taking a long time. We'll be late."

Dan eyed the two men. Neither wore evening attire. "Are you attending?"

"The ball?" Kensington said. "Not a chance. I wouldn't want to be around that crowd. We're all going to the picture show."

That was disappointing. Dan would especially have enjoyed Sam Rothenburg's company. The man had an easy manner that made him seem like an old chum even though they'd just met.

At the moment, Rothenburg's eyes widened with surprise. He then nodded his head toward the other side of the living room. Dan turned to see Jen framed in the doorway. Her willowy figure was highlighted by a shimmering dark red gown that fit her to perfection. Though the dress didn't have any of the usual ornamentation found on evening gowns—beading, lace or bows—its simplicity brought out Jen's exquisite beauty. Her unruly hair had been tamed into a sleek style emulating the popular bob, and the understated headdress completed the outfit.

Dan had seen the most stunning gowns on the most beautiful women, but none of them compared to this. Gradually, he became aware that the room was silent.

"Exquisite," he breathed.

Then she smiled, and every assertion that he'd only invited her to the ball for business purposes went flying out the window.

* * *

Until that instant, Jen had hated every moment of the preparations. In her opinion, she needed ten minutes at most to dress and brush her hair. Her sisters had taken dressing to a new level. Between their fussing, her nerves and the lack of food, she felt shaky. When they finally declared her ready, she hurried downstairs.

Then she saw Dan.

My, oh, my, was he handsome dressed in an elegant black tuxedo and stylish overcoat. His wavy auburn hair had been trimmed and combed, but it was his eyes that captivated her. At first twinkling blue, their color deepened when he saw her. That overly confident smile vanished in what could only be described as shock.

Was her chemise showing? Ruth had carefully pinned the straps to the shoulder seam of the gown so they wouldn't inch into view. Maybe the pin had come undone.

Then his jaw returned to its normal position, and he declared her exquisite.

Not merely pretty or even beautiful, but exquisite!

She about fainted from shock. She didn't dare leave the support of the doorway, even though Beattie, hidden in the kitchen, kept whispering for her to move. All she could manage was a shaky return smile.

Then he crossed the living room until he stood before her. He reached into the pocket of his coat and removed a small box.

A box that was the exact size of a ring box.

Her heart raced. She forgot to breathe.

"I'm honored you agreed to join me tonight." He held out the box. "This is for you."

Oh my, she was going to faint. Right there in front of her sisters and Daring Dan Wagner. Newspapers across the country would display a photograph of her prone form sprawled on the hardwood floor along with the caption: Floored by Proposal.

"Take it," Beattie whispered loud enough for the next-door neighbors to hear.

Dan pressed his lips together in a futile attempt to hide his mirth. He was laughing at her. That brought Jen back to her senses.

She snatched the box from his hands. "Thank you."

Ruth and Beattie appeared over either shoulder.

"Aren't you going to open it?" Beattie asked.

"Yes, we're dying to know what's inside," Ruth seconded.

Even Minnie got in on the disaster. "Do open it. We're all waiting."

Sure enough, she had gathered the children in the parlor doorway.

"Now, girls." Mother swooped in and cleared Jen's sisters away. "Give your sister a little privacy. Sam? Blake? I believe you need to take your lovely brides to the show. I'll take the children, Minnie. Peter is expecting you for supper."

In short order, Jen found herself alone with Dan in the living room. Well, as alone as a girl could be with her mother and three little children within hearing distance.

"You can open it now, if you wish," Dan said. "It's just a small token of appreciation. I planned to get you flowers, too, but I couldn't find a florist in town."

"There isn't one."

"That would explain it."

Jen fingered the small box. A small token definitely did not mean a ring, but the box still looked as if it had come from a jeweler. After all her fuss about not wearing jewelry tonight, she laughed at the irony that he'd brought her a piece of jewelry.

"What's funny?" he asked.

She shook her head. "Something that happened earlier."

She lifted the lid off the box. Nestled on a bed of white cotton was a small medallion. She held it to the light.

"It's to commemorate your role in the polar expedition," he said.

She lifted the silvery medallion from the box. It had the year and the words *Polar Expedition Crewmember* engraved around the edge. In the center was what looked like an iceberg with a tiny flag on top.

"It's wonderful," she breathed.

"You can use it as a pendant."

"How thoughtful." And she meant it. He had gone to a great deal of trouble to have this made just for her. For some ridiculous reason, tears dampened her eyes. She blinked and swallowed against her constricting throat. "Thank you."

"Your contributions are valuable. I mean that. Without your help, we wouldn't stand a chance." He took a breath and shifted his weight, as if nervous.

Daring Dan was anxious around her? That had to be a first. He could win the attention of any woman in the country, maybe the world, yet he was acting like a schoolboy with her. The idea made her both light-headed and overjoyed at the same time.

"Thank you," she whispered.

He looked into her eyes then, and she nearly fell apart. Compassion, understanding, every good thing on earth could be found in those depths. His smile caught and drew her in.

"Even if you do leave for nursing school," he said, "your work won't be forgotten."

Nursing school. She had forgotten about that. His

reminder catapulted her from the heights of joy to the depths of misery. Finally her work had been recognized. Finally a man respected her. Finally she had found someone fascinating enough to consider spending a great deal of time with. At that very moment when the impossible came together, she had to leave.

"We should go," he said gently.

Jen stared at the dark window etched with frost. Years ago, Daddy had promised to walk her down the aisle. He never would. She had promised to write his name in the history of aviation. She never would. Why did everything happen too late?

Chapter Eleven

Despite the incredibly romantic beginning to the evening, the ball ended up just as businesslike as promised. Jen spent the night describing expedition preparations to potential investors. The only highlight was when Dan told those same investors that her assistance had been invaluable. Even with Daring Dan's endorsement, the men hadn't been impressed. They preferred Dan's tales of daring feats and near brushes with disaster to her descriptions of potential commercial and philanthropic applications after the expedition. Even Jack had to take a backseat to the famous aviator. He didn't seem to mind, though, and when the men rejoined their wives for the late supper, he bowed out, saying he wanted to return home to Darcy, who was feeling poorly. Though Darcy's mother was sitting with her, Jack didn't want to keep the elderly woman out too late. They all knew that was just an excuse.

"He sure is devoted to his wife," Dan had commented.

Jen couldn't describe the depth of love Jack and Darcy shared. It reminded her of Mother and Daddy. Or Ruth and Sam. They could communicate without words, considered each other first and clung to the tenderness of their first days together. It was the standard she had held up to any relationship.

She had sighed. "That is true love."

His eyebrows had lifted until he'd considered her statement. "I suppose you're right."

"You don't know anyone that in love?"

"My ma and pa, but in a different way. They accept that life is hard and work comes first."

Jen was still thinking about that statement when Dan helped her out of the hired car and walked her to the front porch. She leaned on his arm up the slippery steps. The dusting of new-fallen snow crunched underfoot. His arm was strong but carried no warmth or tenderness. From his description, his parents saw life as a shared struggle rather than the shared joy she desired. Was that the way Dan saw marriage, too? If so, then she didn't know how they could ever fall in love.

He released her before the door, close enough to shake hands but not so close that Jen would wonder if he intended to kiss her.

"Thank you for joining me." The light from the front window caught both his smile and the cloud of his breath in the still, frigid air. "It made the night more bearable."

More bearable, as if it had been a great hardship to spin tales of daring feats to the rapt attention of wealthy men. As if her presence only made it a little better. Not that he enjoyed being with her and wished they could have had some time alone. Not that he wanted to be with her again. No, she had just made a dreadful evening slightly more tolerable.

Jen mustered a smile. A woman hoping to attract him might gush about how much she had enjoyed the evening. That woman would leave the door open for an invitation. Jen was not that woman. "Good night, Wagner."

"Back to that, are we?" His lips curved into a wry smile. "Well, then, good night, Miss Fox."

The brim of his fedora shadowed his eyes so she couldn't tell if he was disappointed. It didn't matter anyway.

She grabbed the doorknob, and then hesitated. The night could not end so coldly. Mother always said not to go to bed at odds with another person.

"Thank you again for the medallion. It means a lot to me. It would have meant a lot to my father." She ducked inside before he noticed how much that gift had affected her.

The cold, hard door against her back helped calm her shaky nerves. Why did that man do this to her? No one had ever sent her emotions into such a swirling mess. At times he made her so happy that she felt she could touch the stars. Other times he sent her into free fall. That couldn't possibly be love. Love was gentle and kind. It first considered the other.

Dan had shown consideration by giving her the medallion and touting her contributions, but gentle and kind? He had gone behind her back to demand she not be put aboard the expedition plane. That was neither kind nor considerate.

Dan Wagner must feel nothing for her. She did not need emotional turmoil in her life. Not now, when everything was about to change. Tonight had confirmed her decision. The ball had been her swan song. In two weeks she would leave.

She had been accepted into the hospital nursing program.

Something had changed between Jen and him, but Dan couldn't figure out what. Oh, she completed her work as usual over the next week and a half. Her organization skills didn't waver, but she was quieter. The spunk was gone. She no longer questioned everything he said. It felt as if she no longer cared.

"The planes never got off the ground," he said.

She lifted her gaze. "What planes?"

"The ones that were supposed to bring half the diphtheria serum to Nome."

"Oh." This time she didn't bother to look up. Her pencil scratched away at the weight calculations.

"The dogsleds got there a week ago Sunday, the day after the ball."

She didn't even react to the mention of the Valentine's Day Ball. Considering the success of the evening, with three subscribers opening their wallets, she ought to be ecstatic. The polar expedition now had the funding to ship everything to Spitsbergen.

"I thought you were interested in that story," he said. "Thanks to the serum's arrival, the quarantine has been lifted. The rest of the children will survive."

She pursed her lips and tapped the end of the pencil against the paper. "This all weighs too much. Jack wanted the total weight under two tons."

"It is under two tons. I checked the calculations twice."

Instead of arguing, she shoved the paper toward him. "Then where am I making an error?"

He glanced over her calculations and spotted the problem in an instant, but it wasn't fun anymore pointing out her mistakes, knowing she wouldn't come back at him with an equally stinging retort. "A simple transposition of numbers in this column."

She sighed. "Why do I have such trouble with math?"

That surprised him. "If you can pass a navigation exam, you have a good grasp of mathematics. This is a common error, one that's easy to spot. When the difference between your sums comes out to a number divisible by nine, then it's probably a transposed number somewhere."

She looked at him dully. "I knew that, but I forgot."

Something was definitely wrong. "Are you feeling all right? You don't seem your normal self."

"I'm perfectly normal."

The slight acidity in her tone made him smile. "That's my girl. I was beginning to think something terrible had happened."

Instead of chastising him for calling her his girl, she managed a weak smile. "A lot is going on."

Now he was worried. "Do you want to tell me? Maybe I can help."

The old glare returned. "Can you keep our dress shop open?"

He tried to fit together the tidbits she'd shared over the past few weeks. "The dress shop is your family's business. Is it closing? Is that why your mother is selling the house?"

She looked away. For a while he figured she wasn't going to say anything, but just before he gave up, she spoke. "Ruth is moving the shop to New York, and Mother is going with her. They need to help out Sam's mother."

No wonder Jen looked lost. No wonder the spunk was gone. "I'm sorry."

"There's nothing to be done." She squared her shoulders. "Change is inevitable."

"But it's some months away. You said your mother wasn't leaving until after your younger sister's wedding. Wasn't that in May?"

She nodded. "But I can't wait for that."

The last piece fell into place. "You were accepted into nursing school."

She nodded again.

Someone eager to become a nurse would bubble over with joy. Jen looked as if she'd received a life sentence to prison. "I thought that's what you wanted, to fly to remote areas and nurse people back to health."

Her head snapped up. "Maybe I do want that. Are you going to bid on the airmail route?"

Why did she come back to that?

"I did send in the bid," he admitted.

She brightened so much that he couldn't tell her that he'd already decided to turn down the contract if it was offered. Now that Hunter had the necessary support, Dan could put all his efforts into the polar expedition.

"By the time I finish, you'll have an established route," she said. "I can take flight lessons on my days off. There must be a flight school in Grand Rapids."

"Is that where you're going?"

She didn't seem to hear his question. "I'll ask at the hospital. Someone will know where the airfield is and if they offer lessons. Once I receive my first stipend, I'll start lessons."

"You get a stipend?"

"A small amount for necessities, but what could I need?"

Dan could believe that. The woman wore nothing new or even in decent condition. "You do know you're going to have to wear a uniform." He cleared his throat. "With a skirt and starched cap."

Her nose wrinkled. "Sometimes sacrifices must be made."

Dan had to laugh at the idea of her in a nurse's uniform. The night of the ball, she'd looked comfortable in the elegant gown, but that first dinner at the Hunter's house she had chafed in the frilly dress like a misaligned guy wire against a strut. The starched uniform would doubtless bring the latter reaction.

"Do you think this is funny?" she demanded.

He was so happy to hear the challenge in her voice that he took her by the shoulders. "Don't let go of your spirit. Whatever happens, hold on to that."

At first she looked shocked, then her eyes widened.

He'd felt it, too. A sizzle, like an arcing electrical circuit. It had radiated from her to him or vice versa. He wasn't sure which. All he knew was that he couldn't rip his gaze from her face. Those luminous hazel eyes. The expressive lips. The way she nibbled on that lower lip when uncertain, as she was doing at that moment. The unruly cropped hair and the smattering of pale freckles across her nose.

"Jen," he breathed, not able to say more.

She swallowed. "I have to go."

He couldn't bear to break the connection. "I know."

Those eyes of hers sparkled with unshed tears. Jen didn't cry. He'd give her credit for that. Even now, when the tension between them was more than he could bear, she wouldn't let those tears overflow. Instead she looked up at him, waiting.

He could not hold back any longer. Her wild, spruce-like scent undid his resolve to keep his distance. He leaned close and let his lips drift onto hers, soft as landing on clouds. She responded, slowly at first and then with desperation.

Through the fog in his brain came the weak cry of reason. *Stop.* Stop now before he hurt her. He stepped away but didn't let go.

Her eyelids fluttered open, but her lips were still red and parted.

He wanted to kiss her again. He wanted to give her what he'd never given another woman, but Dan Wagner had a rule. As long as he flew airplanes, he would not marry. In fairness to the women, he would not allow a relationship to progress to emotional attachment. This one had already gone too far. Hunter might be willing to leave his wife and unborn baby widowed and fatherless. He would not.

He dropped his hands, breaking the connection completely. "I suppose it's goodbye, then."

Even though Dan was technically correct, Jen wasn't about to say goodbye forever. Her first meaningful kiss wouldn't be her last. She had a plan. Daring Dan Wagner was sure to get the airmail contract. Once she completed the nursing program and received her aviation license, she would join him.

"I'll be back during breaks."

"Maybe I'll see you then." But he didn't say it with any conviction, probably for good reason. The first break wouldn't be until summer or fall. By then Dan would either be in Spitsbergen for the polar attempt or back in Montana.

"If not this summer, then when I finish the program. I won't let you forget about having a nurse copilot on your airmail route."

His taut smile faded. "You sure do have dreams."

That clipped her wings. He had no intention of agreeing to her plan. According to the newspapers, Daring Dan Wagner never made a relationship commitment. She was a fool to think he would start now with her.

He cleared his throat. She stared off into the air. It

was the awkward farewell dance. Her rib cage felt as if it would explode.

"I won't see you, will I?" she whispered.

He looked away and didn't answer.

What could he say? They both knew the truth. No one had to say it aloud. But he didn't need to know how much it hurt her to say goodbye.

"Have a good life, Wagner."

Then she walked out of the flight school for the last time.

Chapter Twelve

By the end of the first day at the hospital nursing school, Jen went into shock. She had never been in a hospital before. Every expectation was soon dashed.

Upon arrival, the supervisor explained to Jen that she would be on probation for three months, during which time she would receive room and board but no stipend. Only if she was accepted after the probationary period would she officially enter the program and receive a small stipend to purchase necessary instruments, including surgical scissors, forceps and thermometer. There would be little or nothing left for flight training until she graduated from the program, received her certification and was hired.

That blow nearly sent her running, but where could she go? She had arrived on the train and hadn't the fare to return. Neither could she face Mother's disappointment or her sisters' scorn. Worst of all, Dan would smirk and tell her that he knew she wasn't fit for nursing. So she swallowed her disappointment and followed the assistant supervisor to the dormitory wing.

Her room consisted of a small cell she shared with three other nurses in training. One was a probationer like her while the other two had advanced into the program. Both of them were first-year students. Two bunks lined each wall. At the base of each was a small dresser with one drawer for each person. A single desk, which they were expected to share, sat beneath the only window. A steam radiator with no control mechanism ran underneath the desk, so the person working there roasted. An open wardrobe to hang their coats and uniforms completed the sparse furnishings.

For three months, she was expected to work twelve-hour shifts performing the most nauseating and menial tasks, from emptying bedpans and urinals to bathing patients and changing soiled bed linens. The moans and cries of suffering patients rang in her ears. An antiseptic odor permeated the air and her dark blue uniform. The nearly silent whisper of the nurses' rubber-heeled shoes filled the corridors. Only upon acceptance to the program would she receive the crisp white-and-sky-blue uniform and a cap. Until then she wore the navy blue skirt and white blouse she'd been asked to bring with her. A clean white apron completed every nurse's ensemble, whether probationer, student nurse or graduate. Her appearance, including spotless starched apron and clean fingernails, must pass inspection every shift.

At the end of the twelve-hour shift, she ate supper and then attended classes, during which her eyelids drooped from fatigue. Finally she had time to sleep, but between her chattering roommates, the brick-hard mattress and the clanging radiator, she could only manage a few hours of slumber. If the memories of the day didn't torment her dreams, Dan Wagner scolded her for entering the program. The dreams would flee only when the watchman pounded on the door and announced the six o'clock hour.

She and those roommates not working the night shift dragged their stiff bodies out of bed to face a new day.

After three weeks, she was exhausted. Home, the flight school and even her sisters had faded to distant memories. Sometimes, when her roommates were gone, she stared out the window and tried to remember Pearlman. She couldn't picture Dan Wagner anymore. His image had paled and yellowed, like an old newspaper clipping. How she would welcome his arrogant grin. It would bring relief from the sheer human anguish that dragged her spirits down each day. She would pull the medallion out of the drawer and run her fingers over the inscription. She hadn't realized the night of the Valentine's Day Ball that he had had her name inscribed on the back. That medallion became her last connection to the outside world and the dream she'd been forced to abandon.

During her allotted time to use the desk, she watched the clouds fly by and dreamed of soaring with them until a roommate chided her to either do her homework or let someone else work. Outside the four brick walls of the hospital, people walked and conversed and went to moving picture shows. They chose where to go and what to do. Jen's life had been ordered into a regimented schedule. Her roommates, all from Grand Rapids, occasionally ate at a diner or visited friends. Jen did not go with them. She never left the building. She couldn't waste a nickel.

In that third week, the supervisor scheduled her in D Ward, which was reserved for expectant mothers. Some arrived when the pains began. Others convalesced, or were "lying in," under the watchful eye of the nurses and staff physicians. According to Mother's last letter, this is where Doc Stevens wanted Darcy to go. It didn't take long for Jen to understand why her friend had refused.

The ward was cheerful compared to most, but it was still in a hospital. Those expectant mothers were often sedated in the effort to prevent seizures. One young woman, named Marie according the card hanging on the end of her bed, suffered from tremendous swelling in her extremities, nausea and headaches.

"Just like my friend Darcy," Jen confided to the head nurse. "At least the swelling and nausea are the same. I'm not certain about the headaches." Though once Jen thought about it, she did recall Darcy rubbing her temple from time to time. Darcy wasn't one to complain, though, so few would know if she suffered. She thought back to Jack's quick departure from the Valentine's Day Ball. Maybe Darcy was having troubles even then. "Nausea is normal, isn't it?"

"Early on, but it usually subsides by the second trimester."

Darcy was much farther along than that.

The nurse continued, "This nausea is more severe. Marie is being treated for toxemia. It can be fatal if seizures begin."

A chill ran through Jen. Daddy had died from a seizure. Could Marie die? Could Darcy? "What is the treatment?"

"The only cure is childbirth. Until then, we need to keep the patients calm to reduce the risk of convulsions, so don't agitate them."

Jen did not ask why the head nurse believed she would agitate anyone. "What if a seizure happens?"

"Call me or the nurse on duty at once and put a gauze-wrapped tongue depressor between the patient's jaws so she doesn't bite her tongue."

Jen drew in a nervous breath.

"Also fetch the head nurse if you notice any changes,"

the nurse continued, "such as the patient has difficulty breathing or complains of severe headache, blurred vision or pain in her upper right abdomen."

If not for Marie and Darcy, Jen might have taken the instructions with complete clarity. Instead, fear muddied the words until all she could recall later was to call the head nurse. Thankfully, no one suffered a seizure during her days in Ward D.

After moving to a different ward, Jen often stopped to see Marie following the evening lecture. One of those nights, another one of the women went into convulsions. The head nurse came running, while the probationer hurried off to get the staff doctor. Marie, tranquil in her sedated state, watched with Jen as the doctor hurried in followed by an intern.

"Get a syringe of magnesium sulfate," he barked to the intern, issuing further instructions that Jen did not fully understand.

Curtains were drawn, so Jen did not see what followed. A gurney was brought, and the patient wheeled away, but the next time Jen visited Marie, the woman's bed was occupied by another expectant mother.

"What happened to the patient in bed eight?" she asked the nurse on duty.

"She didn't make it."

"The baby?"

The nurse shook her head.

Jen shivered. From that day forward, she did not miss an opportunity to visit Marie, despite long days cleaning, bathing and changing beds.

Though Jen was physically strong due to her work with the airplanes, the suffering and dying wore on her. It didn't take long to recognize those patients who would not survive the night. When the final hours drew near, the patient was given privacy with curtains or screens. If a probationer was available, the head nurse would send her to sit with the dying patient.

In the fourth week while on night shift, Jen's turn arrived.

"Go to Ward B," the head nurse instructed, "and sit with the patient in bed three."

Ward B contained those suffering from the effects of influenza, including pneumonia. Jen arrived to find bed three curtained off. Inside lay a man, emaciated from long illness and barely conscious. His skin was already ashen.

At the sound of her arrival, his eyelids flickered open to reveal pale, watery eyes. Jen froze. For an instant, the man reminded her of Daddy, only her father had not awoken when she walked into the room. Instinct told her to flee, to find some closet where she could gather her wits, but she forced herself to walk to the chair positioned bedside.

She sat and took his hand, already cool.

His lips moved, but no sound came out.

She leaned close and barely made out the whispered "thank you."

His eyelids closed again, and he dropped into the shallow breaths marking each limited moment he had left. Where was his family? Where were his loved ones?

She checked the card at the foot of the bed. His name was Herbert Smith. No church or pastor listed. No next of kin. He was alone in this world, but she would not leave him in his final hours on this earth. She returned to the chair and held his hand.

He returned to consciousness once more and asked for prayer. She recited the twenty-third psalm, the only thing that came to mind. It calmed him, and in the wee hours of the morning he passed. She laid his hands upon his chest and said a prayer for his soul.

Jen knew procedure. She was supposed to notify the head nurse, who would call the orderlies. They would cover the deceased with a sheet and remove him from the ward. She would be expected to follow the gurney to the morgue, where she would bathe and cover the body with a dazzling white sheet.

That was procedure, but first she shed a tear for a man who'd had no one to mourn his passing. Then she dried her tears and summoned the head nurse. Like her daddy, Mr. Smith was whisked away.

For most of March, the expedition preparations had proceeded according to plan. Dan supervised packing the supplies for shipment to Spitsbergen. He scheduled the loading of the crates on a train to New York. From there, they would be placed aboard ship for transport to Oslo. Then they would be transferred onto a ship that would carry them to Spitsbergen Island.

All Dan needed was to know which ship, a task that Hunter reserved for himself. Yet as the weeks passed, Hunter would give him no ship name. Whenever Dan asked, he brushed it off, saying he would get to it. In Dan's opinion, the man grew more and more distracted.

Dan missed Jen's organizational skills. She would have had the ship lined up the first week of March. She would have checked and double-checked with the shipping agents for any weather delays or changes in the schedule. She would have gone straight to Hunter and demanded answers in her inimitable way. Dan could have relied on her. Instead he had to deal with a man who looked more worried with each passing day, yet wouldn't tell him why. Dan hoped Hunter wasn't planning to abandon the expedition. A great many people had plunked down large sums to support it. Dan would have to repay the advance he'd gotten from Kensington if the expedition didn't get off the ground. He would not owe anyone, but it would cost him all he had.

"The ship is booked?" Dan asked again.

"The ship is the least of our problems," Hunter said. "What does it take to cross the Atlantic? A couple weeks? We have plenty of time. We can't attempt the arctic until summer anyway."

"Summer? I thought we were doing this in May."

"That's too soon after the baby is born. Darcy will need me at home."

Dan wanted to point out that Jack's wife would doubtless get more help from her mother than her husband, but he had another card to play. "I understand Lieutenant Commander Byrd will be leading the naval flight unit joining the MacMillan polar expedition. They plan an August attempt. If we hope to claim the record, we need to get there first."

His bombshell did not have the desired result.

"Family comes first," Hunter said. "You know that."

Dan's family certainly took top priority when it came to his savings, but this was a once-in-a-lifetime opportunity, one that he was willing to sacrifice a government contract in order to participate in. How he wished Jen was here to talk sense into the man. "There's no reason I can't take charge of arranging the transatlantic shipping. Let me handle it. You have enough on your mind."

"Are you questioning my abilities?" Hunter snapped.

Dan held up his hands in defeat. "I'm only saying that a man needs to stand by his wife first. You take care of her. I'll handle the bookings."

Hunter's defensive posture eased. "I'm sorry. I guess I'm not quite myself these days."

"Understandable." Dan offered a smile of encouragement even though he was worried. Passage to remote Spitsbergen would be difficult to locate if Hunter hadn't done anything yet. Opportunity might have already passed them by. Moreover, Dan had been awarded the airmail contract. The letter from the Post Office was in his pocket. If this expedition fell apart, he preferred it happen now rather than later.

"Just tell me if you're planning to cancel the polar attempt."

Hunter jerked to attention. "Did I say anything about canceling this? It's Darcy's dream."

"Then maybe you should wait until she can participate."

Hunter's gaze narrowed. "Are you bailing out on me?"

"Not at all. Just stating the options."

"There are no options. We're doing this." But Hunter said that with about as much conviction as Jen had mustered for nursing school.

"All right, then." Hunter deserved to know what Dan was laying on the line. "I'll turn down the airmail contract."

Hunter looked him in the eye. "Sorry to make you choose between the two, old sport. I'll understand if you need to take it."

At this rate, nothing would get accomplished. "Look, I'm not planning to bail. I just want to get this process moving. After we cross the pole, I'll have all the contract opportunities I want. Since you're busy with family, let me handle the arrangements."

"All right, but the first order of business is fixing that left engine. Another valve broke."

"What? When? I thought we were done testing."

Hunter raked a hand through his hair. "I wanted one more run-through with Hendrick before we removed the engines from the plane. The last time we ran them, I thought I heard something off."

"You're beginning to sound like Jen."

Hunter grinned. "She has a way with engines, doesn't she?"

Dan didn't want to think about her. If he did, he'd remember that she was stuck in a hospital dumping bedpans. She belonged here, working on the project. He blew out his breath to clear his head. "If we're still having trouble with the valves, we'd better pack plenty of replacements."

"Yep." Hunter scrubbed his whiskered chin. "Trouble is we don't have them."

"What do you mean we don't have them? We can't go to Spitsbergen without spare parts. I was sure Jen had that on the supply list."

"She did, but the spare valves we have packed are the problem according to Hendrick. He is going to machine a set of more durable ones out of a special alloy. If they do the job, he'll make the spares."

"Sounds good to me. When will they be ready to test?"

"When he gets his hands on some of that special alloy."

Dan whistled. "How long to get it?"

"There's some in Grand Rapids."

"Grand Rapids." Dan was beginning to suspect a setup. "Grand Rapids, Michigan, where a certain aspiring aviatrix is attending nursing school."

"She might appreciate an update on the expedition."

Dan groaned. Their parting had been painful. Though she hadn't shed tears, her eyes had welled with hurt. "I don't suppose anyone else could go."

Hunter shrugged. "I can't leave Darcy, and Hendrick has a business to run."

Dan had to give the man credit for first-class manipulation. No doubt he'd convinced the entire town that only Dan could make the run to Grand Rapids. "You aren't giving me any choice, are you?"

"Nope. I will give you the keys to the Model T, though."

Since Jen had spent the night in Ward B, she hadn't visited Marie as usual. Though dead tired, she headed to D Ward after ending her shift.

At this hour, the ward was abuzz while breakfast was being served. Mealtimes were always welcomed in the wards, especially by those patients not on restricted diets.

Jen headed straight for Marie's bed and found another woman in it. "Where's Marie?"

The disheveled brunette glared at her. "I don't see no breakfast tray in your hands."

Jen backed up and looked at the card on the end of the bed. Marie's card was gone. She ran off in search of the head nurse, who was ensuring the proper diet for each patient.

"Where is Marie?" Jen asked breathlessly.

The woman frowned. "I'm busy now, and you're off duty."

"All I want to know is where Marie went. Did someone come for her? Did she have her baby?"

The nurse handed the tray to her assistant and checked her list for the next patient's diet. "Who is Marie?"

"Bed seven."

"Bed seven went into convulsions early this morning and passed."

"Passed?" Jen reeled. "The baby?" she managed to croak out.

"Stillborn." All business, the head nurse resumed directing the junior nurse and probationer.

Somehow Jen left the ward. Nurses, students and staff passed. Someone spoke her name. She heard the faint echo long after the woman had moved on. Marie was dead. Just yesterday she had been brimming with hope. One of the charities had dropped off baby clothes, and she had selected a pretty pink gown in the hope of having a girl. Jen could still see her jubilation, the fervent hope in her eyes. Now she was dead and the baby with her.

Jen stumbled down the corridor, eyes too blurred by tears to see her way. After a few steps, the strength went out of her legs, and she leaned against the wall for support.

"Are you all right, miss?" one of the orderlies asked as he passed by.

She managed a nod. "Just tired."

He didn't look as if he believed her but went on his way rather than cause an uproar by assisting one of the probationers. All she could think about was that she hadn't been with Marie in her hour of need. It wasn't fair. It wasn't right. Marie was younger than her. She had suffered so much pain in her life. The baby had been her first ray of hope for a better future. The breath caught in Jen's throat and squeezed hard.

Vision blurred by tears, she mindlessly wandered the halls and somehow ended up at her room. Thankfully her roommates were gone. Jen closed the door and sank onto the desk chair. The inside of the window had frosted over with delicate feathery patterns. As a child, she had loved to trace the swirls, though they always melted beneath her touch. Life had turned out to be just as fragile.

All the medicine and doctors in the world were powerless to halt death's steady progress.

She laid her head on the desk and wept.

Hours later, a persistent knocking awakened Jen.

"Miss Fox. Miss Fox."

Stiff and groggy, Jen murmured. "Yes?"

"You have a visitor." With the message delivered, the girl, probably another probationer, left, her muffled footsteps echoing down the long dormitory hallway.

A visitor. It took a long time for those words to sink in. Since arriving at the beginning of the month, Jen had not had a single visitor. Her roommates all had. Evelyn, one of her first-year roommates, even had a gentleman caller. The other nurses had teased her about that for days, asking when she was going to get engaged.

Jen stretched her shoulders and moved her head back and forth to loosen her neck. Falling asleep on the desk had not been a brilliant idea, but at least dreams hadn't tormented her.

She stood and smoothed her wrinkled skirt in front of the mirror attached to the back of the door. Hopeless. Moreover her hair stuck out at all angles. She pulled her brush from the dresser drawer and tugged it through her unruly locks.

Who could be paying her a visit? Not a man, certainly. Most likely Mother had taken the train. Or perhaps Ruth. No, Ruth wouldn't be able to leave between nursing Sammy and closing the shop. Minnie was busy planning for her wedding, and Beattie had the children to watch. It must be Mother.

Just as well. Mother might scold her for letting her appearance go, but she would understand when Jen explained that she had been sleeping after a grueling night shift. She would offer a shoulder to cry on and arms that comforted.

In case Mother wanted to step outside for a walk, Jen grabbed her coat and gloves.

Everyone knew that visitors were received in the little waiting room outside the program supervisor's office. It was there that Jen had first arrived and set aside her dreams. She hadn't seen it since.

The distance proved shorter than she remembered. On that first day, the corridors and rooms had seemed endless. Jen had felt that she was walking into a foreign land so far removed from her former life that she could never find her way back.

Today she greeted the stiff-backed receptionist who took her name, noted the time and asked her to sign the log.

"Remember that you must return before nine o'clock curfew," the woman said.

"I doubt I'm going anywhere."

The woman smirked. "I certainly would if I were you."

Jen rubbed the sleep from her eyes but couldn't suppress the yawn. She would tell Mother that she needed her sleep.

The door to the waiting room was solid oak. It stuck slightly, and Jen had to thrust her hip against it to make it move. It gave way all of a sudden, sending Jen stumbling into the small area. Strong, masculine hands caught and set her on her feet.

"You sure know how to make a grand entrance, darling."

Jen sucked in her breath. "Wagner. What are you doing here?"

"Nice to see you, too. I thought you might appreciate lunch in the coffee shop down the street."

Jen glanced at the windows. Frost didn't cover these. She could look out on the busy street. People hurried this way and that. Automobiles chugged past. Horns honked. Police whistles trilled.

The world still existed.

Dan grasped her shoulder. "Are you all right?"

The electricity in his touch startled her. She stepped back and rubbed the shoulder. "Just tired. Thank you. I would enjoy lunch, but I haven't any money with me." Nor did she have enough back in her room, but Dan didn't need to know that.

"Now what sort of gentleman would I be if I didn't offer to buy lunch for an upstanding young woman like you?"

She managed a weak smile. "You don't have to—"

"Now, before you go through all your excuses, let me tell you right off that I won't listen to any of them. I'm taking you to lunch, and that's that." He extended his arm. "Shall we?"

"Well, since I don't have a choice…" She wrapped her arm around his and let his strength carry her the city block to the coffee shop. Along the way, he brought her up to date on her family and the goings-on in Pearlman. Her sisters were all still in town, though the dress shop had announced it would close at the end of the month. Jen bit her lip. She wouldn't see Ruth and family leave.

"Darcy?" she asked with trepidation.

"Fine."

His casual reply told her all was well on that front. She breathed out that worry.

Dan stopped in front of a tiny coffee shop with large windows and a green-and-white awning whose scalloped edge flapped in the light breeze. She'd heard of the place from her roommates, who went there often, but she didn't have money to waste on restaurants.

He pulled open the door and then escorted her to a small table in the front window. "Will this do?"

"It's the only open table."

He cracked a smile. "That's the Jen I missed."

Dan Wagner missed her. That revelation hit harder than it should, considering she was working toward a professional career.

He pulled out her chair and seated her before taking the chair across from her.

A waitress informed them of the day's specials and pointed out the menu scrawled on a chalkboard above the lunch counter. "Coffee?"

"Please," Dan said.

Jen wouldn't spend any more of Dan's money than necessary. "Just water for me."

Several of the student nurses sat at a table within Jen's line of sight. The one they called Country Girl grinned and patted her hair. Jen reached up and discovered her cowlick was standing straight up. She dampened her fingers in the glass of water the waitress deposited in front of her and tried to smooth it down.

Dan looked amused. "Forget to comb your hair?"

"For your information, I brushed it. Moreover—not that it's any of your business—I happened to work the night shift last night and have only had a few hours of sleep."

He looked stricken. "I didn't know, or I would never have woken you."

"It doesn't matter. Sooner or later someone would have come into the room or banged a door, and I would have woken anyway." She took a sip of icy water, which only made her colder. "You didn't answer my question earlier.

You didn't come all the way to Grand Rapids to take me to lunch. What brought you here?"

"I'm here to fetch some special steel that Simmons needs to make new valves for the motors."

She tried to wrap her mind around the project that had once been so vital to her. "The expedition motors? Are you still having problems?"

"On that left engine." He grinned. "I think you rubbed off on us. Hunter said he could hear that something wasn't right, so he ran another test and a valve broke. Simmons figures the new alloy will be stronger." His voice flowed over her like a gentle brook.

Compared to illness, injury and death, a little engine trouble was blissfully easy. "That engine had problems from the start. First the cowling. Now this. If Hendrick hasn't done it already, have him check the cylinders for abnormalities."

"That's my girl." He grinned.

She checked the chalkboard menu. "I'll have a bowl of soup."

"What? No retort that you're not my girl? Or that you're not a girl any longer?"

"I'm too tired to argue."

"That's a shame." He leaned back in that casually dashing manner of his, as if he owned the entire world. "I rather enjoyed our sparring matches."

She looked down at her water, both overcome by Dan's appearance and still reeling from the tragedies of last night. Had Marie teased the man who'd fathered her baby? She was one of those women about whom polite society does not speak. No one had visited her, and no one would mourn her burial. Tears welled. She blinked them away as the waitress arrived to take their orders.

Dan took the lead. "We will have your split pea soup

and roast beef sandwiches. And bring my girl here a cup of hot tea."

Jen glared at him but spoke only after the waitress had gone. "Why did you do that? I only wanted soup."

"Then take the sandwich back with you for supper. It has to be better tasting than what they're feeding you, judging from the number of nursing students here."

Jen stared at her water again, overcome by his consideration. She hadn't been eating well. It wasn't the food, which was nourishing if plain. It simply didn't comfort like her mother's meals. The hospital wasn't home. Most days her roommates talked late into the night. Loralee dreamed of nursing overseas in the military. Norma longed to save lives like Florence Nightingale. Evelyn had the most practical reasons for becoming a nurse. Fourth daughter of nine in an impoverished family, nursing was her best hope for a better life. Jen was no longer sure why she had joined in the program.

"I didn't mean to upset you." Dan covered her clenched fist with his hand and absently stroked her chapped knuckles with his thumb.

She shook her head, unable to speak without bursting into tears.

"If you don't want the sandwich," he said, "I'll take it with me."

Again she shook her head. What was it about men that they always thought they'd caused the problem? She cleared her throat. "A man died last night."

He squeezed her hand.

"He didn't have anyone. No next of kin. No friend. I sat with him until he went."

"That must have been difficult," he said softly.

She shook her head. "It was peaceful, actually." She

had to blink hard to keep back the tears. "But while I was gone, Marie died."

"Marie?"

"A woman in the maternity ward. She didn't have anyone, either. I visited her every day. But I missed yesterday." All the blinking in the world wouldn't stop the tears. She pressed the napkin to her eyes, ashamed that she'd broken down in public but no longer able to hold herself together. "I'm sorry."

She heard a scraping and shuffling sound, and then he put his arm around her shoulders. He didn't say anything, didn't claim it would get better, didn't try to fix things. He just offered his unspoken support and let her finish.

It took a lot of effort to calm down enough to speak. From the security of his presence, she could finally say what had been in her heart since the day she'd arrived.

"Please take me home."

Chapter Thirteen

Dan couldn't leave Jen there. He couldn't walk her back to that forbidding hospital and return her to a life that didn't suit her. So he waited for her to pack her belongings and sign the papers that marked her official withdrawal from the program. Then he carried out her small piece of luggage and helped her into Hunter's car.

She looked exhausted. Her shoulders drooped, and her gaze was hollow.

He said nothing as he cranked the car to a start and began the long drive back to Pearlman. He didn't question her decision. He waited for her to speak first.

She stared blankly out the side window, clutching her handbag as if it would fly away with each bump or jolt.

He had been appalled by her appearance. Yes, her dress was neat, if wrinkled, and she was well scrubbed, but her expression matched that of the soldiers marching back from the front. Shell-shocked. Her cheekbones were more prominent than before, and her cheeks had hollowed. She'd been there less than a month. One more and she would end up in the mental ward.

She needed to go home.

When that tremulous voice had begged him to take

her, it took every ounce of restraint not to sweep her out of the restaurant and put her in the car that moment. Instead, he had promised to bring her home if she ate the soup and drank the tea. Though she'd struggled to down it all, the desire to leave the hospital overcame her apparent queasiness. Though he was famished, he had the sandwiches wrapped in paper for the ride home. Once he'd situated her in the front seat, he had pulled the thick wool blanket over her lap. The old Jen would have snapped at him for coddling her. Today, she let him tuck the blanket around her.

The change made him furious. He wanted to blame someone—the school, her family, even himself—for letting her go. The next moment he wanted to hold her tight and promise she would never have to endure this again.

But he couldn't. He was making an attempt to fly across the North Pole. He might not return alive.

He could make no promises.

So he waited for her to speak first.

Jen stared dully at the bustling city. When she'd first arrived, she'd found it fascinating. After all, she had never been to a city, but the novelty soon wore off. The noises and fumes and overpowering grayness left her longing for Pearlman's quiet streets and tidy yards.

Dan was taking her home.

Her heart quickened. Never had home meant so much, even though that house would soon be put up for sale. Home wasn't a house. It was something more—a comforting mother, sisters' teasing and a bond that could never be broken. Home meant love and acceptance. Mother might be disappointed, but she would still love her. Tears burned in Jen's eyes. How her body could manage another tear was beyond understanding. After last night and the terrible morning hours, she didn't think it possible, yet she had choked up in the coffee shop. Dan had held her, shielded her, though the gossip was sure to fly through the dormitory.

Dan had come to see her.

True, he'd actually come to Grand Rapids to pick up that chunk of steel in the backseat, but he had gone out of his way to see her. Then, against all hopes, he agreed to take her home.

She closed her eyes and let her head drop, but sleep would not come. Yes, the old Model T bumped and jolted over the rutted road, but that wasn't the only thing keeping her awake. Yes, the memories of last night danced in her mind, but that wasn't all that chased away sleep. Dan Wagner had searched her out. Even now he sat beside her, silent as stone, though he was probably bursting to tell her that he'd been right all along.

"You might as well say it," she said.

"Say what?"

"That nursing wasn't for me. That I'm poorly suited to the profession. All of it."

He didn't say anything for a long time. When he did speak, it wasn't with the arrogance she'd expected. "Maybe I was wrong. People could use someone with your compassion and strength."

She stared at her clenched hands. "I'm not strong. Not at all."

"You sat all night with a dying stranger who had no next of kin. You gave your time and affection to a woman who had no one and shed the only tears she'll receive at the end of her life."

Jen's throat swelled and those awful tears came back. She wasn't going to cry again. Jen Fox did not cry in front of others. At least not until the coffee shop. She bit her lip until the tears retreated.

He wasn't finished. "That's real strength. It might not seem like that now because you're tired and hurting, but once you've had a chance to sleep and eat properly your nerves will settle and the strength will come back."

She stared at the bleak landscape. They had left the city and were progressing through farmland. Last year's withered cornstalks and stubbled fields showed no sign of life yet, though the snow was mostly gone. The low spots were wet from early spring rains and melting snow. Even the grass hadn't greened yet.

"Life can be cruel," she whispered.

"Sometimes it can be wonderful, too. I'd forgotten that for a while. I was too busy wallowing in misery." He reached over with his gloved right hand and squeezed hers. "But then I met you. You brought sunshine into my life, Jen Fox."

Maybe the soup had finally warmed her. Perhaps the tea was working wonders. Whatever the reason, hope flickered ever so softly. Dan Wagner thought she had pulled him from despair. In return, she had accused him of gloating that he'd been correct.

"I'm sorry," she choked out.

"For what?"

She wasn't about to point out her flaws and start them on the wrong path again. "I mean, thank you. For listening to me. For not trying to talk me out of leaving the program. For showing up at the right time."

"My pleasure."

Out of the corner of her eye, she saw his lips curve into the grin that she had tried so hard to recall over the past couple weeks. Was he truly pleased or was he secretly smug that he'd been right all along?

"I'm not a quitter," she said. "Until today, I finished everything I started. High school. Work. The written flight examination. I'll complete the flight training, too."

"I'm sure you will." But his grin had dropped into a grim line.

She shivered and squeezed her eyes shut against the cold air swirling through the car. How would she ever get in the flight training? True, Jack had promised to teach her, once the snow melted and the school reopened, but the expedition was due to leave in the coming weeks. "Did the flight school open?"

"Not with Mrs. Hunter confined to bed."

Jen sucked in her breath. Marie had been confined to bed. There probably wasn't any connection. Many of the women in the maternity ward had delivered successfully. So would Darcy. Jen had to believe that.

A more practical implication came to mind. "Then I don't have a job."

"I suppose not," he said, "but you could find another one. Maybe the doctor needs an assistant."

Dan was trying to make light of things, but there was no avoiding the confrontation to come. "Mother will not be pleased. She wanted me to become a nurse. She felt it was my calling."

"Is that why you went into the program?"

"I suppose so. That and the fact that I will need to support myself."

"There are other ways." His fingers thrummed on the steering wheel with a steady rhythm. "You're bright and have a knack with engines. Why not talk to Simmons over at the aeromotor plant?"

That would be interesting work, but the only woman on staff worked in the office. "I'm not sure Hendrick would hire me."

"Have you asked?"

"No. First of all, I had a job. Second, I was so focused on flying that it never crossed my mind to look for work elsewhere."

He chuckled. "I believe that, but there's no reason you can't work at the plant and do your flight training once Mrs. Hunter returns to the school."

There was the rub. Dan Wagner still thought her desire to fly was only a whim. "You could teach me."

He coughed.

For the first time in ages, a smile tugged at her lips. She'd made Dan Wagner uneasy. Teasing him was easier than thinking about what faced her at home. "The snow is pretty much gone, and you must not be leaving for Spitsbergen yet if you still need Hendrick to machine some replacement valves for the engines. You'll have both time and opportunity."

He laughed. "It's good to see you returning to your old self."

"Old?"

"Normal," he corrected. "As for the expedition, the crates are ready for shipping except for the plane and the spare valves. Once we wrap up the engine testing, we can disassemble the plane and ship everything."

"From what port?" It felt good to talk about the polar expedition, even though Dan had clearly brought it up to distract her from flight training.

"I'm not sure yet. Hunter still needs to secure ship passage."

"What? He hasn't done that yet?"

"He's distracted. I think that the prospect of becoming a father has taken his mind off the expedition."

"Then you need to take charge."

He scowled. "I am taking charge, as you so bluntly put it, but this is his expedition. Ultimately he calls the shots."

"I'm sorry," she backtracked. "I knew that."

His frown eased. "I don't suppose you're hungry. Those sandwiches sure smell good."

To Jen's surprise, her stomach rumbled. "I guess I am."

Dan pulled the car onto a grassy patch on the side of the road. A small hill blocked the wind, and the sun shone brightly, warming the interior of the car. Jen unwrapped a sandwich and handed it to him.

"Why, thank you, miss." He gave her a dazzling smile.

"No. Thank you." Impulsively, she kissed him on the cheek.

He looked surprised and maybe even a little shocked, but soon enough the old grin crept back into place. "For buying the sandwich?"

She shook her head and breathed in the fresh air. "For taking me home." Mother's disappointment could never surpass the sheer mass of human suffering that she'd witnessed at the hospital. "I hope I never have to go to a hospital."

"You might if you take up flying. Accidents happen."

"I won't crash."

"Everyone crashes. It's a hazard of the occupation." He took a bite of the sandwich.

Jen unwrapped hers. It did smell delicious, but his statement got her to thinking. He had crashed recently. "That crash of yours last November. Did you go to the hospital?"

He choked, coughed and swallowed. "No."

Clearly that was one topic he did not want to discuss, but that only made her more curious. "You sound like you have been in the hospital."

His jaw tightened. "In the war."

"You were in the Great War? Was your airplane shot down?"

"The engine lost power at the wrong time. The plane hit a tree."

She winced. "You were hurt?"

"Broken leg and arm. I spent plenty of time in the hospital and sure appreciated the care the nurses gave me."

She laughed. "Something tells me you had them eating out of your hand."

"I wasn't Daring Dan back then."

"No, but you were just as handsome and charming."

That grin of his could light a city block. "Why, thank you, Miss Genevieve."

She gagged on a bite of sandwich.

He pulled a vacuum bottle from behind the seat and poured some tepid coffee into a tin cup. He held it out to her. "This will help."

She waved it off. "I'm better now. Just don't call me Genevieve."

He laughed, eyes sparkling. "Ah, Miss Fox, you have just handed me live ammunition."

"What do you mean?"

"If you don't know, then I'm not about to tell you." He swallowed the coffee. "Ready to finish the trip home?"

Home, where Mother waited. This would not be a pleasant reunion.

Jen looked nervous. Dan couldn't imagine why. This is what she wanted.

Her brow was creased, and her lips curved downward as she stared out the windshield.

"We can wait a little longer," he offered, "but I would like to get back before nightfall."

She shook her head. "Go ahead. I just need to figure out what to tell my mother."

"Tell her that nursing wasn't the right course for you."

"That will get me nowhere. She seems to think that nursing is my calling because Doc Stevens thought I would make a good nurse. But I wasn't." She bit her lip. "I was afraid."

"I think we're all afraid we'll fail."

She shook her head. "I did fail. Don't you see? I failed at home and I failed at the hospital. People died. I can't do anything that might hurt people."

"Then you don't want to fly airplanes."

Her head snapped toward him. "What do you mean? I can fly by myself."

"What of the instructor? Your copilot? The person you're training? The crowds at an air show? Aviation is not a solitary venture."

Before she could respond, he hopped out and cranked to start the car. When he slid into the driver's seat, he found her in exactly the same position, her jaw set.

"You don't want a partner on your airmail route." Her statement hung like a dark cloud between them.

He searched for the right thing to say. "You don't have the experience." He put the car in gear and resumed their drive back to Pearlman.

The bouncing and creaking was loud, but not loud enough to drown Jen's retort. "I don't have the experience for anything, since no one will show me how to fly."

If he wasn't holding on to the steering wheel, he'd throw his hands in the air. Whatever argument he used, it always led back to him teaching her to fly. He opted to let her stew in silence the rest of the drive. She obliged with the same stony expression.

When they coasted into town well over an hour later,

she finally came to life. "You should drop off the steel first rather than backtrack."

"Are you sure?" Of course she was sure. She didn't want to face her mother. He could give her that bit of time to gather herself.

After giving the steel to Simmons, he drove the short distance to Jen's family home. Cozy. That's the word he would use to describe it. Yes, he'd been there the night of the ball, but it had been dark then. In the daylight, he noticed how tiny the house was, even with the second story. The porch looked more dilapidated than he remembered, and the shutters sagged. If he was staying the summer, he would repair and paint that porch.

He slowed and parked the car. "I'll bring your bag."

"I can get it." But she didn't move.

He hopped out, grabbed her small bag from the back-seat and opened the passenger door.

She still didn't move.

"You will have to face her eventually. She's probably realized you're here." He nodded toward the curtained windows.

She blew out a sigh. "I'm sorry." She pivoted, accepted his hand and stood.

He squeezed her hand, conscious that he was right in front of her mother's house. "She's your mother. She'll understand. Even people who make their living off you eventually understand."

"Make their living off you?"

"My manager nearly keeled over when I told him I was leaving stunt flying. But he got over it. Still tries to convince me to do a show, but I don't hold it against him."

The corners of her mouth inched up.

"Your mother isn't depending on your income," he

pointed out, "and she loves you a whole lot more than my manager loved me."

She laughed. My, how he loved to hear her laugh. He loved the spark in her eye and the way she completely abandoned herself to the moment. "All right, Mr. Wagner. Let's face Mother." She wrapped her arm around his.

He wasn't sure how he'd ended up part of this confrontation, but he wouldn't let Jen down. She needed to know he would support her no matter what happened, though he doubted her mother would throw a fit in front of a virtual stranger, especially since she'd been so charmed the night of the ball.

The front door was unlocked, as were all front doors in Pearlman according to what he'd seen. Jen pushed it open and stepped inside.

No one met them.

"Mother?" she called out.

No answer.

"She's probably at the dress shop," Jen said with evident relief. "Ruth must be finishing packing up everything." She blinked rapidly. "You did say it was still open."

"As far as I know."

"Genevieve?" The silver-haired woman that Dan had met the night of the ball stepped into the parlor. Her hands were flour-covered. Apparently she was baking. She looked from her daughter to Dan and back again. "You have a break from school already?"

"No." Jen looked horribly guilty. If she didn't say this with confidence and conviction, her mother would not believe it.

"Then what happened?" Again Mrs. Fox looked to Dan. "Why is Mr. Wagner here?" Her eyes rounded. "Do you have an announcement?"

"No," Jen squeaked. "No, Dan just drove me back."

"All the way from Grand Rapids?"

"He was there to pick up some steel for the aeromotor factory."

Mrs. Fox frowned. "But how did you find each other and why did you come home—" she paused "—with a gentleman?"

Dan had the distinct impression that Pearlman held to stricter rules of behavior than the more liberal city populations. "It was only a drive, ma'am."

Her grim expression didn't budge. "Genevieve Fox. Explain yourself."

Jen began to tremble, something so unusual that Dan feared she would collapse. He gently guided her to the nearby sofa. She sank onto it but said nothing.

Dan ought to leave. He wanted to leave, but he couldn't abandon Jen. "Pardon me, ma'am, but I believe your daughter was eager to see you after what she's been through."

Mrs. Fox wiped her hands on her apron and then tenderly touched her daughter's shoulder. "What happened, dear?"

Jen shook her head, clearly fighting back tears, and in fits and starts managed to spit out that two patients had died. "I wasn't even there for her," she whispered in a ragged voice. "I was poor Marie's only visitor, and when she really needed someone I wasn't there."

"You were doing your job. Another nurse would have stayed with her."

"You don't understand. I failed her just like I failed Daddy."

Dan slipped silently away. This had gotten far too personal. Thankfully, neither woman noticed him head for the door. He grasped the doorknob.

"I left him, Mama." Jen's voice shook. "I left Daddy because I wanted to get my study materials from the flight school. I left him, and he died all alone."

"Hush now, dearest," Mrs. Fox consoled. "You are not to blame, and your father was never all alone. Our Lord was by his side."

Dan slipped out the door. He had heard too much.

Chapter Fourteen

Mother didn't understand. Oh, she accepted Jen's decision, but she didn't understand why Jen had to leave the nursing program.

"Perhaps after a little break they will take you back."

Jen couldn't let her cling to that hope. "No, Mother. I signed papers withdrawing from the program."

Mother gasped, ever so softly, before recovering. "There are other hospital programs. The Battle Creek Sanitarium has one, and you might not face the same traumas there."

In the end, Jen had agreed to consider other programs, but her mind had not changed after a long night's sleep. Nor would it change on this sunny beginning to the rest of her life. She pulled the pillow to her face, reveling in the familiar fresh scent. How she'd missed that. She'd even missed her sisters. Minnie must have gotten up already. Her bed was made, but with so little care that Jen rose and tucked the corners properly. She then made her bed, stretching the sheets so tightly that every wrinkle disappeared. The assistant nurse supervisor made anyone remake a bed that didn't follow the guidelines exactly.

After dressing, Jen wandered downstairs.

"Good morning," Mother said as she bounced baby Sammy on her lap. "Did you sleep well?"

"Yes, Mother."

The baby giggled, and Mother tickled his chin. "You must not have gotten much sleep there. I wondered if you would sleep all morning."

Jen glanced at the clock. It read nearly ten o'clock. She had never slept that late in her life. "I was tired."

"You were exhausted, dear. Do you feel better?"

Jen poured a cup of coffee. "I will once I drink this."

"It's not hot."

"I don't care." Jen tickled Sammy under the chin.

He squealed and reached for her.

Mother relinquished him without hesitation. "Have you thought about what we discussed last night?"

"I just woke up." Jen walked around the kitchen, Sammy on her hip, showing the baby the view through the window and all the cups lined up on the cupboard shelves.

"Well, I've been giving it some thought. I searched the week's newspapers and found two other hospital nursing programs accepting students. One is in Detroit. That would be very far away, but as I suspected the Battle Creek Sanitarium is advertising." She pushed a newspaper, folded to expose only the advertisement, across the table.

Jen didn't bother looking. "Nursing is not for me, Mother. I can fix a sewing machine or an airplane motor, but I can't fix people. I never felt so helpless. I couldn't do anything but hold people's hands."

"You were there for Mr. Smith. That is a gift and a calling. We all have our time, dear. A nurse can help ease the passing to the next life."

"I thought they healed people."

"God heals. We can only give comfort and hope."

Jen had no response for that. Nor could she have answered Dan's insistence that flying also put others at risk. Fortunately, Sammy distracted her by grabbing for the coffee cup. She moved it far from his reach. Naturally he screamed his displeasure, so she gave him a wooden spoon. He immediately stuck it in his mouth. "When are Ruth and Sam leaving? I didn't see them last night."

"Ruth is busy with the shop." Mother sighed. "It's sad to see it close. Your father opened it soon after Beatrice was born. It took a while before business picked up. My, we struggled in those days."

"But you're smiling. It couldn't have been that bad."

"When you're with someone you love, even the struggles are bearable. Remember that, Genevieve."

Jen wiped the drool from Sammy's chin.

"That young man who brought you home," Mother said. "Mr. Wagner. Other than his poor judgment in driving you here without a chaperone, he seems to be a gentleman."

Jen felt the beginnings of a matchmaking attempt coming on. "He has a reputation for short-lived relationships with women."

Mother frowned. "And you agreed to ride from Grand Rapids with him?"

"He is a friend, Mother, nothing more."

"But people will talk." Her frown deepened by the minute. "The neighbors would have seen him arrive. By now, everyone will know."

"By now, all of Pearlman knows I worked with Mr. Wagner on the polar expedition for over a month. I doubt seeing him bring me home in Jack's car was any surprise at all. Moreover, I attended the Valentine's Day Ball with him. I'm sure the gossips have us engaged by now."

Mother reached for Sammy, who had begun fussing. "How can you be so cavalier? A ruined reputation is no laughing matter. I must have a word with Mr. Wagner."

"No! Please don't." The last thing Jen needed was her mother's interference. "I'm sure no one thought a thing of it. I promise it won't happen again."

"No, it won't." Mother tapped the newspaper advertisement. "If you aren't to marry, you need to go to school. Since we can't afford college, a hospital nursing program is your only chance to learn a skill that will carry you through life."

Jen cut a slice from the loaf of fresh bread and recalled what Dan had told her. "Maybe my skills lie elsewhere."

"Where? You can't tinker around at the flight school forever. That will not earn you enough to let a room, least of all put food on the table."

Jen knew her mother was right, but the thought of returning to nursing made her nauseous. "I will find something before you leave for New York. I promise." She finished buttering the bread and took a bite.

"I'm leaving with Ruth and Sammy next week."

Jen choked on the mouthful of bread and washed it down with lukewarm coffee. "I thought you were waiting for Minnie's wedding."

"I was, but the house sold."

"So soon?" Jen cried. "I didn't know you even had it on the market."

"It is a blessing, especially since Sam's father has taken a turn for the worse. Sam left for New York Monday. Ruth, Sammy and I will take the train there next week."

"But the wedding. Minnie will be devastated."

Mother smiled indulgently. "I won't miss your sister's wedding. Ruth and Sam will return for that, so I can come with them."

Jen tried to sort it all out in her head. "But what about Minnie? Is she going to New York, too?"

"Of course not. She is going to stay with Beatrice until the wedding. She can help out with the cleaning and the children."

Jen leaned against the counter. "Then everything is accounted for."

"Except you. We expected you to be at the hospital for two years. We had no idea you planned to resign. I didn't receive a single letter from you."

"I'm sorry. There was no time between the twelve-hour shifts and the studying. I barely managed a few hours of sleep a day."

Mother simply nodded. "Well, that's water under the bridge, but it does leave us at a bit of a loss. You might ask Beatrice if she would be willing to take you in, too."

"If I had known..." Jen mused.

"You would have stayed at the hospital?"

Jen shook her head. "No. I knew from the start that I didn't belong there, but I might have found a job in the city. When were you planning to tell me this?"

"I sent a letter on Monday, the moment the sale was official."

Jen looked around the familiar kitchen, stuffed with the belongings of a lifetime. "What will we do with everything?"

"Ruth suggested we hold a sale in the dress shop, now that it's empty. Whatever doesn't sell, Beatrice offered to store in her attic."

Jen's head spun. Her childhood home had sold. Someone else would move in and change things around. Her mother and Ruth were leaving next week. She would have nowhere to live. Just when life was beginning to return to normal, the rug had been yanked out from under her feet.

Dan stared at Simmons. The barn was still cold at midday, but the man's admission sure heated things up. "Are you saying Jen was right?"

The man shuffled his feet, something he did when uncomfortable. "I didn't know that was her idea."

"Didn't I mention that?"

Dan tried to recall exactly what he had said to Simmons. Yesterday had been a blur. After leaving Jen and her mother in painful conversation, he had gone straight to the flight school hoping to talk to Hunter. The place had been locked up. Then he'd returned to the plant, where he mentioned Jen's idea of checking the cylinders, but he couldn't recall if he'd specifically told Simmons that Jen had suggested that.

"You just said to check the cylinder bore. I took a look last night and found some flaws. Cleaned them up early this morning. All we gotta do now is test the motor."

Dan blew out his breath. "We need some cold weather then, or we'll have to go into this attempt without the additional testing." That did not make him feel comfortable at all.

"Guess that's somethin' to pray for."

"For the weather? Do you really think God controls the weather?"

Simmons shrugged. "Can't hurt."

"What can't hurt?" said the very woman on Dan's mind.

He had to grin when he saw the faded old trousers and ragged mackinaw. "Back to your old self, I see."

She ignored him. "What's happening, Hendrick? Did we bring you the right kind of steel?"

Dan noticed she'd managed to put herself into the equation. To his surprise, he didn't mind.

"It'll work," Simmons said. "Gotta go."

"Wait!" Jen flagged him down. "I had something to ask you. I was wondering if there are any openings at the plant."

Simmons blinked. "No, uh, only— Nope. Not right now."

"Only what?" She snagged the single faint hope amid all those negatives. "I can work anywhere. I'm good with my hands."

Simmons shook his head. "There's nothing right now. I hafta get back."

She looked disappointed but rallied. "Be sure to keep me in mind if a job opens up."

Though Simmons muttered that he would, Dan suspected he wouldn't. Simmons came from the same traditional stock as Dan. He was not going to hire a woman to work on the assembly line. Dan didn't exactly blame him. With all that machinery, accidents happened. Fingers were lost. Occasionally a belt snapped. Fatalities were not out of the question. Still, women worked in a great many industries, especially in textiles. Dan could hardly believe he was thinking this, but Jen Fox would do well at Simmons Aeromotor. He wasn't quite ready to say that in front of her, though.

Her mouth had twisted into that determined frown that he had come to know—and end up on the receiving end of—all too often. Jen Fox would not let a little refusal stop her.

He chuckled as she watched Simmons walk away.

She spun around to face him. "What are you laughing at, Wagner?"

"The prettiest sight in the world."

Her head jerked back in surprise. Her mouth dropped open, and the loveliest color infused her cheeks. "You mean the airplane."

Dan roared. "Definitely not, though it is a fine-looking machine."

As usual, she turned the conversation away from her. "I see the left engine is still torn apart. Did Hendrick bring news?"

"He thinks he found the problem."

"Great. Was it the cylinder?"

Dan was not going to swell her pride by admitting she'd been right. "Simmons thinks he's found the problem, but we need to test the motor to be sure. Unfortunately the weather is too warm to cause icing." He shook his head. "I don't see it cooling off before we need to pack up and ship it all off to Europe."

She pursed her lips and scrunched her forehead. Her toe tapped the ground as seconds and then minutes passed.

He waited.

At last she grinned. "I think I have an idea."

"Great. Let's hear it."

She got a smug look on her face. "Only if you agree to teach me to fly."

Dan had not seen that coming. "That's blackmail."

"That's my price."

"You would jeopardize the polar attempt for selfish reasons?"

She flinched. "No, but I would at least like to start before you leave for Europe."

"What about Jack Hunter? He promised to teach you."

She shook her head. "I couldn't take him away from Darcy." She tilted her head in that incredibly alluring manner. "All I'm asking is to do a little grass cutting.

Show me the controls. Let me practice. Not dangerous at all."

Dan sighed. She had pegged his fears, but even grass cutting had its dangers. She might not brake sufficiently and plow into a tree or building. The wing could clip practically anything in a turn. He scrubbed his bristled jaw, trying to figure a way out of this.

"Please?" She gave him such a dazzling smile that he nearly gave in.

Then he remembered that Agnes had done the very same thing. She'd pleaded and promised him the world if only he would show her how a plane worked. He had caved in to her pressure, and look what happened. Her sudden movement, the loss of control, the tumbling plane, the fire. He'd carried her twisted body away. He'd known at once that she was dead, but still he carried her. He'd stumbled, and her limp body had dropped to the ground. He would never forget that waxen face, her eyes staring at nothing. In his mind, Jen's face replaced Agnes's. Those beautiful hazel eyes lifeless. He felt sick.

"No," he said. "I do not teach students. Period."

He walked away before she could change his mind.

"Dan Wagner is the most stubborn man alive," Jen complained to Minnie as they packed dishes into a crate to bring over to the dress shop. "Why don't we hold the sale here? It's so much work carting everything over there only to bring half of it back. You know most of this won't sell."

"I suppose we're having the sale there so we don't have to pack up the things we're using. You wouldn't want someone to buy the book on Shackleton that Daddy gave you for Christmas, would you? Or Ruthie's elephants. Or

Mother's Bible. Or that precious mackinaw that you rescued out of the rag bin."

"I suppose not." But ever since the unsuccessful talk with Dan yesterday, she'd been in a terrible mood. "I thought Wagner had changed."

"Don't you mean Dan?" Minnie said coyly. "I thought he'd graduated in your esteem."

So Jen's little sister was still playing matchmaker. She'd put an end to that. "No, I don't mean Dan. I mean Wagner. He's irritating, arrogant and stubborn as a mule."

Minnie laughed. "Sounds perfect for you."

Jen tossed a dishcloth at her sister.

"Why would you think he had changed?" Minnie said more soberly.

Jen recalled his tender consideration two days ago, when she'd broken down and begged him to take her home. He hadn't refused her then. "If he would drive me home, why won't he take me on a little training flight? Automobiles are at least as dangerous as airplanes, and you can't tell me he's more comfortable driving a car than a plane. He's the best aviator on earth."

Minnie lifted an eyebrow. "The whole earth?"

"Well, this half of it anyway. He's famous. He's done every stunt invented and added more of his own."

"Maybe he's not comfortable teaching."

Jen brushed that idea aside. "Why not? If he can do it, surely he can teach it."

"Maybe he's not comfortable teaching *you*."

Jen stared at her little sister. Could a girl who'd just turned twenty years old be right? "Why would it make any difference who he's teaching?"

Minnie barked out a laugh. "Because he likes you. Guys want to protect the gals they like."

Dan liked her? Was it possible? Jen felt the heat rise.

How could she forget that kiss? It wasn't stormy and filled with unquenchable passion like in the moving picture shows. It was more restrained, more of a promise, but she'd felt depth behind it. Was Minnie right? Was Dan afraid to teach her because he was falling for her?

"And then there's the accident," Minnie added.

"What accident?"

"The one last November. The one where that woman died."

"What?" The air punched from Jen's lungs. "A woman died?"

"Uh-huh. I clipped out the article because I thought you might want it later, after you came out of mourning. I found it last night and read it again. Her name was Agnes Something-or-other. I think it started with an *F*. Fineman or something like that. Anyway, they were supposedly getting serious. At least that's what the newspaper said. According to the article, the people closest to them figured they were going to marry within the year."

Jen sank onto a kitchen chair. Dan Wagner had been in love, had been ready to marry, and the woman he'd loved had died. "He was flying the plane?"

Minnie nodded. "The article said she was learning, and he was showing her how to work the controls. The plane got off the ground fine. Then someone saw it tilt. A wing caught a tree branch. The plane flipped, crashed and caught on fire. There was a photograph of a smoking wreck. The article said he carried her from the wreckage and was found kneeling beside her lifeless body, distraught."

Jen had no trouble imagining every step of that terrible day. She had held a dying man's hand. She had witnessed his last breath. It had affected her terribly, and she didn't even know the man. She had found Daddy dead in his bed, had tried to wake him even though she knew he was gone. Even the memory of that day made her tremble.

No wonder Dan had refused to teach her. His steadfast refusal to show her even the safest maneuver now made sense. It even explained why he'd made Jack promise to keep her from the expedition cockpit. It must mean he cared for her. Perhaps he was even falling for her. If she was just another gal, he wouldn't be so adamant.

"Why didn't he tell me?"

Minnie shrugged. "He's a man. Why didn't Peter tell me that his old friend was caught up in a bootlegging ring?"

"Because he didn't want you to get hurt."

Minnie nodded. "They're so busy trying to protect us, that they don't realize we can help them."

"Help them. Of course." The light dawned. "You helped Peter."

"And we found our way forward together. Well, some things he had to do himself. That's always the case, but a guy is stronger knowing that his gal is standing by his side."

That made perfect sense. Now Jen knew exactly what she had to do.

Chapter Fifteen

Jen arrived at the Hunter home after the lunch hour the next day. Darcy looked weak, and her hands were so swollen that Jen barely recognized them. Her face was also puffy, especially around the eyes. Similar to Marie. Jen shoved the thought away. Darcy wasn't Marie.

"Are you feeling all right?" Jen settled on the chair next to Darcy's sofa.

Her friend smiled weakly. "Tired all the time. I think it's the sedative Doc Stevens prescribed. It makes me sleepy, but he says I need to stay still and quiet until the baby is ready to be born."

"I heard that he also said you should go to a hospital."

"That's right." Jack stuck his head into the room. "Hello, Jen. Welcome back. Maybe you can talk some sense into my wife. She refuses to consider going to the hospital. Tell her to follow the doctor's advice. Maybe she'll listen to you."

Jen swallowed the growing flame of worry and gave Darcy what she hoped was an encouraging smile. "Maybe Jack is right. Maybe you should go to the hospital. They can monitor you and the baby day and night."

"See?" Jack said. "Even Jen agrees, and she should know. She's been a nurse at a hospital."

"Not quite a nurse yet," Jen corrected. "Not even a nurse in training. Just a probationer, but I did spend time in the maternity ward. There were a goodly number of women lying in."

Darcy waved a hand. "I'm perfectly fine right here. Besides, you didn't come here today to talk about me. What's on your mind?"

Jen struggled to surface from the flood of hospital memories.

"Before you two get started," Jack interjected, "would you mind staying with Darcy this afternoon? I need to go to Holland to meet with a subscriber."

"You didn't mention that before," Darcy said with a frown.

"I didn't want to worry you." Jack kissed his wife. "You know what the doctor said. No excitement or agitation. It'll only be for a few hours, and Mr. Kensington is going with me."

Darcy lifted an eyebrow. "I suppose that means you will be testing the golf course or shooting range."

Jack placed a hand over his heart. "It's not my way to do business, but some subscribers insist. I'll do my best to despise it."

Darcy laughed. "Go on, then. Jen and I will have a nice long visit and plan our arrival at Spitsbergen for the takeoff."

Jack didn't even argue. He thanked Jen and left.

She didn't recall agreeing to stay, but if Darcy could help her come up with a way to break through Dan's reserves, it would be worth the time. After all, what else did she have to do but pack dishes and linens? With Jack gone and the winds fresh, Dan wouldn't take the plane on a test flight.

"All right now," Darcy said. "What's on your mind?"

"Dan Wagner."

Darcy laughed. "How did I know that's what you would say? He is quite the looker, isn't he? Reminds me a lot of Jack. Full of charm, yet underneath that winsome act is a whole lot of hurt."

"Do you really think so?" Until yesterday's conversation with Minnie, Jen had never considered that Dan might be hurting. She figured he could brush off any problem, even that disastrous crash. "He always seems so sure of himself."

"So was Jack when I met him." She sighed, lost in memory. "My, he was handsome. Took my breath away. And so confident."

"Just like Dan."

Darcy smiled. "Just like Dan."

"Do you think he's hurting from November's accident?"

"Jack says he won't discuss it."

"That was my experience, too," Jen said. "When I brought it up, he changed the subject. Minnie told me a woman died."

Darcy nodded. "That's the kind of thing a top-notch aviator takes to heart."

"Anyone would, especially if they were planning to marry."

Darcy peered at her. "Is that what's got you concerned? You think that Dan is still in love with the woman who died?"

When spoken aloud, it sounded rather foolish. "He might be, but I would never know because he doesn't talk much about himself."

"Most men are like that. Women enjoy sharing their joys and hurts. Men keep them bottled up inside. Jack certainly did. I had no idea his sister had been crippled by polio. I didn't even know he had a sister for the longest time. What a surprise."

Jen was a little relieved. She knew a bit more about her favorite aviator. "Dan has brothers, and his parents are still living out in Montana on a ranch."

"Well, it seems he has told you a great deal."

"Except about the accident."

Darcy nodded. "That might still be difficult, especially if he did love her. It's only been a few months."

Jen heaved a sigh. "But I don't see why it should make any difference in teaching me to fly."

"Don't you?"

"You obviously know the answer, so tell me."

"You know the answer, too, better than anyone else." Darcy rubbed her temple.

"Minnie said it's because a guy wants to protect the gal he likes."

"True."

"That would mean Dan likes me, but how do I know?"

"Has he given you any idea that he cares? A little extra consideration, for instance. A gift perhaps." Darcy stopped rubbing her temple, but the frown didn't leave.

Jen pulled the medal from around her neck. "He did give me this to commemorate my part in the expedition." She wasn't about to mention the kiss.

Darcy examined the medal. "Lovely. And crafted by hand. That's not an insignificant gift. I would say he likes you very much."

Jen tried to take it in. He liked her. A lot. Even Darcy thought the evidence led to that conclusion. "He likes me." Saying it aloud felt foolish. "But then why won't he tell me that?"

"It might be difficult, with the memory of the crash so recent."

Until Darcy said that, Jen could have floated out the door and danced down the street. She wouldn't have even cared what people said. Dan Wagner liked her, but he hadn't gotten over the death of the woman he'd loved. She clutched the medal, as if it would vanish into thin air.

"I'm not sure." Panic gripped Jen's chest and squeezed hard. "What do I do now?"

Dan supposed a squeamish subscriber was reason enough for Hunter to leave town, but he had hoped to talk the man into giving Jen an initial lesson. Maybe then she would divulge her idea for testing the engine for carburetor icing.

Since Hunter's wife was a good friend of Jen's, he also figured the man could answer the lingering question of her father's death. Based on her reaction the day he brought her home, that event had devastated her. She'd held out her father as the reason she had to be part of the polar expedition, but it was her agonized confession that stuck in his head. For some reason, she blamed herself and that blame had somehow gotten wrapped up into the whole idea that she ought to become a nurse.

When Blake Kensington appeared with the news that Hunter had gone to Holland with his father, Dan had to grit his teeth. Another day lost. True, the winds had been brisk early on, but they were dying down. By late afternoon, they would have no trouble flying. Unfortunately, Hunter wouldn't be there.

"So this is the bird," Blake said as he walked around

the expedition airplane. "It's a lot bigger than the one Hunter built for the transatlantic attempt."

The night of the ball, Dan had found Blake Kensington bitter. Today, he wasn't sure if the man was truly appreciative or for some reason measuring this plane against the one that had failed to cross the Atlantic.

He decided to take the man at face value for now. "Were you involved with that flight?"

Kensington grinned. "I was the top backer."

So that was it. The son measured himself against his father. "You could join us for the polar attempt. We welcome all supporters."

That bitter look reappeared for a moment. "Not this time, old sport. Just wanted to see what the old man has gotten himself into." He stopped next to the ladder and looked up at the left engine. "Problems?"

"Fixed." At least Dan hoped they were. He'd checked the forecast for the next few days, and the springtime warmth was increasing. Chance of thunderstorms, starting today, but that wasn't the weather problem he needed. Ice and snow were apparently a thing of the past.

"That's good." Kensington made another circuit of the plane, as if looking for something.

"Anything I can do for you?"

Blake Kensington scanned from the fuselage to the wheels they'd installed in place of the skids. "Doesn't look like it carries much gear."

"Only safety equipment, fuel and oil. The necessities."

"Then the trip will be nonstop."

"That's the idea."

Kensington looked up at the cockpit. "The expedition will last awhile, though."

Dan had no idea what he was getting at. "As much as a month or so, depending on the weather."

"Then you'll need food and supplies for the ground crew."

"Yes." Something tickled the edge of his memory. Kensington clearly had a vested interest, but what was it? Dan searched his memory. Blake was married to Jen's oldest sister. Though Mayor Kensington's only son, the two had had a falling-out over something. Yet Dan seemed to recall that Blake was still involved in the family's businesses. The mercantile! That was it.

"Of course we'll be placing an order with you once we settle on the number of crew we're bringing to Spitsbergen." Dan hoped Jack wouldn't be upset that he'd committed to use the mercantile, even though it was probably more expensive. Where was Jen when he needed her? She would have known instantly whether they should buy local, from large-scale suppliers or abroad.

Blake looked pleased. "Be sure to give us enough lead time. Some of the suppliers can take their time."

"I'm sure the large quantity will spur them into action."

Blake stuck out his hand. "Pleasure doing business with you, Wagner."

Against his better judgment, Dan shook on the deal. If he was going to commit the expedition to buying locally, he might at least pry a little information out of Kensington. "I wonder if you could enlighten me on the Fox family."

The wariness returned. "How?"

"Could you tell me a little about their father?"

Blake looked surprised. "What do you want to know? He passed away last October."

"Was Jen close to him?"

Blake shrugged. "They all were. He had a weak heart

since childhood, but he was a gentle man and a good listener."

"It sounds like you knew him well."

"It didn't take long to figure out he was the opposite of my father. Good old Dad wasn't too pleased when I married a Fox."

"Oh?" Dan thought he knew why, but Blake looked eager to tell him.

"Wrong side of the tracks and all." He grinned. "She's a beauty, though. Still takes my breath away." He shook his head. "Don't know what she's doing with someone like me, but then that's what we all wonder."

"You're right about that." Dan had trouble imagining why Jen would be interested in him. "They're a fine family. Too bad everyone's going in different directions."

"It's a great opportunity. Ruth is a talented dress designer. She will do well in New York. Her father would be proud of her."

"I'm sure he would be proud of all of his daughters." Yet Dan suspected Jen didn't feel that way. Like Blake, she seemed to be trying to prove something. Unlike Blake, her father was no longer alive to acknowledge her success. "Would you like a tour of the plane?"

Blake brightened. "Boy, would I."

That was the first time Dan had seen any excitement in the man. Maybe buying from his mercantile would do more than support a local merchant. "Ever been up in one?"

Blake ran a hand over the fuselage. "Sure. With Jack Hunter. He let me take the controls." He whistled. "I wanted to get my license. Should have."

"Why didn't you?"

Kensington sighed. "Life. A wife and children. Responsibilities." He winced. "And bad choices."

Maybe that's what had estranged father from son. Dan couldn't believe that marrying one of the Fox girls was enough to set his father against him. "We all make bad choices now and then." Dan made a split-second decision. "Would you like to take her up today? I'd like to make a test flight."

That spark ignited again. "Are you joking? Sure."

"It'll take a little while before we can take off. I need to do the full preflight check. Say half an hour. If you have something to do—"

"Nothing that can't wait. Show me everything." Every trace of bitterness had vanished, replaced by eager excitement.

Who knew an airplane could do that? Dan had made the right decision. One flight could make a difference in a man's life. He handed Kensington the clipboard with the preflight procedure. "Read out each item and check them off when I tell you to."

Dan would take his time. This flight had to go perfectly since he had no one aboard who could help in the event of trouble.

Darcy pressed both hands to her temples and squeezed her eyes shut.

"Headache?" Jen asked.

"It'll pass." But she sounded breathless and weak.

Jen hopped up. "I'll get a cold compress. That might help."

She had been at the Hunters' house often enough to know her way around their kitchen. She was surprised to see a telephone installed on the kitchen wall. The Hunters weren't well-off. Maybe Darcy's parents had insisted she have a telephone. Her father was the bank manager.

Jen grabbed a small washcloth from the drawer and

began pumping water with the hand pump. This time of year, the well water was ice-cold, but the old pump took a little muscle to get going. She wondered how Darcy managed since she was supposed to be confined to bed. Even if Jack filled a container of fresh water in the morning, she might need more throughout the day. They certainly didn't have a maid.

They could use a housekeeper and nurse.

Jen's hand stilled. She wasn't good at either, but she knew how to clean and cook. She also knew more about nursing than the average person. Since she needed a place to stay starting next week, maybe Darcy would let her live with them in exchange for housekeeping services. Knowing Darcy, she would insist on paying Jen or complain that the guest bedroom wasn't ready for a boarder. No, it would be better to go through Jack. She would talk to him when he returned.

She squeezed the excess water from the cloth and brought it to the parlor. "Here." She applied the compress to Darcy's forehead. "Does that feel any better?"

Darcy murmured her thanks. "You should be a nurse."

Jen chuckled. "I discovered I wasn't tough enough. It takes a strong woman to be a nurse."

"I believe that." Darcy leaned her head against the pillow and gasped softly.

Jen's pulse accelerated. "Is it time for more medicine?"

"No. Please. I would rather the pain than that dreadful sedative." She smiled wanly, though her eyes didn't open. "It's just this pain under my rib cage. It must be the baby kicking." She rubbed her right side. "He is certainly strong."

"He? How do you know it's a boy?"

"I don't, of course, but my mother insists I'm going to have a boy from the way I'm carrying the baby. We shall see." She pulled the compress from her forehead. "Now, what were we discussing?"

"How to convince Dan to teach me to fly."

"Ah, that's right." Darcy's fingers kneaded her brow. "You need to show him that you aren't a piece of porcelain."

Jen snorted. "Look at me. Who could ever think I'm fragile? That's Beattie and Ruth and maybe even Minnie, but not me."

"You would be surprised. Jack thought I was. He still hovers over me in the worst way. Sometimes I want to scream."

"But you convinced him to teach you to fly."

"I convinced him that if he wouldn't teach me, I would find someone who would."

"But of course you didn't."

"No." A faint smile lifted her lips for a moment before the pain stole it away. "He taught me. We had our problems. That first crash bothered him terribly."

"You hit your head in that one, right?"

She nodded. "He was so upset. I thought he would never take me up in a plane again, but that wasn't it. He'd begun to realize he was falling in love with me and couldn't bear losing me. That's when I had to use some extra persuasion. I rallied the town to fix his plane. When he saw what we'd done, why, he loved me more than ever."

Jen's mind whirred. If she could fix that bothersome left engine, maybe Dan would realize she wasn't a fragile flower. She leaped to her feet and paced the room. Hendrick had fixed the cowling and the cylinder bore. That should do it, but they needed that test. Perhaps instead of bargaining one against the other, she should offer the solution she'd come up with and trust Dan to follow

through with lessons. He was a gentleman. He appreciated her mechanical skills. That might just do it.

"That's it! Thank you, Darcy. That's exactly what I
needed."

Instead of hearing Darcy's agreement, only deathly
silence came from the direction of the sofa.

"Darcy?" Jen hurried across the dim room.

Her friend's entire body shuddered with the same ter-
rifying convulsions Jen had witnessed in the hospital's
maternity ward.

Chapter Sixteen

Jen froze.

It was happening again. Her father. The woman in the maternity ward. Marie. They'd all died.

But not Darcy. *Please, Lord, not Darcy.* She was finally going to have the baby she'd wanted for years. All those miscarriages. All that heartache. It couldn't end now. It couldn't end this way.

A nurse leaps into action with a calm mind and a sure hand. The nursing instructor's admonition rang in Jen's mind.

Calm down. She took a deep breath. Darcy needed help, not panic.

Put a padded tongue depressor between her jaws. The instruction flashed into Jen's mind, but she didn't have a tongue depressor. She didn't have any wood at all. She looked around the room. All sorts of bric-a-brac but nothing that would work.

The compress. Jen rolled it tightly. Thankfully, the cloth was small and thin enough that it rolled into a size that fit between Darcy's upper and lower jaws while leaving room to breathe.

Now what? Darcy was breathing, but the seizure

hadn't stopped. Jen fought panic. What should she do? What could she do? She was alone here, and the nearest hospital was in Grand Rapids. Think. Think.

What had the nurses done in the ward? After ensuring the patient could breathe and couldn't bite her tongue, they had made sure a thrashing patient didn't injure herself. But Darcy wasn't thrashing. Her muscles quivered, but her limbs didn't jerk. Then they had summoned the staff physician on duty. Jen should fetch Doc Stevens. But that meant leaving Darcy. Jen had left her father, and he'd died. She couldn't leave Darcy.

Then she remembered the telephone in the kitchen. She would have to leave Darcy for a moment, but she had to do something.

"Hold on, Darcy, I'm calling for Doc Stevens." Jen stroked her arm and noticed the spasms were easing. She was coming out of the convulsion. That gave her just enough time.

She ran into the kitchen and rang the operator. Cora Williams took her sweet time answering.

Jen didn't wait for her to finish asking what she could do for her. "Get me Doc Stevens. Now. It's an emergency."

"Doctor Stevens is at the Buncton farm. There was a terrible accident with the—"

"Do they have a telephone? I need medical advice immediately. Mrs. Hunter has gone into convulsions."

Jen regretted giving that information to the town gossip, but it did spur Cora into action.

"Please wait while I make the connection."

It probably took only seconds, but it felt like minutes before someone's scratchy voice came on the line.

"Get me Doc Stevens," Jen shouted. "It's an emergency."

"It's an emergency here, too," the woman snapped. "Doc is preparing for surgery."

Jen gathered herself. "I'm sorry. Could you ask him for some advice? Mrs. Hunter has gone into convulsions. I know from my time at the hospital that this could be fatal."

The woman didn't answer. Jen heard only static. Had the woman hung up?

Then Doc Stevens came on the line. "What are the symptoms?"

Jen repeated what she had observed.

"Is she in labor?" he asked.

"I don't know."

"Find out. If she gives birth, she may make it."

Jen's knees went weak. Then she remembered. "She did complain about some abdominal pain. Maybe she is starting labor. I'll check."

"You may not have much time. Did you birth any babies at the hospital?"

"No, sir, but I did witness a birth."

"It'll have to do. You could send for Mollie Humphries."

Jen recognized the midwife's name. "I'm alone. Does she have a telephone?"

"No. Don't leave the patient. You need to stay with her. Now listen carefully. If she's in labor and dilated sufficiently, you may need to hurry the baby along by breaking the membranes. Understand? If Mrs. Hunter is conscious, have her push. Even so, you might need to ease the baby out the birth canal. Since you don't have forceps, use your hands. Be sure to scrub them thoroughly."

Jen felt sick, but Darcy needed her to be strong and keep her wits about her. "What do I do if she's not in labor?"

"She needs to get to a hospital at once. Have Jack drive her there." The connection crackled.

"Doctor Stevens? Doc?" she cried into the telephone mouthpiece. "Jack's not here."

With a click, the line disconnected.

"I'm sorry, Jen," the operator, Cora Williams, said. "I'll try to reconnect the call."

"No. I got the information I needed." Jen hung up.

Please God, let Darcy be in labor.

If not, she needed to find another way to get Darcy to the hospital. Who could drive the distance fast enough?

The answer came in a flash, so obvious. He wouldn't be near a telephone, though. She picked up the telephone receiver again.

Cora came on the line so quickly that she must have been waiting.

Jen rushed past formalities. "Try the flight school. If there's no answer, send someone fast as you can to the airfield and have him bring Dan Wagner to the Hunters' house."

Blake Kensington seemed truly interested in the workings of the airplane. He asked questions about every checklist item, absorbed the information and asked more questions. A student couldn't have done better. The man would have made a fine aviator, but he had chosen the responsible path of raising a family.

Dan knew he was being unfair to Jen. If he was going to take any novice on a test run, it ought to be her. She at least knew how the plane worked. Kensington didn't. This rash decision of his didn't look fair on the surface, but Dan didn't trust himself at the controls with Jen on board. It was too much like that bad decision to teach Agnes—only worse. He hadn't loved Agnes. Jen, on the other hand, occupied his thoughts day in and day out. Maybe it wasn't love, but it was getting close.

No, this little flight would last only minutes. Dan would take the plane up, circle the airfield and come down. Simple. Quick. Jen wouldn't even know. Except the Hunters lived across the road from the airfield and Jack said Jen was staying with his wife today.

She'd know.

And he'd hear about it tomorrow.

For a second, Dan considered canceling the flight. He could claim the winds weren't right. Kensington wouldn't know. But the man had come alive at the prospect of flying. Dan could explain things to Jen, and the flight wouldn't last long enough to put a family man in danger.

"Elevator," Kensington called out.

Dan verified its operation from the controls, and then checked it visually while explaining its function.

Kensington took it all in. "You sure have the life. Sometimes I wish I hadn't married."

The comment shivered through Dan. "Sometimes I wish I had, but the right woman never came along."

"Why not have both? The Hunters are married."

"That might work for them but not for me. Not with stunt flying, anyway. I had to comfort too many widows to ever put a woman through that." Dan's hand stilled. "Sometimes I envy guys like you. You get to come home every night to a woman who loves you and children eager to see you. I've spent years going from hotel to hotel. Not the fine ones, either. This is the longest I've been in any one place since I started flying, but a boardinghouse is not a home. My brothers have families, children to carry on their name. That's what's important."

"It's a burden sometimes."

Dan sensed the man's chafing against circumstances.

He had to make Kensington see what a treasure he had. "Everything has its downside, believe me. Flying isn't all glory. There's a lot of loneliness and heartache. At the end of the day, a plane can't love you. It can only perform or not perform."

Kensington considered his words. "You sound like a man ready to retire."

"I'm done with stunt flying." Dan crawled down from the ladder. "I'd like what you have. A family. Time at home. Maybe children someday."

"With Jen Fox?"

The pointed question hit Dan hard. Was Jen the deciding factor? He'd given up stunt flying before he met her, but if she hadn't captured his interest, he would probably be starting the airmail route about now. Yes, he cared for her. A lot. Maybe even loved her, but he wasn't sure she felt the same. That impulsive hug and kiss had come from gratitude, not love. She never talked about having a family or children. She bristled whenever he got too close.

"I doubt she'd have me," Dan joked. "I manage to set her off pretty much every time I open my mouth."

Kensington laughed, but not harshly like the night of the ball. Today it held a surprising measure of sympathy. "I know the feeling, old sport. They're pretty much all like that. At least the Fox women. Good through and through. Maybe too good for the average guy and pretty near impossible to figure out."

"I can't disagree with you there." Dan wiped his hands on a rag, more than ready to turn back to business. "That should be the last thing on the preflight checklist. I fueled her earlier."

Blake handed him the clipboard, and Dan looked it over.

"Mister Wagner. Mister Kensington." A boy's breathless cries drew Dan's attention away from the airplane.

Dan looked up to see a dark-haired, olive-skinned boy of perhaps fourteen or fifteen running toward them.

"Luke? What are you doing here?" Kensington asked.

"Missus Hunter is sick, and Miss Jen needs help. She needs Mister Wagner to go to Mister Hunter's house right away."

Dan didn't hear anything past "Miss Jen needs help." He threw the clipboard on the table and sprinted from the barn, Blake Kensington on his heels.

Darcy came out of the convulsion confused and angry. She yanked the rolled cloth out of her mouth and flung it to the floor. "What is that doing in my mouth? What are you doing to me?"

Jen imitated the calm yet firm tone the head nurse always used. "You had a seizure. The cloth was to prevent you from injuring yourself."

"What are you talking about? I'm right here and perfectly fine."

Darcy didn't know what had happened.

Jen's heart pounded in her throat, and her palms sweated. She had to follow Doc's instructions, even though she knew nothing about birthing a baby. She had only witnessed the early pangs from a distance. Those women had screamed as if being torn in half.

Darcy wasn't screaming. Yelling at her, yes, but not screaming.

On the other hand, many of the women suffering the pangs leading up to childbirth had done so in silence or with only the faintest of moans. Jen had mopped their foreheads and consoled them that their time would come soon. It seldom did. Hours would pass. Sometimes a day, leaving the woman exhausted.

Darcy looked uncomfortable, but her face didn't twist with pain.

Jen picked up the rolled compress and set it on the end table while she figured out how to ask the question Doc Stevens had posed to her. In the end, she decided asking straight out was best. "Are you having labor pains?"

Darcy stared before squeezing her eyes shut. "Of course not."

That was not good. They would have to get Darcy to the hospital at once. In this mood, she would put up a fight.

Maybe Jen could convince her she might be in labor. "You mentioned pain earlier. Maybe it's the start."

"I suppose we could call Doc Stevens." Darcy was starting to sound more normal. "He has been here far too often, though. I hate to bring him here for nothing."

"I already talked to him on the telephone."

"You did? When? We've been talking the entire time."

"Well, no. You drifted off for a couple minutes." That sounded innocuous enough.

Darcy heaved an irritated sigh. "Then, he is on his way."

"Well, no. He's out at the Buncton farm. Apparently there was an accident requiring surgery."

"Oh, dear."

Jen tried not to panic. What if Darcy had another convulsion? She hoped Cora reached Dan by telephone or sent someone right away. She hoped he was at the flight school. If not…

Her stomach churned. "Lord, help us."

Darcy's eyes flickered open. "What did you say?"

Jen didn't realize she'd said that prayer aloud. "Just praying for the Lord to watch over us."

"And the injured at the Buncton farm," Darcy added.

That was it. Prayer calmed the worst agitation. Jen knelt by Darcy's side. "Let's pray together."

The act of concentrating on prayer calmed Jen, and she could feel Darcy relax, too. After praying for the injured person that Doc Stevens was treating, they prayed for Jack's travels and Ruth and Mother's train trip and even the safety of the polar expedition crew. Naturally Darcy did not mention her own need.

That fell to Jen. "Lord, bring this little one safely into this world. Give Darcy strength to see this birth through."

The front door burst open, cutting off their prayer.

Dan charged into the room. "What happened?"

Behind him came Blake Kensington, of all people. Jen briefly wondered why he was there, but there would be time to ask that question later.

Jen stood. "Doc Stevens wants us to get Darcy to the hospital right away."

"What?" Darcy cried. "I don't need to go to a hospital. I'm fine."

Jen wheeled about, the firmness of her few weeks of nurse training taking over. "No, you're not. Doc Stevens confirmed it. You need to get to a hospital now. No debate."

"But Jack," Darcy said. "I need Jack with me."

"I'll get him," Blake volunteered. "I know who they were meeting, and I have a pretty good idea where they would have met." He looked to Jen. "Do I bring him here?"

"No. That will take too long. Bring him to Memorial Southwest in Grand Rapids." The hospital where she'd trained was closest and the care excellent.

"Then, who is bringing Mrs. Hunter to the hospital?" Dan asked.

"We are," Jen answered. "Darcy, do you have a bag packed?"

"Yes, it's in the bedroom, but there's no reason for this fuss."

"Yes, there is." The nurses hadn't taken any guff, and neither would Jen.

"Wait a minute, Miss Fox," Dan interjected. "You are forgetting something important. Neither one of us has an automobile."

She looked him square in the eye. "We have a plane."

Chapter Seventeen

"A what?" Dan must have heard wrong. She expected him to fly Mrs. Hunter to the hospital? Was she out of her mind? "Doesn't this town have an ambulance?"

"We don't have a hospital. We surely don't have an ambulance. Prepare the plane. Blake, I'll need your assistance getting Darcy to the airfield. Do you have your car?"

"I'll be back before you're ready to go." Blake shot off at a run.

Fortunate man. He wasn't the one who had to fly an overconfident and underexperienced nurse-aviatrix and her patient to an airfield he had never seen.

"Slow down, Jen. Let's think this through."

Her glare could have frozen a steaming geyser. "Get the plane ready."

"It is ready. I've done a preflight check today, but is this the best method to get Mrs. Hunter to the hospital?"

"I don't need to go the hospital," Darcy insisted, though she squeezed her eyes shut in evident pain and began taking short, shallow breaths. "Why is everyone insisting I go?"

Jen grabbed Dan's arm and hauled him into the

kitchen. Standing painfully close, so her nose nearly touched his, she hissed, "Listen, Wagner. I am not over-reacting. Darcy had a seizure. I called Doc Stevens, and he said she has to get to a hospital now or she will die. Understand? Now go get that plane."

Dan didn't hesitate. He obeyed. In fact, he ran.

As his feet pounded the dirt road, he vaguely noted how glorious Jen was in command. In a crisis, she had risen to take charge. The brokenness he'd observed the day he'd brought her back from the hospital was gone. This Jen was strong and firm and in control. This Jen knew exactly what to do and woe to anyone who questioned her. If he wasn't so panicked, he would have enjoyed the moment. But the fact was that a woman depended on his aviation skills. Two women, if he knew Jen Fox. She would insist on joining her patient. Two women and a baby.

It was three times worse than the day with Agnes.

He went to the flight school first to find any notes Jack had made about the Grand Rapids airfield. He then placed a telephone call to Memorial Southwest hospital and requested an ambulance meet them at the airfield.

Then he raced to the barn. He pulled open the doors and ran to the plane.

The checklist. One more look to make sure he had everything. It would be a few minutes before Blake arrived with the women. He picked up the clipboard, but his hand was shaking so much that he couldn't read the list.

Frustrated, he set it down. Flaps, ailerons, elevator, pedals, fuel, oil, everything checked out. Except they would be using an untested left engine.

He closed his eyes and took one deep breath. Two. Three. The doubts had started. Once an aviator lost confidence, his career was over. He'd seen it over and over.

The polar expedition had been the perfect solution, because Jack Hunter took the lead. He would fly the plane. Dan was copilot and navigator. Simple. In an emergency, he could step in. In an emergency, he wouldn't have time to think about the crash. Then why was he thinking of it now? This was surely an emergency.

This flight risked three lives. No one could help him. He had no one to turn to except God, but he'd dismissed Him years ago. Dan was a man of science.

He barked out a bitter laugh. Science failed. He only had to look at the engine troubles and his crash for evidence.

God never fails.

That assertion came from some deep recess in his mind, that part of him that had memorized scripture as a youth. King David had believed it with all his heart, and God had rewarded that faith with success. Could Dan put his trust in that which couldn't be proved by scientific means? It came down to faith. Could Dan make that leap? Jen had. He'd heard their prayer, had seen the change in her. Maybe he could.

What choice did he have?

Lord, I don't know how to pray. Years of neglect had left him clueless. *Please help. Get us there safely. Only You can save Mrs. Hunter and her baby.*

He could not imagine what Jack would do if his wife perished.

Dan pulled on the thick sweaters he wore under his leather jacket. He donned the leather helmet and grabbed a blanket from one of the expedition crates to make Mrs. Hunter more comfortable. Then he faced the airplane and the flight that would either kill him or make him strong.

"I'll need you to help me start the engines," Jen told Blake as he drove them the short distance to the barn. "And get Darcy in the plane."

"I don't need to go," Darcy repeated, though her protests were getting weaker.

Jen hoped the convulsions wouldn't return. She didn't know much about them except that the result was usually bad. Since Darcy didn't appear to be in labor yet, maybe giving her a purpose would keep her mind occupied enough that she wouldn't shut down.

"We need you in the cockpit," Jen said firmly. "You are the only person in Pearlman qualified to be copilot, and the expedition plane definitely needs a copilot."

As Jen had suspected, the prospect of flying gave Darcy a burst of energy. "The preflight needs to be done."

"Dan said he already did that."

"We did," Blake concurred. "We had just finished when Luke Meeks came running in with the message that you needed help."

Blake had helped Dan perform the preflight check? Why? That had to have taken place before they knew she needed Dan to fly them to the closest hospital. It made no sense. She tucked that nugget away for later. She couldn't dwell on it now when every moment was critical.

Blake sped onto the pitted and rutted airfield. The Cadillac was better built than many automobiles, but the jolts still threw Jen into the air. Darcy moaned.

"Slow down," Jen demanded. "We don't want her to have the baby in your car." Though Doc Stevens had said that giving birth would remedy the situation, the thought of actually birthing a baby made her queasy.

Blake must have felt the same way, because he braked the car to a more comfortable pace.

Now that she could talk without her teeth slamming together over every bump, Jen tried to keep Darcy focused. "Which engine do we start first?"

"The right." Darcy's voice sounded faint.

Jen's palms began sweating again. What if Darcy had another seizure? The copilot's seat might not be the best place for her. The plane was large, with enough room between the seats for a person to slip into the back. That was so the navigator could access supplies in the cargo area and make drift calculations through a small trapdoor. Maybe she should have Darcy lie down in the cargo area.

"Are you having any labor pangs?" she asked Darcy again.

"No, just this pain on my right side."

That sounded familiar. The head nurse in maternity said that was one of the signs of progressing toxemia. Seizures came next. In the hospital, they injected magnesium something or other. That remedy was not in Jen's grasp. Other than preventing Darcy from biting her tongue and ensuring she could breathe, Jen could offer little but prayer and a comforting, calm presence. The rest was in God's hands.

Preventing a seizure was the best option. That meant keeping Darcy calm and focused on something other than her condition. That meant the copilot's seat. She would also rest easier once Jack was with her. He could get there sooner if Blake's father drove him straight to the hospital.

"Blake, can your father and Jack be reached by telephone?"

"Not where I figure they went. I'll try, though."

"Use the telephone in the flight school office." If the school was open. "If it's locked, Dan will have a key."

"Right." He drove around a huge pothole and approached the barn, whose doors were wide-open. "Darcy, I'll pick up your parents on the way."

"That's thoughtful," Jen said. Surprisingly thoughtful. She had always found Blake self-absorbed and still clinging to his days as a college football star. He had never seemed to consider anyone else before, yet today he'd thought of a source of comfort that Jen had forgotten.

"I'll get everyone to the hospital as soon as I can." Blake pulled the car into the barn and as close to the plane as possible.

Dan whipped open the passenger door, and the next minutes were consumed with getting Darcy out of the automobile and into the airplane. When Jen had come up with this plan, she'd forgotten that the cockpit was five feet above the ground. To get Darcy inside, she must climb a ladder. She was in no condition to climb one rung, least of all five feet. Then she would have to crawl into the copilot seat.

"How?" Jen mouthed to Dan.

He had it figured out. "Blake, you take Darcy's left arm, and I'll take the right. He had placed three ladders side by side leading up to the cockpit.

Jen followed, carrying the wool blanket from the car and Darcy's bag. She helped Darcy place each foot securely on a rung. The two men pretty much carried her up the ladder and then tucked her into the seat. To Jen's surprise, the plane was equipped with seat belts. That was unusual except for stunt planes and trainers. Considering this plane was enclosed due to the arctic cold, she hadn't expected to find seat belts. It must be Dan's influence. Jack hadn't had them originally. Unfortunately, even at its maximum extension, it wouldn't fit around Darcy. She wrapped the car blanket around Darcy's legs to shield them from the cold.

"Pull the ladders into the plane," Dan barked. "We don't know what they'll have at the airfield."

Blake and Jen followed orders. It was better than thinking about what might happen. The ladders took up most of the cargo space. Jen spread out one of the expedition blankets in the remaining area in case she had to get Darcy into a lying position.

"Blake, Jen, I want you each on a propeller. Jen, show Blake what to do."

Blake crawled down onto the wing and then hopped off. Jen got out onto the wing.

"Close the door," Dan commanded.

"I'll need to get back in," Jen pointed out.

"I can do this without you."

"What? Are you a nurse? Do you have the slightest idea what to do if there's an emergency? Darcy needs me, and I intend to stay with her the entire flight."

"I'm fine," Darcy said again. "I don't need to go to the hospital."

"You're going," Jen reiterated, "and I'm going with you."

Dan didn't look pleased, but he had the sense not to argue. "All right, but hurry."

Jen bit back the retort that they would be a lot further along if he hadn't asked her to leave. Now was no time to feud with Dan Wagner.

"I'll help you turn the props," she shouted to Blake.

"I can do it," he shouted back. "I've done it before for Jack."

"Right one first." After pointing to the correct propeller, Jen crawled back in the plane and closed the door.

She'd forgotten cotton for Darcy's ears and hers, but Dan handed a wad to her. While she helped Darcy with the cotton earplugs, Dan started the engines.

Blake backed his car out of the garage, and then Dan inched the plane out of the barn.

Darcy looked pale. Soon Jen wouldn't be able to communicate with her. Already the drone of the engines was loud. When Dan brought them up to speed, it would be deafening.

Jen leaned over her so she could see her patient's face. "How do you feel?"

Darcy smiled and squeezed Jen's hand. Her normally strong grip was weak. Knowing Darcy, she was putting on a good front when she really felt awful. Jen pulled her watch from her trouser pocket and took Darcy's pulse. Not good.

Please let her make it to the hospital, Lord.

Dan had reached the head of the runway. The ground was sloppy, and dark clouds lined the western horizon. Foggy haze had settled low over the fields. This combination signaled storms on the way. They had to complete the flight before the storm arrived.

When the engines accelerated, Jen shoved the cotton into her ears. The roar and vibration sank clear to the roots of her teeth. The length of flight required for the polar attempt meant hours upon hours—twenty or more—in that din. She shook her head. By the time the pilots returned, they would be practically deaf.

Dan brought the lumbering plane down the runway. Jen knelt on the blanket, which did little to ease the hardness of the floor. Thankfully, the flight shouldn't take long, maybe a half hour or so in this powerful plane.

They sped past the bare trees and familiar houses of Pearlman. The pitted runway jolted her side to side and pitched her forward. She braced herself against the seats so she wouldn't get thrown onto the controls and instruments. The end of the runway loomed closer and closer. Then, when it seemed certain they would not get into the air, the plane rose. The jolting and bumping stopped, replaced by the glorious sight of her town far below.

Pearlman. Jen squeezed Darcy's hand. Her friend

pulled it away and grabbed her abdomen. Her face was contorted with pain.

Oh, no. Darcy was in labor.

Dan vaguely noticed that Jen was doing something with Mrs. Hunter. He hated to admit she'd been right. Again. If Mrs. Hunter went into labor, he sure didn't want to birth the baby. Yes, he'd birthed his share of calves growing up, but a baby was different. Much different.

Moreover, he had plenty of trouble in store just handling the airplane. They'd taken off in virtual calm, but that cloud bank to the west did not bode well. Neither did the soaring ground temperatures and thick haze. If he'd wanted to test the plane's reliability under adverse conditions, he was about to get the chance.

Only he didn't want to test anything. He wanted a quick and easy flight to the Grand Rapids airfield. It wasn't far. A direct shot. Definitely faster than by automobile. Jen had that right. They should touch down in thirty minutes, more or less.

Then the left engine coughed.

Dan clenched his jaw. That engine had better hold out for this short distance. The plane would be impossible to control with just one engine. He could probably land in a farmer's field. There were plenty beneath him, but that wouldn't get Mrs. Hunter to the hospital.

It coughed again.

Dan thought madly. The fix should have worked. It wasn't cold enough for icing, especially since they were on the warm side of the coming storm. That left the fuel mixture as the likely culprit. Jen had noticed that earlier, and they hadn't adjusted the mix since fixing the engine.

He adjusted the mix a little at a time until the sputtering stopped.

Jen shot him a grin.

He gave her a thumbs-up, but she had again focused on Mrs. Hunter. Whatever was going on there could not be good.

Dan eyed the storm front again. It was moving fast. Ugly black clouds trailed misty fingers toward the ground. He gripped the control wheel. Tornadoes. He'd seen them sweep across the open plains. He glanced again. There wasn't any rotation to the clouds. No, those fingers weren't tornadoes. More likely they were dense cloudbursts. Maybe even hail.

He accelerated as fast as the motors would go.

Jen gave him a questioning look. Then she must have spotted the storm, for she nodded and turned back to her patient.

If this storm caught him, he'd never see the field. Cloudburst and hail meant strong updrafts and downdrafts. They would be tossed around like a child's rubber ball.

He scanned the fields below, hoping to spot the airfield. The storm was getting closer. This plane could fly high, especially light, but those cloud tops were too high to get above. He needed to outrace it.

Then he spotted the airfield. It lay immediately in the path of the storm. Even pushed to maximum velocity, the plane might not get there before the storm.

Lightning crackled to the ground.

"Come on, God," he muttered. "I have two women and an unborn baby on board. We could use some help here."

His answer was a boom of thunder followed by a bolt of lightning off to his right.

Dan could have used any number of choice expressions, but he was in the presence of ladies—even if they couldn't hear—and appealing to God for deliverance.

Sweat dripped down his forehead despite the cooler air at this altitude.

He had to begin the descent. The storm would arrive at the same time. He might not see the runway until the last moment. He decided to bring the plane in low and slow, on an even trajectory that would give the softest landing.

Down they went. He eased off the fuel and used every trick he knew to slow the speed.

The first raindrop splattered on the windshield. Then the next and the next. The black sky blotted out the light. He couldn't see the runway, so he brought the plane lower.

Lightning exploded close by. Its blue light revealed trees ahead.

Trees!

He was too low. Just like in November's accident. The scrape of branches echoed from that fatal day. He pulled on the control wheel to lift the nose. It wouldn't budge. He tried again. It was jammed.

They were going to crash.

Chapter Eighteen

Dan Wagner flew as one with the plane. Jen had to admire his skill and instinct. He'd fixed the sputtering in the left engine with no problem. He looked as calm as a man sitting down to read the evening newspaper.

But even Dan Wagner couldn't fix this dilemma.

Once the labor pangs began, Jen attempted to get Darcy to move to the back. She didn't respond. Judging from her expression, the pains weren't close together yet. Jen decided to leave Darcy in place for the short flight.

Then another seizure struck. Jen pulled off her belt and shoved the leather between Darcy's jaws. In the meantime, Darcy grabbed the copilot's wheel and pulled it with shocking strength. Jen pushed with all her might just to keep the plane level.

Jen saw the trees approach, saw Dan attempt to lift the nose. The wheel didn't budge because of the tug-of-war Jen was having with Darcy. She could let go, but that would send them into a steep climb.

Dan tried again to lift the nose. If he would just yank harder, it might be enough, but he didn't. He stared at the approaching trees with an expression of horror.

The accident. Of course. According to the newspaper article, a wing had clipped the trees. He was reliving the accident.

Please, God, give Dan strength. Help him realize it wasn't his fault.

Just as it wasn't her fault that Daddy had died? The thought startled her. She looked down at Darcy, still locked in the seizure. Jen was here, but she could not prevent Darcy's convulsion. If she'd been with her father, she wouldn't have been able to save him, either.

Mother had told her over and over that it was simply his time. Jen hadn't understood until now. No amount of nurse training would have changed what had happened.

The seizure eased and with it Darcy's grip. The wheel shot forward, but the nose didn't dive. In fact, they cleared the trees and began a proper descent to the runway. Dan must have disconnected the copilot's controls somehow. Maybe Jack had installed the same sort of mechanism they used in the trainers. However, Dan had done it, Jen was relieved beyond words.

At that moment, the storm hit. The gusts pushed against the plane, threatening to drive them sideways, but Dan kept it in line with the runway. That took strength and nerve, more than she would have had in the same situation. Seconds later, he nestled the plane on the ground as easily as if it was a calm summer afternoon.

What skill! No wonder Dan Wagner was famous. He was also heroic. She could have flung her arms around him with joy. Then she felt another contraction beneath her hands. Darcy cried out.

Dan taxied the plane to a waiting ambulance and stopped. By now, rain lashed the plane, and the wind buffeted them.

Jen wrapped an arm around Darcy's shoulders. "We're here."

Darcy said something that Jen couldn't make out over the drone of the engines.

"Hold on," Jen yelled. "You'll be at the hospital soon."

Darcy didn't say anything, but at least she wasn't combative like the last time. Another labor pang twisted her features, and she gasped with the pain. Jen held on, doing her best to comfort her.

After the engine noise died down, Jen removed the cotton from Darcy's ears. The ambulance men hovered below. Somehow she and Dan would have to carry Darcy down the ladders to the ground. After that, they would load Darcy into the ambulance and race to the hospital. Was there enough time?

Dan stepped over her and opened the door. The wind whipped rain into the cabin as he slid out the ladders. Jen instinctively shielded Darcy with her coat. In seconds, Jen was drenched. Icy water ran down her face, dripped off her nose and trickled down her back. She started shaking. The flight must have been cold, but she hadn't noticed, focused as she was on Darcy.

Another man joined Dan. He picked up Darcy's wrist to take her pulse. Darcy yanked it away.

"There's no time," Jen shouted. She gave him her latest reading. "She just came out of a convulsion. Labor pains have begun." In no order whatever, she barked out everything she'd observed during the flight.

The man didn't ask for her credentials. He didn't question her information. "Let's get her into the ambulance."

He and Dan lifted Darcy and carried her off the plane to the waiting attendants. In short order, Darcy was put into the ambulance, and it left, siren howling.

Jen didn't move. She knelt on the cold floor of the plane, numb.

Dan touched her on the shoulder. "You did great."

She hadn't even seen him return. "Was it enough?"

He pulled her close, whispering into her cotton-plugged ears. "With God's help."

Something inside Jen began to break. It started slow, like a trickle leaking through an earthen dam. She could bury that hint of emotion in Dan's cold wet leather coat, but a leaky dam eventually breaks. As the memories of her father and Marie and the dying man at the hospital mixed with thoughts of Darcy, she lost the last bit of control and sobbed.

"She'll be all right," he whispered into her ear. "You have to believe that."

Jen couldn't. She had seen death, knew when it was about to visit. "I found my father dead."

His hand, which had been rubbing her back, stilled.

"I went to the flight school." She choked on the memory, yet for some reason she had to get it out or drown under the weight of it. "The flight school of all places! I was supposed to stay with him, but I'd left my study materials at the school. I wanted to show him what I was learning." This was the hardest thing to admit. "When I returned, he was dead."

"You couldn't have known that would happen."

She squeezed her eyelids shut. "That doesn't matter. I didn't do what I was supposed to do. I left him for something trivial."

"It wasn't trivial. You shared an interest in aviation. He loved you. He would have wanted to hear all about your studies." He lifted her chin. "Is that why you want to fly on the polar expedition? Because of your father?"

She didn't dare look into those blue eyes or she'd lose control. "I did. I thought it would change things, that I would feel better, but it won't, will it?"

"No."

"Just like all this." She waved at the plane. "All this work, all our efforts, and it doesn't mean a thing, not without Darcy." She shook uncontrollably. "What if it's not enough? What if we were too late?"

Dan pulled her close again and held her.

The memories of the crash that had plagued Dan since November disappeared tonight. He held Jen and let her cry out her pain, but he had never seen her more courageous. She had taken charge in a crisis. The broken girl he'd brought home from the hospital had become a strong woman. Her compassion shone. She cared deeply, and he loved her more for that. Maybe that depth of compassion was why she'd put up the prickly barrier that few could break through.

Dan hoped he was one of those few. Her arms around his waist felt so good. Her clean, spruce scent was better than sunshine.

"I'm sorry," she mumbled into his shoulder. "I don't usually fall apart like this."

"It's all right. I was scared, too." It felt good to admit that.

Everyone thought Daring Dan was fearless, and he'd had to maintain that image. Jen had always seen through the smoke screen. She knew the daredevil flier was a charade, that deep at heart he was still a country boy. He liked small towns and Sunday chicken dinner, boots and a cowboy hat. The spotlight had been fun for a while, but he'd discovered its cold shallowness soon enough. Jen knew that. Jen had always seen who he really was.

"You stayed so calm." She sniffled, and he dug out a handkerchief, clean but not exactly dry after all the rain. She wiped her eyes and blew her nose.

Funny how even that made him smile. "I wasn't calm.

I was probably just as scared as you. In fact, I thought you were the calm one."

She shook her head.

He wiped a stray tear from her cheek. "I'm starting to think that I might have been wrong about you."

"Oh?" That perked her up. "Dan Wagner, wrong?"

My, how he loved that side of her. "Once. Just a little." He held his fingers an inch apart.

"Confess, Wagner." Her feistiness was returning, and along with it came the grin he'd grown to love.

"You would make a fine nurse."

She barked out a laugh. "No, no, no. You were not wrong about that. I like to fix things, but I can't fix people."

He cupped her face in his hands, never more sure. "Only God can heal."

Her mouth opened in surprise and then closed. "I didn't know you believed in God. You never mention your faith. I've never seen you in church."

"I took the wrong course for a while but I'm navigating my way back."

She smiled. "I like that."

He traced the curve of her chin with his thumb. "And I like you."

She gasped, ever so softly. Her eyes softened, and her lips parted slightly.

He wanted to kiss those expressive lips, to ask her to share a life together, but that was selfish. What could he offer? She needed a home right away. He couldn't give her that. He'd carefully orchestrated a solitary life. After the polar expedition—if it pulled off—he would go to whatever remote outpost needed a supply or airmail route.

Between now and then, he was homeless. Well, he

could always go back to the family ranch, but it was bursting at the seams with his parents and two brothers' families. Sure, they'd gladly accept her, but he couldn't drag her away from everyone she loved and leave her with strangers while he started a business capable of supporting a wife and family. He most especially couldn't do that while she was so vulnerable.

So, rather than give in to the selfish desire to kiss her, he looked out the windshield. The rains had stopped, and the skies were growing lighter. "It looks like the storm is over."

Her disappointment was palpable.

He tried to hold on, but she broke free and skittered toward the door.

"We should go to the hospital." She crawled onto the wing. "If we can find a way to get there."

This time Dan had to rein in disappointment. He had blown his chance.

Jen's emotions were running out of control. It was easier to move, to do something, than to think about what Dan had said. He liked her. Only he hadn't said it like one friend to another or a brother to a sister. No, his words had carried deeper meaning. Then, instead of kissing her, which she'd expected, he looked away and talked about the weather. That man was too infuriating to deal with when a greater crisis was underway.

She had to know if their efforts had saved Darcy.

Fortunately, they found a taxicab near the airfield and within minutes arrived at the familiar brick edifice that Jen had called home not that long ago. In the dreary light of a storm-filled late afternoon, it looked no more hospitable than the day she had left. The little coffee shop down the street was nearly empty. Student nurses would be hard at work at this hour preparing the supper trays.

This time Jen and Dan went in the main entrance and checked with the nurse on duty. No word on Mrs. Hunter had come to her yet, but she directed them to the waiting area. Though that room was filled with people, Jen saw no one she recognized. Blake hadn't arrived yet with Darcy's parents. Jen suspected Mr. Kensington would drive Jack to Grand Rapids. It was anyone's guess whether father or son would get there first.

Jen had never been in this portion of the hospital. Her training had been confined to the wards and the nursing program wing. The elegant waiting area could have been from a posh hotel except for the faint scent of disinfectant that hung in the air. Crystal chandeliers graced the high ceiling with its sculpted molding. Wingback chairs and plush wool rugs dotted the marble floor. The room hummed with anxious whispers. All eyes trained on the massive doors leading to the emergency ward and operating room and the nurse sitting guard at the little table in front of those doors. When a white-coated doctor emerged from behind the doors, the hum turned to an expectant hush. All hoped the nurse would call for the family or friends of their loved one.

Jen was no different. She clasped and unclasped her hands. She shifted in the chair. She stood and paced to the windows, looking for Jack or Blake or Mr. and Mrs. Shea. Seeing nothing, she returned to her chair.

She only made the mistake of checking with the nurse once. After being informed that the patient's family would be called only when news arrived, Jen returned dissatisfied.

"She didn't care that I was a probationer here."

"Probationer?" Dan looked up from the book he had

taken from the ample bookshelves beside the unlit fireplace. He sat with one leg crossed over the other, the very model of calm.

"When a girl applies to the nursing program, she is on probation for three months before she can be accepted into the program."

"Sensible." He returned to his reading.

"How can you be so calm when a woman's life hangs in the balance?"

He looked up again. "What do you propose I do? I'm not a doctor."

She gnawed a fingernail, a disgusting habit she'd broken at the age of fourteen, and glanced at the doors again. "What's taking so long?"

"You said Mrs. Hunter is in labor. How long does that take?"

Jen thought back to her experiences at the hospital. "It can be quick, or it can take hours and hours. Sometimes a day or more. But I don't think it'll be that long. Doc Stevens told me to…" She really oughtn't talk about such things to a man. "He suggested I might have to hurry it along."

"Then there's no reason to worry."

Jen blew out her breath. She knew too well the number of things that could go wrong. Marie hadn't survived. Her lifeless body and that of the unborn child would have been placed on a gurney. The lowest-ranking attending nurse, generally a probationer, would accompany the body to the morgue where it would be bathed and shrouded.

She choked back a sob. That couldn't happen to Darcy. *Please, God, not Darcy.* That would be too much to bear.

"It's all right." Dan squeezed her hand. "She's in good hands now."

"I don't know how you can be so unconcerned."

"I'm concerned, but there's nothing we can do but wait."

"You're right." She did hate admitting that. When had Dan Wagner started being right about things?

He laughed. "I love the ring of that."

His calm was driving her to tears. "I guess I'm not very patient. I need to do something."

He had the grace not to mention that she'd given up the opportunity to work on the opposite side of those massive doors. "Have you prayed?"

Her jaw dropped. Dan Wagner suggesting prayer? "You want to pray?"

"I just wondered if you had."

Jen was embarrassed to admit that she hadn't prayed for Darcy since arriving at the hospital. "I can't seem to settle my mind. Maybe we could pray together. You could start."

"Me? I don't have the proper words."

"I don't think it matters much. At least that's what Pastor Gabe says. Just talk to God like you'd talk to a friend."

Dan looked surprised. "That doesn't sound like any pastor I've ever known."

"You should come to our church. Pastor Gabe is very down-to-earth. You would like him."

"Maybe I will."

Now Jen was truly surprised. Maybe he really had changed. "You can sit with us. Mother, Ruthie, Minnie and I."

He gave her a questioning look, and then she remembered that her mother and Ruth would be leaving soon.

"Well, at least with Minnie and me. If she doesn't sit with Peter." She hopped to her feet, intending to go to the windows again so Dan wouldn't see how much the coming changes bothered her, but he snagged her hand.

"I thought we were going to pray."

Jen sat back down and tried to focus on Darcy instead of her own worries. How could she even think about such trivial matters when her friend and the baby were in danger?

Dan squeezed her hands. "Why don't you begin?"

"Dear Lord," Darcy took a breath and imagined her friend lying in the operating room. A shudder ran through her. Her friend's life hung in the balance. She clung to Dan's hands as to a lifeline. "Lord, we love Darcy and Jack and want the best for them. They will be good parents, wonderful parents. Please give them that chance. Please spare Darcy and the baby. Please don't take them home to You yet."

She imagined how Jack would feel if Darcy and their unborn baby perished, and her throat closed as the tears threatened. She tried to hold them back but failed. Instead they trickled down her cheeks.

Dan drew her close. "Amen."

Her daddy's death had hurt terribly, but they'd known for years that his health was declining and he would eventually leave them. That wasn't the case with Darcy. She was young and vibrant and filled with life. Darcy's sister had borne four children. Why couldn't Darcy have just one? Jack wanted children so badly. Darcy had once said he was probably glad she was with child since she wouldn't be in danger any longer. But now her life was in more peril than she had faced in years of flying.

"I don't understand why some people die," she murmured.

"Me, either." Dan handed her the handkerchief again.

"But I'm starting to realize that life and death are in God's hands. We do our best. The rest is up to Him."

"Like the accident you were in last November?"

Every other time she'd brought up the topic, he had flinched and changed the subject. This time he didn't blink.

"Like that," he said. "No one had ever died before on a plane I was flying. It didn't seem right that I walked away while she died."

"You loved her," she whispered.

He jerked back. "Why would you think that? We spent some time together, true, but she was more interested in the glamour and thrill of accompanying a flying ace than in a relationship."

"I didn't say that she loved you. I said that you loved her."

He shook his head. "No more than any other gal. Why would you think I loved her?"

"The newspapers—"

"The newspapers?" He snorted. "They make up stories to sell papers. A dying lover makes for better business than a novice eager to make a name for herself. Please don't base your opinion of me on what you read in the newspapers. Very little of it is accurate."

"Even when they discussed relationships?"

"Especially relationships. I was never serious about any woman, and I never will be as long as I fly airplanes."

Jen gasped. Dan had made himself perfectly clear. He would never have a serious relationship with a woman as long as he flew. That meant forever, as far as she could see. "You can't mean that."

"I won't risk making a woman a widow."

Now he was making her angry. "Don't you think she ought to have a say in that?"

"No." The man didn't even have the grace to hesitate. "A relationship can't last unless both partners work together. Until I stop flying, that can't happen."

"Why not? Jack and Darcy have made it work."

"Oh?"

That simple question infuriated her. "We are not here because both Jack and Darcy fly airplanes. This could happen to anyone. At any time." That reality finally sank in. "No one can remove all risk from life."

"Perhaps, but I can minimize it. I won't make a woman suffer from losing her husband."

"That sounds to me like you're afraid of losing someone you love."

His expression darkened, all sense of calm gone.

She had finally pushed him too far.

"If that's true, Miss Fox," he growled, "then we both are."

He hadn't denied it. He hadn't protested that he loved her too much to risk her happiness. No, he had reverted to formality and charged her with the same crime. In his eyes, they were both afraid to love. But that wasn't true. It couldn't be. Yes, she'd lost her father, but she was getting over that. The problem wasn't on her side. It was entirely on his.

He wasn't telling her the whole truth about that crash last November. For him to shy away from any relationship, he must have cared deeply for the woman who had died. The newspapers had been right. They were in love. They would have married.

That meant he was not ready to love another woman. He might never be ready. A stolen kiss or a tender word meant nothing. He could never give his heart. She'd better forget about Dan Wagner. He had summarily dismissed her.

Chapter Nineteen

Why did Jen have to bring up Agnes? Just when Dan thought he was getting past the memory of that horrific accident, Jen pushed it in his face. She, of all people, must understand that guilt was difficult to overcome. He would live with it forever, but he didn't want to think about it now. And he didn't appreciate Jen pushing him where he couldn't go.

The kind of relationship she wanted was impossible. She would never give up her dream of flying. Even that attempt at nursing school had been tied to aviation. She wanted to partner on an airmail route. Impossible. He couldn't carry another woman out of an airplane. He sure couldn't carry Jen's lifeless body. That would kill him. The flight today had confirmed it. He would never risk her life again.

She was bright sunshine on a cloudy day, a brilliant flower in the midst of a desert. Except for these maddening moments, she made him feel glad to be alive. Such a woman deserved a long life. Better he step away than snuff out the light in those hazel eyes.

Jen didn't hide her feelings behind a wall of artifice. Every emotion played openly across her face. He could see her reason out his words and come to the unhappy resolution he'd intended. That expressive mouth of hers turned downward, and the hazel eyes dulled. Her hands fisted, but she didn't fling out the usual retort. Instead, she stalked to the window, probably in an attempt to hide her disappointment.

It didn't work.

He felt her anguish to the marrow, yet he couldn't look away.

The window was cracked open, and the late-day breeze ruffled her short hair. How he'd grown to love those tousled locks that could never quite be tamed. Just like her. His pa would call her a wild mustang. When Dan was young, he'd asked his pa if they could catch one and tame it so he could have a horse of his own.

His pa had looked him in the eye. "Son, a mustang is meant to run wild. Tame 'em, and you take the life out of 'em."

Funny how those words still stuck with him. Odd how aptly they fit Jen Fox. Turning her into a common house-wife would drive the life out of her. She needed to run wild and free. Man could only admire such a creature. He could never possess her.

That was the trouble. He wanted to give her exactly what she wanted—a life together. Yet that was impossible. Dan Wagner knew only one thing—flying. His brothers had the ranch. He couldn't waltz in and take it from them. Nor did he want to. After all this time, he wouldn't remember the first thing about ranching. He couldn't rope a calf or ride a horse all day. He had no idea how to mend a fence. The thought of birthing a calf or sitting with a sick cow didn't sit well. No, he was no rancher. He was an aviator through and through.

That meant no wife. No family. It was the trade-off

he had been willing to accept when he took up flying. Never before had walking away from a woman hurt the way it did with Jen.

She looked in his direction, and a smile flickered to life.

For a moment, Dan's pulse quickened. She didn't despise him.

Then he noticed she wasn't looking at him. She was looking past him to the other side of the room. He turned to see what had pushed aside her disappointment.

Hunter had arrived.

"Jen. Dan." Jack Hunter, Darcy's parents and both Kensingtons clattered across the waiting room floor. Jen couldn't help but notice the change between father and son. They walked together, shoulder to shoulder, united in their concern for Darcy.

Jack looked frantic.

Jen intercepted him. "Darcy is in labor. The ambulance took her here the moment we landed. We haven't had any word since."

He barely registered her words.

"How is she, son?" the elder Kensington asked Dan, who had joined them in the center of the considerably emptier waiting room.

"You should ask Jen," Dan deferred. "She's the one who was with Darcy every step of the way. If not for her quick thinking, this might have ended badly."

Jen appreciated his nod of confidence even though his words had made Jack pale.

The Sheas looked equally shaken. "Please tell us all you know."

She couldn't mention the additional convulsions. She couldn't crack everyone's hope when all might still end well. She said a quick prayer and then smiled. "The labor pains began during the flight. We got here around five o'clock." It was now past six-thirty.

Mrs. Shea audibly sighed. "It could be a while. Amelia endured twenty hours before Frederick was born." Amelia was Darcy's older sister.

"When I was here as a student nurse, one of the births took thirty-four hours."

"Poor woman," Mrs. Shea said.

Jack was getting paler by the moment.

"Have a seat, sport," Blake said, drawing Jack to a chair. "When you hear that you have a son or daughter, you'll feel a lot better. Until then, all we men can do is wait."

For Jack's sake, Jen added that the long-laboring woman had a healthy baby boy.

His color got a little better. "What do we do? Can I see her?"

The two Kensington men and Mr. Shea chuckled.

The latter clapped Jack on the shoulder. "We wait, son. Darcy is in good hands."

Jen would not tell them of Marie or any of the other heart-wrenching cases. This was a time for hope, not fear.

"Blake really surprised us," the elder Kensington began, his hand firmly on the shoulder of his son. "I don't know how he found us. That's some sharp thinking, I tell you. The way he drove. Why, he navigated those roads like a race-car driver. I could barely keep up."

Blake's grin got wider and wider, and he added his own embellishments to the tale. The men had pulled chairs into a tight circle around Jack, each trying to top the next in storytelling.

"At least that will keep their minds off things," Mrs. Shea said.

Jen had forgotten that Darcy's mother was there. As the only other woman, she had naturally stayed at Jen's side. "Funny how men and women invariably split into separate groups."

"It's the natural order of things, I suppose. We do find it rather odd when a woman attempts to join the men or a man attempts to converse with a group of women."

Jen supposed she was right, but it felt like a subtle hint that Jen had overstepped her place by wanting to be with the men. On the other hand, Darcy had done the same by flying airplanes with Jack. She worked mostly with male students. Only a few women came to the school. Jen looked down at her trousers and mackinaw. No one at the hospital had frowned at her or refused to let her enter, but a few of the dwindling family members in the waiting room did stare. Jen crossed her arms and turned her back to them.

The massive doors swung open. Everyone's attention shifted to see whose family would be called. Instead of the usual physician, a nurse came out and spoke to the nurse on duty. The new nurse looked familiar. Jen moved closer. It was Evelyn, her old roommate.

The nurse on duty pointed to her logbook, and Evelyn nodded.

Jen glanced at the large clock. Seven o'clock. The night shift was coming on duty.

"Change of shifts," she said, "but I recognize the incoming nurse. Maybe she knows something."

Jen headed for the little table where Evelyn now sat. To her dismay, Mrs. Shea followed. She sure hoped the men didn't join them. Evelyn would never tell her anything with everyone around her. She wasn't supposed to give out information without authorization.

Unfortunately, Jen's movement toward Evelyn inspired

the other families to press toward the nurse station. Most arrived ahead of Jen. This did not bode well. Evelyn would be frustrated before Jen even arrived.

She hung back.

"Shouldn't we wait in line?" Mrs. Shea asked a bit anxiously.

Jen drew her aside. "She won't be able to give any information other than what's authorized. I hoped that she might remember me and tell me something, but she won't while everyone else is there." She looked back. "At least the men haven't noticed yet. She'll never tell me anything if they're here."

"I'll keep them occupied." Having a task to accomplish seemed to energize Mrs. Shea. "Let me know what you find out."

She trundled off and soon blocked the men's view. Jen could hear Evelyn tell each anxious relative that she had no news but would inform them the moment she learned anything. Jen approached her only when the crowd had completely departed.

"I'm sorry, but I don't have any information on the patients," Evelyn said without lifting her gaze from the logbook.

Jen could tell at a glance that the log listed all the patients currently in emergency care. Some also listed a next of kin. Darcy Hunter's name was on the log with Jack listed beside it.

Jen smoothed her hair. "Evelyn, don't you remember me?"

The woman looked up, and her jaw dropped. "Jen? Is that you? You look so…different."

She must mean Jen's trousers and mackinaw.

"Oh, these." Jen was suddenly self-conscious. Everyone in Pearlman expected to see her in such attire, but in the city—and in the hospital especially—it no longer fit. For the first time in a long while, she wished she'd worn a skirt and blouse.

Evelyn leaned close. "I thought you were a boy."

Jen bit her lip. "We had to fly my friend here. Trousers are more practical for that." She didn't mention that she wasn't flying the plane. "My friend's name is Darcy Hunter. She came in by ambulance. I think she has toxemia, but she was in labor."

"I believe the doctor is with her, but I don't have any word from obstetrics."

"That could be good news." At least Jen would take it that way.

"Did you say you *flew* her here? In an airplane? I didn't know you were an aviator."

"Aviatrix," Jen corrected. "Though, actually Dan was the pilot. I stayed with Mrs. Hunter. She is a licensed pilot."

Evelyn couldn't seem to wrap her mind around this. "She flies airplanes?"

"She teaches aviation down in Pearlman. I help out and intend to get my license." If tonight turned out well. If not, she couldn't imagine Jack setting foot in another airplane.

"Why would you ever want to go into nursing?"

Why indeed. Jen had tossed the question around since first setting foot in the hospital's nursing program. She hadn't particularly wanted to do it, but she had seen its value. After tonight, she saw the possibilities she had begun to imagine before that first day in school. "I think someday doctors and nurses will use airplanes to get to people who need medical attention."

Evelyn shook her head. "You're a dreamer, Jen Fox.

Why would a doctor risk his life going here and there in an airplane? Better he set up practice nearby."

Jen couldn't explain further because Mrs. Shea had lost control of the men, and they were now approaching en masse.

She hurried to intercept them. "No news yet."

Jack looked like the delirious and feverish patients she'd tended in the wards. Desperate, bleak and despairing.

She had to give him hope. "That's a good thing. It can take many hours to birth a first baby. It's only been a few."

That settled him for the moment, but it wouldn't last. Doubt and anxiety would creep in, filling the gaps between desperate hope.

Dan had to admire Jen. When everyone around her was falling apart, she stayed calm. She seemed to know the exact moment to boost spirits and the precise thing to say or do that would accomplish that task. She was a marvel, and he'd chased her away.

For her sake, he reminded himself.

Yet as the minutes ticked past, he began to doubt that rock-solid intent. Jen might have been right. He was afraid of losing her. One look at Jack told him how agonizing that would be.

Dan joined the aviator. "Sorry about the wait."

Jack mustered a wan smile. "Thanks to you, Darcy has a chance."

No one dared think how Jack would feel if they managed to save the baby yet lost the mother. No man wanted to consider that option. Dan sure wouldn't. At times like that, bachelorhood made sense. However, a bachelor had no one to help him through trouble. Look how badly he'd managed Agnes's death. It would have been easier with someone like Jen at his side.

Two are better than one...for if they fall, the one will lift up his fellow.

Dan shook his head. Where had that come from? He hadn't recalled memorized scripture in years, and yet fragments of verses had come to mind twice now.

"She's a lot like Darcy," Jack said.

Dan blinked. "Who?"

"Jen."

Had the man read his mind? Dan looked down at the loosely clasped hands between his knees. "This is tougher than any aerial maneuver."

Jack nodded. He also leaned on his elbows, hands clasped between his knees. "Darcy always said love's a risk worth taking."

Dan wasn't so sure. "Do you still believe that?"

"Absolutely."

Dan had doubts, but Jack looked sincere.

"None of us know the future," Jack said. "Each day could be our last. When you love someone, don't waste a single moment. That's what Darcy taught me." He cleared his throat. "That's what I'll always remember."

Dan clapped Jack on the back. What could he say? The night would probably get longer.

"Go to her, old chum," Jack said. "Don't waste a moment."

"I don't think she feels the same."

Jack shook his head, a wry smile on his face. "You're fooling yourself. She might act aloof, but she keeps glancing at you."

That observation sent a tingle of hope into Dan. He hadn't ruined his only chance. "I don't have anything to offer. Not yet."

"None of us do, and yet they let us into their hearts anyway." Jack shook his head. "When I proposed, I'd lost my plane and my only source of income. I was in debt way over my head. She should have told me to go back to New York. Instead, she wanted to work with me, to make a life together." He blinked and swiped his face with his sleeve before clearing his throat. "Best day of my life."

Today might end up the worst, but Dan wasn't going to let that thinking rule. He would hold out hope the way that everyone else did. At the moment, Jack expected him to mend things with Jen. She sat alone, knees drawn up to her chin, staring out the black window. The Kensingtons had gone to fetch supper. The Sheas murmured softly and held hands, probably in prayer.

Jack gave him a push. "If you waste another moment, you'll regret it the rest of your life."

"All right. You win." Dan rose and ventured across the room. By now, few people waited. No one was within hearing distance of Jen. "Mind if I join you?"

She looked up with red eyes. Without answering, she went back to staring out the window.

Dan sat gingerly on the chair next to hers. Red eyes meant she'd shed tears. Jen Fox wasn't as strong and calm as she appeared to be, but that knowledge didn't make his job easier.

"I, um, might have been a little hasty earlier tonight." He waited for her comment.

She made no indication she'd even heard him.

He scrubbed the whiskers that were starting to appear at this late hour. "You're not making this easy on me. I suppose I deserve that." He swallowed hard. "I shouldn't have kissed you back when you were leaving for school. I didn't mean to mislead you."

Her shoulders tensed. She obviously didn't want to hear what he had to say.

But he had to say it. "I'm sorry. I'm starting to realize that every day is a risk. We can only do our best with the time we've got."

"There's no need to explain," she said bitterly. "I understand perfectly."

But she didn't. He hadn't said what he truly wanted to say.

"Mr. Hunter?" The authoritative voice drew everyone's attention.

Jen hopped to her feet. "Doctor."

Jack got to the man first. "I'm Jack Hunter."

"Congratulations, Mr. Hunter. You have a baby boy."

Hunter began to tremble. "My wife?"

"Resting. She and the baby will need to stay here for a week or so for observation." The doctor looked around at the crowd gathered near. "I understand someone flew Mrs. Hunter here in an airplane."

Dan nodded.

"That was some clear thinking, young man. If it had taken much longer to get here, the outcome might have been different."

"Miss Fox was the one who thought of it," Dan said, but the tears and the congratulations blotted out his words.

Jack gave him a bear hug followed by a whoop. "A boy. I have a son." He then hugged Mr. and Mrs. Shea.

"Would you like to see the baby?" the doctor asked.

Jack and the Sheas followed the doctor through the massive doors into the hospital proper. Dan and Jen hung back.

"Thank You, God," Jen prayed, her eyes closed with reverence and probably exhaustion.

Dan hugged her close. "And thank you. You gave me the confidence to make that flight."

She melted against him, and he realized she must be as exhausted as he was.

"Would you like some coffee?" he asked.

She dropped into a chair, somber. "I suppose we should try to get some sleep. Come morning you'll have to fly the plane back. Maybe Blake will go with you."

"He has a car to drive." Dan sank into the chair beside her and grasped her hand. It was cold. "I'd rather have you in the copilot's seat."

She finally looked at him, a hint of hope brightening those luminous eyes. "You would?"

"Absolutely."

Chapter Twenty

Riding as copilot was merely a parting gift. That was what Jen told herself. Dan hadn't said he wanted anything beyond that. He'd actually apologized for kissing her. Clearly he was cutting all ties. Fine. She would move on.

They flew back to Pearlman early the following morning. Jen was exhausted and yet exhilarated. From the navigator's seat, she saw the world as she'd never seen it before. All her dreams had been wrapped up in that experience, and it didn't fail her. She arrived even hungrier to fly.

That wouldn't happen for a while. Darcy had to stay at the hospital for a week or so to make sure she didn't have more convulsions. Though childbirth was the only cure, the danger didn't pass until her health improved. The baby, on the other hand, was doing famously. Though he had arrived early, he was strong and with good, sound lungs, as Jack had pointed out with delight.

Naturally they had expected Jack to delay the polar expedition, but he strode into the flight school a few days later and announced they were not going to attempt it this year.

"Sorry, old chum," Jack said to Dan. "Didn't mean to

string you along. The offer stands for next year if you're not occupied elsewhere."

Dan's tight smile told Jen all she needed to know. He would not return. That realization hurt more than it should, seeing as he'd made it perfectly clear that he would not consider a relationship or a partnership.

"I suppose you're going to take the airmail route now," she said after Jack left.

Dan gathered his charts and papers from the table. "It's already been awarded to someone else."

She felt for him. "That's too bad. Maybe you can get another."

"First I have a debt to repay," he snapped, not looking at her.

"What debt?"

He glared.

She'd asked too personal a question. "I'm sorry."

He shook his head. "No, I am. I should have seen this coming." He plunked the papers down on the table. "I should never have requested an advance from Kensington."

"But he won't expect to be repaid," Jen blurted out.

"I don't care what he expects. Dan Wagner honors his word. No expedition means I need to repay him. Period."

"But you worked for months. That counts for something. Without your efforts, the expedition won't get off the ground next year."

"Don't try to talk me out of this."

She should have paid attention to his growl, but she clung to faint hope. "You could come back."

"I have responsibilities. My family depends on the income I earn to keep the ranch going."

She cringed. "I'm sorry." She'd forgotten that he sent money home. "The newspapers make it sound like…"

His instruction not to believe the newspapers popped into her mind, and she stopped.

"Like I'm rich? The newspapers write what will sell. An honest man trying to help his family doesn't make a good story."

"It should."

The corner of his mouth jerked upward for a second before the scowl returned. "I have no choice now."

"Air shows." Suddenly those didn't sound so glamorous anymore. "I don't want you to die."

That brought a grim smile. "Me, either." He pressed down on the stack of papers. "Thanks to you, I've got to thinking how a man needs to use the talents God gave him to do good in the world. I'm praying He shows me how."

How could she deny a righteous cause? That was what she'd wanted when she began the nursing program. It was the only thing that could have kept her there.

"My mother always says that if God wants you to do something, He'll clear the path."

He gathered up his papers again. "I hope your mother is right—for both of us. What do you plan to do, Jen?"

"See if I can help Darcy with the baby in exchange for room and board." That was the only idea she'd had since learning that the house had sold and Mother would soon leave with Ruth.

He nodded. "That makes sense. And then after that? Do you still plan to take the flight training?"

"Yes." Though the desire had waned now that Dan was leaving. She couldn't bear the gloom that had settled over them. Dan was leaving, and she'd never see him again. She took one final shot. "Maybe Jack will put me in the cockpit next year for the polar attempt." It was worth saying just to see Dan's horrified expression.

He reined it in quickly. "You'll make a fine navigator. You're definitely calm under pressure. That's a key quality in an aviator."

"I never thought I'd hear Dan Wagner say that."

"Maybe I've changed." He paused. "I don't suppose you would be willing to let me take you to supper tonight at the restaurant in town."

Jen's stomach fluttered. That sounded an awful lot like a date, but supper together would only increase the pain when he left. "That might not be a good idea."

His eyes were dark as the deepest waters and gave her no idea how he felt. He merely nodded. "Maybe you're right."

Then he walked out of the flight school and out of her life.

"You did what?" Minnie cried when Jen explained that she'd turned down Dan's offer of supper at Lily's Restaurant.

Ruth and Beatrice, who had joined the family tonight in order to hear all the details of the daring flight, joined Minnie with so many protests that Jen had to cover her ears.

"Stop it. He's leaving anyway. What possible reason could I have to go out with him now? Besides, Mother would not want me to appear alone in public with a gentleman."

"Nonsense," her mother said as she bustled into the kitchen, supposedly to check the chicken roasting in the oven, but more likely to insert her advice. "You should have invited Mr. Wagner to supper here."

"But—"

"No 'buts.' Three roasters are more chicken than we

could possibly eat. I don't want leftovers since Ruth, Sammy and I are leaving the day after tomorrow."

That was the hardest part to swallow. In less than two days, everyone would leave, the house would be stripped of the last of their belongings, and new owners would arrive. Jen needed to find someplace to stay. Darcy should be arriving home on the same day that Mother and Ruth would leave. With Jack's approval, Jen could help out until she found a job that paid enough to afford a room.

It all made sense in her head, but her heart still ached for what would be lost.

"I'll send Blake," Beattie was saying. "He can get Mr. Wagner before he's ordered."

"No, wait," Jen said, but no one paid her the slightest attention. Having Dan join them would only make the hurt worse. She wasn't sure she could bear it.

Beatrice hurried from the room, beaming at the idea of furthering a romance. Since the day Blake returned from driving the Sheas to the hospital, Beatrice had changed. She now looked at her husband with deep respect. The article in the newspaper practically made Blake and Jen and Dan into heroes, and Beattie reveled in the accolades. She'd gone on and on about which women went out of their way to congratulate her. Business was even up at the mercantile. Best of all, the reconciliation between father and son brought peace. Mrs. Kensington even suggested Beatrice run for president of the Ladies' Aid Society.

Jen was happy for her sisters, truly she was. All of them had found joy in marriage—or soon would in Minnie's case. Jen, however, had to watch the only interesting man she'd ever met walk away. It didn't seem fair. Hadn't Daddy stood right here and promised to walk her down the aisle one day?

That would never happen, and it seemed that any chance at marriage had vanished, too.

"Jen?" Mother touched her arm. "You were a million miles away just then. What's bothering you?"

She shook her head, not willing to burden her mother with memories from the past. "It's just so much upheaval at once."

"You have a solid plan, one that will be a great relief to Mr. and Mrs. Hunter." She kissed Jen's cheek. "I'm proud of you, dear."

Jen smoothed her skirt and stood on first one foot then the other to ease the discomfort of the heeled shoes. Her feet hurt almost as much as those days in the hospital ward, when she wouldn't have a chance to sit for more than ten minutes in the twelve-hour shift.

"What do I say to him?"

Mother blinked. "Who, dear?"

"Dan. Mr. Wagner."

Mother smiled. "*Hello* is a good start. My dear, you have spent so much time together, surely you have something in common that you can discuss. His plans perhaps?"

There was nothing left to discuss. Dan was leaving, either for an airmail route somewhere or to the air-show circuit. In either case, he was leaving and wouldn't consider a partner in business or life so long as he flew. She couldn't handle a minute more in his presence, much less an entire meal.

Surely Dan would refuse the invitation. He was a solitary man, the lone wolf that the newspapers portrayed. No woman could capture Daring Dan Wagner. The only one who had come close had died.

Yet some fifteen or twenty minutes later, after she had carved the birds and Minnie had mashed the potatoes and put the green beans into a large bowl and the gravy into a small one, she heard Dan thank her mother at the front door. "I've been longing for a home-cooked meal for ages. I'm sorry I don't have a hostess gift."

"Nonsense," Mother replied. "None is needed. You're practically family now."

With Peter's arrival at the kitchen door, they were now complete. Jen squeezed one more mismatched place setting at the only spot available around the crowded table—Daddy's seat. The children would eat at the little folding table Blake had set up on the other side of the room. That left the four sisters, Mother, two husbands—Sam being in New York already—and Dan. Eight at their tiny table, not including Sammy, who was too little to eat with the children yet too excited to sleep in his crib. Elbows were bound to bang. Cups could very well spill. There was no room to even breathe.

Mother beamed. "Your father would be so pleased. He loved to see family together."

Jen swallowed the lump in her throat and looked away when Dan entered. Though shorter than Sam and Peter, his presence filled a room. You couldn't help knowing he was there.

"Nice place, Mrs. Fox," he said. "I only saw the front room the last time I was here. How many rooms in total?"

"Three bedrooms upstairs, the parlor, the living room and this kitchen."

While Mother described the house in minute detail, Jen drew Beattie aside. "After everyone is seated, I'll pass around the serving dishes one at a time, starting with you. There's no room for them on the table."

"Who carved the chicken?"

"I did. Daddy taught me." That lump came back.

Beattie looked between the table and the warming

oven. "I can do the serving. You don't want to miss talking to Mr. Wagner."

Sure enough, Mother and her sisters had managed to place Dan next to her chair.

Jen shook her head. "I'll do it. Do sit down next to your husband."

Beattie blushed and hurried over like a newlywed. Once she was seated, Mother said grace, and then Jen handed the platter of chicken to Beattie.

"You look very pretty, Jen," Dan said from the vicinity of her left elbow.

"It's just an everyday skirt and blouse."

"On you they shine."

That compliment sent heat rushing to her cheeks. Jen turned away so no one would notice.

Blake cleared his throat. "Do I smell mashed potatoes?"

Jen fetched the potatoes. Why did Dan Wagner always throw her off-kilter? Well, soon enough she wouldn't have to worry about that. He would be gone, and life would return to its dull and monotonous norm. She handed the potatoes to Beatrice and headed back for the gravy.

Mother joined the conversation. "Where are you headed next, Mr. Wagner? Jen told me the polar expedition is postponed for a year. Will you be staying on at the flight school?"

Jen paused, waiting to hear his answer.

"No, ma'am. I'm planning to head west to see my folks first. Then I'll fly in air shows until I can get a contract to deliver mail by airplane."

Jen's hands shook. He really was leaving, never to return. She leaned against the counter to steady herself.

Mother didn't notice the effect Dan's news had on Jen.

"How interesting. Why would anyone need airplanes to deliver mail?"

"To remote areas, ma'am. Places that don't have good roads or roads at all."

Jen picked up the gravy bowl and handed it to Blake. Before anyone could notice her distress, she returned to the warming oven to fetch the green beans.

"What would you like, Jen?" Dan asked. "Dark meat or white?"

She couldn't look at him, or she'd lose the tiny bit of control she'd managed to regain. "Either. I'm not particular."

"At last I've found something you're not particular about."

Everyone chuckled except Jen. Did he really think her that persnickety? No wonder he was leaving. Well, good riddance. She set the bowl of green beans on the table with a thud. "I might have my opinions, but at least no one has to wonder what I think."

Dan grinned. "That's one thing I liked about you from the start."

Ruth and Minnie gave each other a knowing look, which Beatrice seconded. Well, they were wrong. Dan clearly had no interest in a relationship. He'd stated it flat out. Jen put the half-empty serving dishes in the warming oven and then pulled her chair as far away from Dan as possible before sitting down to eat. Since eight people were crammed at the table, that wasn't very far. She could feel his presence like the hum of an airplane engine.

"Mighty fine dinner, Mrs. Fox," Dan said. "Reminds me of home."

"Tell me again where home is."

"Montana, ma'am. Boynton, Montana. Ranching

country. Rolling plains as far as you can see. Sky so
wide it seems to go on forever. Fresh air and sunshine."

"That sounds lovely. Does your family own a ranch?"
Before long Mother had extracted Dan's entire history,
including that his parents were still living and his two
younger brothers and their families ran the ranch alongside their father. "What a wonderful life."

"It's a hard life, ma'am." Dan set down his fork before
Jen had finished half her dinner. "Every year brings a
trial or two. This winter we lost fifty head in a blizzard,
and a barn roof collapsed."

Jen didn't know that. "Why didn't you tell me?"

He shrugged. "You didn't need my troubles on top of
your own. Besides, you couldn't help."

That sounded a lot like her reasoning, which she was
beginning to realize was flawed. Two people who cared
about each other shared not only the joys but the diffi-
culties. "I could have listened. And prayed."

His smile was hollow. "That's thoughtful, but everything is taken care of."

She looked down at her plate of food, no longer hungry. As a master of hiding her troubles, she recognized
when her concerns were being brushed off. Things were
not as rosy as Dan was saying. That was why he had to
return home. He'd also made it perfectly clear that he
alone would handle the problem. No help or sympathy
was needed. No partnership—in life or business—for
Dan Wagner.

Jen's quiet resignation plagued Dan long after he said
goodbye to the family and returned to the boardinghouse.
He missed the spunk that she'd shown at the flight school.
Other than a brief moment following his deliberate attempt to spur her to protest, she'd been too reserved.

That was in stark contrast to her declaration that she still hoped to get in the cockpit of the polar attempt next year. Rather than mourn the postponed expedition, she'd turned the disappointment into a challenge to make her dream come true. He admired that about her. Jen Fox let nothing stop her.

Maybe that was why her change of mood got to him. It was so uncharacteristic. She'd barely looked up during the entire meal.

It took every bit of restraint not to lift that determined little chin of hers and wipe away whatever had made her spirits plummet. Had something happened with the family? They had all seemed happy, even Beatrice. She and Blake had acted like newlyweds, whispering and exchanging little glances and touches that they thought no one noticed. Ruth talked about rejoining her husband in a few days. Minnie and her fiancé barely took their eyes off each other. Even Mrs. Fox seemed pleased to journey to New York. Only Jen dwelled in a melancholic haze.

After the meal, he'd tried to speak with her, but she walked away after delivering a glare that would melt the Arctic.

He'd drawn Mrs. Fox aside to ask if she knew why Jen was in such a sour mood.

The woman sighed. "She is not accepting the changes easily. I think she still sees her father in these walls. She doesn't realize that he's inside her heart, not in an old house. I wish I could make her understand, but I fear it will take time." She'd squeezed his hand. "Pray for her. She thinks highly of you. Your prayers would mean a lot."

Prayer wasn't something Dan had done much until lately. Prayer meant baring his soul before God. That soul was rusty and full of holes. He'd lived the life of an aviation star. Women, parties, greed. He'd done it all.

Until last November's crash, he hadn't wanted to let go of any of it. Even afterward, he'd only nominally relinquished the lifestyle. The decision to bid on an airmail route would keep him from that wild life and begin to scour away the stains on his soul. But that wasn't enough. He couldn't just run from his past. He had to admit that his vow to remain a bachelor was rooted in his selfish refusal to risk giving away any of himself. He had to declare his faults and start fresh.

But how?

That pastor in Jen's church had said it came down to giving total control to God.

Dan blew out his breath. Whew, that was a tough one. Until the crash, Dan Wagner had always been in control. He was known for it. He kept aloof from any entanglement, whether in business or relationships. Family was his only exception.

The crash changed everything. He thought he'd lost all control until the flight to bring Mrs. Hunter to the hospital. That success had given control back to him. If that preacher was right, he had to turn over the reins to everything—flying career, family, even his future. He hadn't come close to wanting to do that until now.

Until Jen Fox. The idea of losing her hurt a thousand times more than anything he'd faced up until now. No one made him feel more alive. The peaks and valleys became an adventure with her, not a trial. That mischievous grin and tart tongue could get him through the worst trouble with laughter in his heart.

What could he do? He had no answers—except one.

For the first time since he was a boy, he knelt on the hard wood floor and prayed.

Chapter Twenty-One

~∽~

Three months later

Jen circled the old trainer plane and brought it in line for the approach. Below her, the grass runway—brilliant green from recent rainfall—stretched straight and narrow between the unmowed fields. She'd landed many times before, but none had mattered as much as this one.

A large circle, marked with white chalk dust, was her target. Hit that, and the license was hers. Jack and Darcy, holding baby John, stood to the side, ready to score her landing.

She checked speed, wind direction and velocity for the umpteenth time. She slowed to the right descent speed, had the perfect angle and could do this in her sleep. Yet the added pressure of the license made her palms sweat.

Concentrate.

She brought the plane lower, held it steady despite a gust of wind and dropped it onto the runway. The plane bounced and slowed as she applied the brake, but she wasn't sure if she hit the target. Jack was walking toward her. She couldn't have hit it dead-on, then.

Disappointment coursed through her veins. The test

could be retaken, but how would Jack ever gain confidence in her as a navigator and pilot if she failed the flight test?

She killed the engine. After the propeller slowed to a stop, she pulled off her goggles and helmet and then removed the cotton from her ears.

Jack climbed onto the wing just outside the cockpit. "How do you think you did?"

"A gust of wind sent me sideways, but I brought it back in line for the landing."

His mouth twitched. "I didn't ask about the weather conditions. Do you think you passed?"

Jen squared her shoulders. "I believe I earned my license."

"So do I." He held out the oh-so-precious license in the leather folder with Hunter School of Aviation embossed in gold on the front.

Jen's hand trembled. "I did? I hit the target?"

He nodded.

How long she'd wanted this. How difficult the path. Her throat constricted. "My father would be proud."

Jack clapped her on the shoulder. "He is." He looked upward into the limitless blue. "I'm sure of it. Well now, how do you plan to celebrate?"

"By bringing the plane into the hangar and completing the postflight check."

Jack laughed. "'Atta girl. You'll make a first-class pilot, after all."

Relief buoyed into elation. "Good enough for the polar attempt?"

"We'll see. You know how much Darcy wants to do that." He hopped off. "Meet you in the hangar."

He gave the propeller a tug, and the motor came to life. Jen taxied ahead before turning the plane. Only then did she see that she had indeed hit the target. Maybe not dead-center, but within the boundary. It would take only a few minutes to reach the hangar, but that was long enough for the emptiness to creep in again.

Over the past three months, the changes in her life had left a deep hole. First Mother boarded the train with Ruth and Sammy. Jen had hugged her mother until the conductor called out that all passengers had to be on board. Then she'd waved until the train disappeared from sight.

Then she and Minnie had removed their belongings from the house. Though Minnie had intended to move in with Beattie and Blake, that plan got changed when Peter's sister-in-law, Mariah Simmons, needed help at the orphanage. Though Peter had moved into the apartment he was remodeling for them once they married, Jen suspected he went to the orphanage for supper and to see Minnie each evening. Jen moved into the second bedroom in Jack and Darcy's house. One day soon, this would be the baby's room, and Jen would have to move out.

She'd saved her wages from running the classroom training for Darcy. The new job came with an increase in wage. That should have lifted her spirits, but every day that she went to the flight school, she remembered Dan's wavy auburn hair and twinkling blue eyes. His grin and the way he teased her could bring a smile to her face. Then she remembered the comfort of his embrace and the hope it had once given her.

Gone.

Every day she walked by the old house. Every day she expected to see new tenants but it remained sadly vacant, like a child's abandoned playhouse longing for the joy of family.

Minnie's wedding brought Mother and Ruth and Sam

back for a week, but they weren't in the old house. They stayed at the boardinghouse, and Jen didn't get to spend as much time with them as she wanted. They brought good news. Sam's father, despite lingering paralysis of his left side from the stroke, had regained the ability to speak. The two reconciled, and though Sam refused any inheritance, his father insisted he would receive the library Sam had always enjoyed. In addition, the dress-shop business was booming, and Ruth's designs had been picked up by a major manufacturer. Ironically, the ready-made gowns would soon appear in Hutton's Department Stores nationwide as well as their new catalog.

Beatrice and Blake, using profits from their greatly improved mercantile business, planned a summer holiday to the Lake Michigan shore far north in Petoskey so little Tillie and Branford could enjoy building sandcastles and splashing in the cool waters.

All too soon, Ruth, Sam and Mother returned to New York. Minnie moved into the apartment with Peter. Beatrice and Blake left for their holiday. Jen had never felt more alone. True, she was busy at the flight school and helping Darcy with the housework and the baby, but busyness couldn't fill the hole in her heart.

Celebrate? Jen patted her pocket where she'd tucked the license. Maybe she'd walk to the cemetery and show her daddy that she'd finally made it. Except of course he wasn't there, any more than the family was in the old house.

She eased the plane into the hangar and killed the motor. Then she climbed out. Even though she knew the procedure by heart, she walked to the office, where the postflight checklist hung on a clipboard.

Except the clipboard wasn't there.

"Who forgot to put it back?" Jen groused. Every student knew the clipboard was supposed to go back to the same spot so the next person could use it.

Except it was Saturday, so none of the students were there. All the planes were in place. None had gone out earlier.

"What on earth?" Jen shook her head. Jack must have taken it into the office or classroom. It was the only answer.

"Jack?"

He didn't answer. In fact, the school was deafeningly quiet. He and Darcy must have gone home.

She heaved a sigh. "Some celebration."

She pushed open the door to the office, and a snowstorm of little pieces of paper rained down on her.

"Congratulations!" cried a roomful of people, half of them with noisemaking rattles and whistles.

Jen brushed the paper from her hair.

Minnie threw her arms around her. "You did it."

"We're so proud of you," Mother said.

"Mother. When did you get here?"

"On this morning's train," said Sam, extending his hand. "Congratulations."

Ruth butted in, Sammy on one hip, yet still managing to look radiant in one of her latest designs. "When Jack told us you were going to get your license this weekend, we had to come west."

"Jack knew I would get my license?" Jen said.

"Of course." Darcy hugged her. "We believed in you from the start. I might even be able to talk Jack into letting you on the polar expedition team."

"Providing the MacMillan expedition doesn't succeed."

"How dare they? That accolade belongs right here

in Pearlman." Beattie kissed her on the cheek. "I'm so happy for you."

"I thought you were at the lakeshore," Jen marveled.

"We had to come back for this."

Indeed, Beattie's whole family was there.

"You came back for me?" Jen couldn't quite believe it.

"Come along now." Darcy wrapped her arm around Jen's. "The cake is in the classroom. Lily baked it especially for you."

The entire group proceeded next door to the classroom, where seemingly the rest of Pearlman greeted her. From the elder Kensingtons to Hendrick and Mariah Simmons, practically everyone Jen had ever known was there.

Darcy led her to the instructor's desk, where a large cake with vanilla buttercream icing sported the words *Jen Fox, Ace Aviatrix*, along with a piped icing depiction of an airplane.

"It's perfect. Beautiful," Jen told Lily, owner of the town's restaurant and bakery.

The woman beamed at the compliment.

Jen looked around the room at all the well-wishers. Pastor Gabe and his wife and children were there. So were Brandon and Anna Landers, Peter's foster sister. This was her family. This entire town. Emotions welled, and she had to blink back tears.

"Thank you," she managed to choke out.

"Let's see the license," Peter said.

For the next few minutes, Jen showed everyone her new license. Then she cut the cake while Minnie ladled punch into little glass cups that looked suspiciously like the ones used at the Valentine's Day Ball. Jen didn't even ask Minnie how she'd talked Mrs. Neidecker into loaning her punch set.

It was all too wonderful, and for several precious minutes, Jen felt whole again. Then, after the cake was eaten and the first people drifted away, the emptiness began to return. The day had been perfect except for one thing. Dan wasn't there.

Dan paced back and forth in front of his plane. The mowed hayfield crunched underfoot as the sun blazed overhead. A light breeze barely ruffled the seed tops that had missed the reaper. Perfect conditions for flying.

All his sacrifices and preparations had come together in time. He'd set off with excitement coursing through his veins, more alive than ever. Then a cylinder started missing, and he had to bring the plane down. Of all the days to run into trouble, why did it have to be today? If he didn't know deep inside that he was doing the first right thing he'd done in years, he would start thinking he wasn't supposed to make it to his destination today.

Instead, he urged the mechanic to hurry. "I need to get there this afternoon."

The man, standing on a ladder, snapped back, "It'll be done when it's done and not a minute sooner."

Frustrated, Dan raked a hand through his hair and strode to the edge of the field. Fortunately, the man who farmed this field was also a mechanic of sorts, but if the engine had major problems, he wouldn't be able to fix it.

How else could Dan get there? He was miles from the nearest town and even farther from a passenger rail route. He doubted Harrison, the mechanically inclined farmer, would loan him an automobile. Everything rested on his plane.

"Please, God," he prayed aloud.

The farmer grunted. "Never heard anyone pray for a motor before, but seems your prayers are answered."

Dan sprinted back to the plane. "It works?"

Harrison wiped his hands on his overalls. "Cleaned up a sticking valve. Should run fine now."

"Thank You, God," he shouted into the heavens. "And thank you, Mr. Harrison." He drew out a healthy number of bills and handed the money to the farmer. "You've saved my day."

Harrison whistled. "Guess this was a big deal to you."

"Yes, sir. The biggest. The rest of my life depends on it."

He got back in the cockpit, pulled on the helmet and goggles and waited for Harrison to give the propeller a pull. Sure enough. The motor sprang to life. No miss. Smooth as silk.

Dan turned the plane and bumped down the field until he could lift into the air and set course once again toward the east and the only thing in life that truly mattered.

Since Darcy looked tired, Jen sent her home with Jack. She then rejoined her mother and sisters, grabbed a broom and began sweeping up crumbs.

"You're not supposed to clean up," Ruth protested. "Let us do this. You should go and enjoy this moment with your friends."

"I'd rather be with my family."

"Oh, sis." Ruthie hugged her, tears in her eyes. "I miss you all, too. It's like old times being together here, even if it's only for a couple days. Tell me everything that's gone on since Minnie's wedding."

Jen shrugged. "Nothing much. The mercantile is doing a booming business since Blake started the discount program. City hall got a new clock."

"I don't want to hear about that, silly. I want to hear

about you." Ruth took the broom from Jen and swept the crumbs into a dustpan.

"I've been busy teaching classroom instruction at the flight school and getting flight training so I could take the license test."

"That I could figure out. Tell me if a special man has come into your life. Have you heard from Mr. Wagner?"

"No and no." Jen certainly didn't want to talk about Dan. Bad enough they'd parted on such icy terms. She had no doubt she'd seen the last of Dan Wagner. "I'm resolved to live a solitary life."

Ruth laughed. "Then you're in the perfect place for marriage. That's exactly how I felt when Sam appeared. Watch out—your future husband might be right around the corner."

"Or right next door," Minnie added.

Naturally she would say that. Like Beatrice, she had married a man she'd known in school. Unlike Beatrice, Minnie hadn't fallen in love with Peter until they were grown. Jen had neither prospect to consider. Only one man had ever captured her heart, and he had left with no intent of ever returning.

Ruth frowned. "What's that buzzing sound I hear?"

"A bee?" Minnie yelped. "There's a bee in here?"

Only then did Jen notice the drone. She recognized it at once. "It's not a bee. It's an airplane, and it's getting closer. That's odd. Who could it be? None of the students are flying today. I wonder who would fly into Pearlman."

Minnie glanced at Ruth. "Maybe you should go check. We can handle things here."

Apparently they wanted rid of her out of some misguided idea that she shouldn't help clean up.

"Go." Ruth shooed her out of the classroom with the broom.

"All right, but only because I'm curious." Jen walked through the hangar and out the open doors onto the airfield. It didn't take long to locate the low-flying biplane. It was an old Curtiss Jenny, the type popular with stunt fliers and private pilots because the army surplus models were so inexpensive to purchase. This one sounded as if it had a more powerful engine than the old surplus models, and by the looks of it, had undergone considerable modifications. The flashy red-and-yellow plane appeared to be lining up to land.

How unusual. Few planes ever landed in Pearlman. Occasionally an old friend of Jack's would drop in, but they usually notified him ahead of time. Usually. This one clearly hadn't, or Jack wouldn't have gone home.

Jen squinted against the high sun, following the plane as it made a perfect landing and rolled to the far end of the runway. Then it turned and coasted toward the hangar before pulling to a halt near her.

The plane wasn't nearly as shiny up close as it had appeared from the distance. The usual grease and oil splattered the fuselage near the motor. The wings bore the scars of a long flight, including a coating of smashed insects. The solitary pilot—a man, considering the breadth of the shoulders—hopped out of the plane without removing his helmet and goggles.

He strode toward her with the arrogant swagger of an ace pilot, a stride that struck a familiar and tantalizing chord. The build, the height all pointed to one man. Her heart raced at the thought. Could it be? She couldn't tell for certain without a glimpse of his hair and eyes, but the gloves looked like his. All that was lacking was the tattered Stetson.

He stopped in front of her. "Where's the old mackinaw, Miss Fox?"

"Dan?" She choked out his name, hardly daring to believe it could be him. After not writing or sending any word for three months, why had he suddenly shown up today of all days?

He pulled off the goggles and helmet. Sure enough, there was that gorgeous auburn hair and those bright blue eyes.

"Dan, is it?" He grinned, those eyes twinkling. "You must not be angry with me anymore."

"Angry?" Maybe she was. Maybe she wasn't. She didn't know what to feel. "You didn't write. You didn't even let us know that you'd arrived safely."

"Neither did you."

"I didn't know where to write."

He called her lame excuse. "Boynton is small enough to know everyone. You only had to post a letter to general delivery. They would know where to find me."

The words were factual, but the tone was hard. He'd expected to hear from her, too. The blame didn't land on one set of shoulders.

She set her jaw. Nothing he could say would send her off-kilter. Now she was a licensed aviator. She had accomplished the one thing he had refused to believe she could do. "Why are you here?"

"Nice to see you, too."

She whipped around, sick of playing this game.

He caught her arm. "I missed you, Jen. Darcy wrote that you were flying for your license today. I couldn't miss it."

"You came all the way from Montana just to see me take my flight test? Or did you expect me to fail?"

"No."

She tossed her head. "You're too late anyway. I took the exam hours ago."

"You passed, of course." He didn't ask. He knew she'd done it.

She made the mistake of looking into his eyes. His gaze held her to the spot. Something had happened to those blue eyes of his. They'd deepened, darkened and yet softened. She couldn't seem to look away.

He swallowed, making his Adam's apple bob. "I brought something for you...for later, actually." He dug in his jacket pocket until he came up with something round and flat and metal. He pressed it into her hand. "For the polar attempt."

It was a medallion, just like the one he'd given her the night of the ball. "But I still have the other one you gave me."

He motioned for her to turn it over.

She did, and the tears rose. Engraved on the back was her father's name.

"Carry it with you," he said. "Bring him to the Pole with you."

She pressed a hand to her lips, trying to control the trembling that had set in. "Thank you." It came out soft and ragged and filled with emotion.

"It's the least I could do." His gaze never left hers, never flickered.

She could no longer hold back the surging emotions. She threw her arms around his neck and hugged tightly. "I missed you."

His arms wrapped around her. "I missed you, too."

"You did?" She gazed into those eyes again, and this time she saw it—the reflection of her looking at him. Love curled around that image, unspoken yet unwavering.

"Every moment of every day." He leaned close and brushed her lips. "How I missed that."

She could not bear his teasing. "Please tell me you're staying. Please tell me you're not just flying through en route to an air show."

"I'm not going to an air show."

But she noticed he didn't say he would stay.

"I'm starting an airmail route."

She hardly dared ask where. No, she knew. In Montana. She squeezed her eyes shut and leaned against his strong chest. "Congratulations." It hurt to say it. He'd only just arrived. Now he would leave again. Better he had never tortured her with his presence.

He smoothed a hand over her hair. "I'm looking for a copilot."

Oh, these tears were bitter. "Jack would never leave Pearlman."

He kissed the top of her head. "I'm not talking about Jack."

Startled, she pulled back to look him in the eye. "Who, then?"

"Is it that difficult to figure out? You did get your license today."

The shock nearly killed her, but he wasn't finished.

"Now I'm not fool enough to think that arrangement would pass muster with either your mother or mine, so I'm proposing another partnership, something more permanent."

He had lost her. "You want to sign a contract?"

He grinned. "In a manner of speaking, I guess I do." He dropped to one knee and took her hand. "I love you, and I want to spend my life with you."

Jen could not breathe. Was he saying what she thought he was?

"Will you be my copilot through life, Jen Fox? Will you marry me?"

At some point her family must have sneaked up behind her, for when she didn't answer right away, Minnie called out, "Say yes."

Ruth and Beatrice seconded that. Even Mother got in on the advice. When Darcy added her voice, Jen turned to see her friend had returned, not nearly as tired as she'd seemed less than an hour before.

"Where?" was all she could squeak out.

Her sisters groaned, but Dan grinned.

He stood and brushed the dust from his knee. "I suppose I ought to give you all the details. I've gotten a route flying north from Grand Rapids to the Upper Peninsula of Michigan. If it's all right with you, I figured we could stay right here in Pearlman."

How could this be? How could everything she'd ever wanted come together on a single day?

"Well?" her sisters chimed in chorus.

Jen looked into Dan's eyes again and knew the answer. She'd known it for months, since the first time she'd set eyes on him. "Yes. Yes, I'll marry you. Yes to all of it."

Dan whooped and grabbed her in a bear hug. Then he spun her around and kissed her, joyous and intense and filled with promise. Jen wished it would never end, and when it did, she looked into those wonderful eyes, marveling that she would get to see them every day of the rest of her life.

Then her sisters ran to her, showering the pair with congratulations and tears and hugs until Jen felt she would burst from it all.

"When should we get married? Will we fly this plane? Will Jack let us keep the plane in the hangar? How often do we fly? Should we talk to Pastor Gabe today?" The questions flowed from her lips faster than water from a spigot.

"Whoa now," Dan said. "There is one little thing I need to pass by you before you go getting the preacher."

His serious demeanor made her heart sink. What hadn't he told her?

This time he looked nervous. He kicked at the dirt and watched the bits of gravel fly. "Now, I know how much you like to have the final say on things, but this was such a deal that I went ahead and did it without asking." He sneaked a peek at her. "I went and made a down payment on a house for us."

Jen gulped. "You did what?" She didn't want to think about the size of the mortgage. "How could you manage that? I thought you had to pay off debts, and then were planning to put the rest into your plane."

"I was, but I figured we'd have half a year before we'd need to consider whether or not to get the engine outfitted for cold weather. And I kinda hoped that Mr. Simmons might give us a deal." He raised a hand before she could protest. "The debts are paid off, darling. The way I see it, a house is more important than a plane."

"No, it's not. The plane is your means to earn a living. Our means." If Dan was one of those men who spent money faster than he made it, she was going to have to get control of that little habit right now.

"Whoa now." Again he held up his hand. "What do

you say you have a look at the place first before making any decisions? The payments are well within reach, but if you don't like it, we'll put it back on the market."

Mollified, Jen consented to at least look at the house. "But you certainly were sure that I would agree to marry you."

That grin came back. "I had a good feeling about it, especially after talking to Jack and Darcy."

Jen could just imagine what they'd told him. That she'd been moping around and asking if they'd heard anything. "They never told me they'd talked to you."

"I asked them to keep it a surprise. Do you want to see the place now? It's not all that big, but I think you'll like it. Maybe Blake could drive us there."

Within minutes, practically the entire family had piled into Blake's Cadillac. They were squeezed in so tightly that Jen had to sit on Dan's lap. Blake drove up Old State and then turned on Third.

"How do you know where this is?" Jen asked, suddenly realizing Dan hadn't said a word to Blake.

"My dad's the one who sold it to Dan." Blake turned left onto Oak.

"Does everyone but me know what's going on?"

"Yes," shouted a chorus of voices.

Blake slowed the car.

"That's our house," Jen cried.

"Yes, it is," Dan confirmed.

"You bought our house?"

"I took a little look around the day I had dinner with your family. I found the place charming. After getting the airmail route, I made inquiries and learned it was back on the market. Since I needed a place to live, I made an offer."

"Then you weren't certain I would agree to marry you."

He wrapped his arms around her. "I hoped you would, but I was prepared to battle it out—for years if necessary."

"Then you really do love me."

"I really do." He kissed the nape of her neck. "Is the house all right?"

Jen bubbled over with emotion. This wonderful, incredible man had given her everything she had ever wanted. She didn't even care that everyone could see her tears flow. "It's perfect. It's absolutely perfect."

* * * * *

Dear Reader,

I have long been fascinated by Alaska's Iditarod dogsled race, which is run in commemoration of the diphtheria outbreak mentioned in Jen's story. The airplanes of the era never got off the ground, while the heroic efforts of a dogsled relay got the antitoxin to Nome. Great feats in aviation lay just ahead, though, including Lindbergh's solo transatlantic flight in 1927. Though the MacMillan expedition mentioned in the book did not reach the pole in 1925, both Byrd and Amundsen did fly over it just three days apart in May of the following year.

I did move one timeline forward a little in the interest of the story. The first private contractor to fly the mail for the US Post Office began in 1926. Before that the Post Office hired and trained their own pilots. Airmail service was too perfect a solution for Dan and Jen for me to pass it up when less than a year separated fact from fiction.

I hope you have enjoyed the Fox sisters' stories in this series. They are like family to me now. I do love to hear from readers. You may write me in care of Love Inspired or through my website at:
http://christineelizabethjohnson.com.

Blessings,
Christine Johnson

REQUEST YOUR FREE BOOKS!

2 FREE INSPIRATIONAL NOVELS
PLUS 2 *FREE* MYSTERY GIFTS

Love Inspired® HISTORICAL

YES! Please send me 2 FREE Love Inspired® Historical novels and my 2 FREE mystery gifts (gifts are worth about $10). After receiving them, if I don't wish to receive any more books, I can return the shipping statement marked "cancel." If I don't cancel, I will receive 4 brand-new novels every month and be billed just $4.99 per book in the U.S. or $5.49 per book in Canada. That's a saving of at least 17% off the cover price. It's quite a bargain! Shipping and handling is just 50¢ per book in the U.S. and 75¢ per book in Canada.* I understand that accepting the 2 free books and gifts places me under no obligation to buy anything. I can always return a shipment and cancel at any time. Even if I never buy another book, the two free books and gifts are mine to keep forever.

102/302 IDN GH6Z

Name	(PLEASE PRINT)	
Address		Apt. #
City	State/Prov.	Zip/Postal Code

Signature (if under 18, a parent or guardian must sign)

Mail to the **Reader Service:**
IN U.S.A.: P.O. Box 1867, Buffalo, NY 14240-1867
IN CANADA: P.O. Box 609, Fort Erie, Ontario L2A 5X3

Want to try two free books from another series?
Call 1-800-873-8635 or visit www.ReaderService.com.

* Terms and prices subject to change without notice. Prices do not include applicable taxes. Sales tax applicable in N.Y. Canadian residents will be charged applicable taxes. Offer not valid in Quebec. This offer is limited to one order per household. Not valid for current subscribers to Love Inspired Historical books. All orders subject to credit approval. Credit or debit balances in a customer's account(s) may be offset by any other outstanding balance owed by or to the customer. Please allow 4 to 6 weeks for delivery. Offer available while quantities last.

Your Privacy—The Reader Service is committed to protecting your privacy. Our Privacy Policy is available online at www.ReaderService.com or upon request from the Reader Service.

We make a portion of our mailing list available to reputable third parties that offer products we believe may interest you. If you prefer that we not exchange your name with third parties, or if you wish to clarify or modify your communication preferences, please visit us at www.ReaderService.com/consumerchoice or write to us at Reader Service Preference Service, P.O. Box 9062, Buffalo, NY 14240-9062. Include your complete name and address.

LIH15

*Rachel Hewitt survived the journey to Oregon, but
arriving in her new home brings new challenges—like
three adorable girls who need a nanny, and their sheriff
father, who needs a second chance at love...*

Read on for a sneak preview of Renee Ryan's
WAGON TRAIN PROPOSAL,
the heartwarming conclusion of the series
JOURNEY WEST.

"Are you my new mommy?"

Rachel blinked in stunned silence at the child staring
back at her. She saw a lot of herself in the precocious six-
year-old. In the determined angle of her tiny shoulders. In
the bold tilt of her head. In the desperate hope simmering
in her big, sorrowful blue eyes.

For a dangerous moment, Rachel had a powerful urge
to tug the little girl into her arms and give her the answer
she so clearly wanted.

Careful, she warned herself. *Think before you speak.*

"Well?" Hands still perched on her hips, Daisy's small
mouth turned down at the corners. "Are you my new
mommy or not?"

"I'm sorry, Daisy, no. I'm not your new mommy.
However, I am your new neighbor, and I'll certainly see
you often, perhaps even daily."

Tristan cut in then, touching his daughter's shoulder to
gain her attention. "Daisy, my darling girl, we've talked

about this before. You cannot go around asking every woman you meet if she's your mommy."

"But, Da—" the little girl's lower lip jutted out "—you said you were bringing us back a new mommy when you got home."

"No, baby." He pulled his hand away from her shoulder then shoved it into his pocket. "I said I *might* bring you home a new mommy."

When tears formed in the little girl's eyes, Rachel found herself interceding. "I may not be your new mommy," she began, taming a stray wisp of the child's hair behind her ear, "but I can be your very good friend."

The little girl's eyes lit up and she plopped into Rachel's lap. No longer able to resist, Rachel wrapped her arms around the child and hugged her close. Lily attempted to join her sister on Rachel's lap. When Daisy refused to budge, the little girl settled for pulling on Rachel's sleeve. "You don't want to be our new mommy?"

The poor child sounded so despondent Rachel's heart twisted. "Oh, Lily, it's not a matter of want. You see, I'm already committed to—"

She cut off her own words, realizing she had no other commitments now that her brother was married. He didn't need her to run his household. *No one* needed her. Except, maybe, this tiny family.

Don't miss
WAGON TRAIN PROPOSAL
by Renee Ryan,
available June 2015 wherever
Love Inspired® *Historical books and ebooks are sold.*

SPECIAL EXCERPT FROM

Love Inspired®

Can a widow and widower ever leave their grief in the past and forge a new future—and a family—together?

Read on for a sneak preview of
THE AMISH WIDOW'S SECRET.

"Wait, before you go. I have an important question to ask you."

Sarah nodded her head and sat back down.

"I stayed up until late last night, thinking about your situation and mine. I prayed, and *Gott* kept pushing this thought at me." He took a deep breath. "I wonder, would you consider becoming my *frau*?"

Sarah held up her hand, as if to stop his words. "I…"

"Before you speak, let me explain." Mose took another deep breath. "I know you still love Joseph, just as I still love my Greta. But I have *kinder* who need a mother to guide and love them. Now that Joseph's gone and the farm's being sold, you need a place to call home, people who care about you, a family. We can join forces and help each other." He saw a panicked expression forming in her eyes. "It would only be a marriage of convenience. The girls need a loving mother and you've already proven you can be that. What do you say, Sarah Nolt? Will you be my wife?"

Sarah sat silent, her face turned away. She looked into Mose's eyes. "You'd do this for me? But…you don't know me."

"I'd do this for us," Mose corrected, and smiled.

The tips of Sarah's fingers nervously pleated and un-pleated a scrap of her skirt. "But we hardly know each other. What would people think? They will say I took advantage of your good nature."

Mose smiled. "So, let them talk. They'd be wrong and we'd know it. I want this marriage for both of us, for the *kinder*. We can't let others decide what is best for our lives. I believe this marriage is *Gott*'s plan for us."

Sarah's face cleared and she seemed to come to a decision. She smoothed out the fabric of her skirt and tidied her hair, then finally took Mose's outstretched hand with a smile. "You're right. This is our life. I accept your proposal, Mose Fisher. I will be your *frau* and your *kinder*'s mother."

Don't miss
THE AMISH WIDOW'S SECRET
by Cheryl Williford,
available June 2015 wherever
Love Inspired® books and ebooks are sold.

LIEXP0515

SPECIAL EXCERPT FROM

*Could an intruder at the White House be the break the
Capitol K-9 Unit needs to track down a killer?*

*Read on for a sneak preview of
SECURITY BREACH,
the fourth book in the exciting new series
CAPITOL K-9 UNIT.*

Nicholas Cole hurried toward the White House special in-house security chief's office in the West Wing, gripping the leash for his K-9 partner, Max. General Margaret Meyer stood behind her oak desk, a fierce expression on her face.

The general moved from behind her desk. "This office has been searched."

He came to attention in front of his boss, having a hard time shaking his military training as a navy SEAL. "Anything missing?"

"No, but someone had searched through the Jeffries file, and it would be easy to take pictures of the papers and evidence the team has uncovered so far."

"What do you want me to do, ma'am?" Nicholas knew the murder of Michael Jeffries, son of the prominent congressman Harland Jeffries, was important to the general as well as his unit captain, Gavin McCord.

"I want to know who was in my office. It could be the break we've needed on this case. With the Easter Egg Roll today, the White House has been crawling with visitors since early this morning, so it won't be easy." She shook her head. "Especially with the Oval Office and the Situation Room here in the West Wing being used for the festivities. If you discover anything, find me right away."

"Yes, ma'am." Nicholas exited the West Wing by the West Colonnade and cut across the Rose Garden toward where the Easter Egg Roll was taking place.

He scanned the people gathered. His survey came to rest upon Selena Barrow, the White House tour director, who was responsible for planning this event. Even from a distance, Selena commanded a person's attention. She was tall and slender with long, wavy brown hair and the bluest eyes, but what drew him to Selena was her air of integrity and compassion.

Selena would have an updated list of the people who were invited to the party. It might save him a trip to the front gate if he asked her for it. And it would give him a reason to talk to her.

Don't miss
SECURITY BREACH by Margaret Daley,
available June 2015 wherever
Love Inspired® Suspense books and ebooks are sold.

LISEXP0515